SINGER

SINGER

Memoir of a Christian Sniper

A NOVEL

CAP DANIELS
with
PASTORS DAVE MASON
and JOHN GROSSMANN

ANCHOR WATCH
PUBLISHING
** USA **

Singer
Memoir of a Christian Sniper

Published by:

** USA **

13 Digit ISBN: 978-1-951021-44-3
Library of Congress Control Number: 2023937798
Copyright © 2023 Cap Daniels – All Rights Reserved

Cover Design: German Creative

Printed in the United States of America

SINGER

Memoir of a Christian Sniper

CAP DANIELS
with
Pastors DAVE MASON
and JOHN GROSSMANN

Part I
Young Guns

Chapter 1

Sons of Thunder

Mark 3:17 NASB
*". . . and James, the son of Zebedee, and John the brother of James
(to them He gave the name Boanerges, which means
'Sons of Thunder.')"*

* * *

My name is Jimmy Grossmann, but please call me Singer. Everybody does. The first two things I want you to know about me may sound like stark contradictions, but please believe me when I tell you they're not. Both of them are, in fact, the God's honest truth. First, I'm an ordained Southern Baptist minister who leads the choir and occasionally takes to the pulpit to teach and preach the beloved Word of God. Second, I've been a serial killer since I was nine years old.

When I began writing this story, I dug deep into my soul, trying to find the perfect place to start, and no matter how hard I fought it, the same fateful day kept pouring into my mind, time after time. So, you'll have to forgive the tearstains on the coming pages as I tell you the agonizing, true story of how I became one of the Sons of Thunder.

I've only told this story to one other living soul in all the days of my life, so don't expect my words to come easily. I will stutter and pause to gather myself more than once before we've reached the end, but stay with me, and we'll find a way to get through it together.

Before He was arrested, tried, and crucified, Jesus fell on His face in the Garden of Gethsemane and prayed, "*My Father, if it is possible, let this cup pass from Me; yet not as I will, but as You will.*"

I wish the story of my life began on some other day, in some other place, and at some other time, but like Jesus, that cup couldn't pass from me. That's how it had to be, and if you're to understand why I was placed on Earth, I must begin on that horrible night so long ago.

I grew up just outside a little town called Sumter, South Carolina. It's a military town built around Shaw Air Force Base, and other than the base, there's not much there.

My father . . .

Forgive me while I take a moment to gather the courage to continue.

My father was not a good man. He was an alcoholic and an addict. My mother, on the other hand, was a godly woman of enormous faith. I'm sure fear made her think about taking my brother and me and escaping the old man's abuse and the poverty in which we lived, but something made her stay one day too long. Other kids played hide-and-seek, but my brother and I just played hide.

I was nine, and he was eleven when it happened. Momma was crying, and Daddy was yelling . . . again. He was drunk or high on something . . . again. He'd hit her before, but never like that. It was different that night. He was enraged like we'd never seen.

That's when Momma quit screaming. My brother and I both heard the blow that stopped her tears. We were scared, but in times like that, fear isn't enough to stop two boys from checking on their mother. We ran down the hallway of our trailer and saw Daddy standing over Momma's body. She looked dead to me, but my father was too drunk or too high to stop beating her. My brother Billy ran into the living room and shoved the drunken animal away from Momma. Daddy stumbled and crashed into the bar that separated the living room from the kitchen. When he staggered back to his feet, he was gripping a kitchen knife in his hand and aiming it at Billy. His old single-shot twenty-gauge was propped in the corner by a threadbare recliner, where our father usually slept off the hangovers.

I can't tell you what it was, but something inside my little nine-year-old head made me pick up that shotgun. I remember thinking, *I've got to stop him before he kills Billy, too.* I don't remember the thunder of the shotgun that filled the tiny space and echoed from the paper-thin walls, but I'll never forget the red spatter on the ceiling and the walls of that run-down, rotten trailer.

Momma lived a few more days until the aneurism he'd caused inside her brain claimed her mortal body and freed her timeless soul. I'd stopped him before he could physically hurt Billy, but physical injuries are the easy ones to overcome.

Billy didn't talk after that. It was like he wasn't in there anymore. He just stared into space with blank, empty eyes and didn't react to anything. He was like that for nearly a year. We didn't have any family, so a preacher and his wife took Billy and me in and treated us like we were their own boys. They were good people, but they didn't know how to help Billy. In those days, in rural South Carolina, there wasn't any help for a boy who'd been through what Billy had endured. We went to see a man the preacher called "a shrink" a few times. I suppose he did his best, and I learned to cope with what happened and with what I'd done, but Billy never did.

One day, the preacher put us in the cab of his truck, and we drove for what felt like hours. When we finally stopped, we were at a Trappist monastery. I'd never heard of monks or monasteries, but we left Billy there with those monks on that unforgettable day so long ago.

I never asked the preacher why Billy had to stay in that strange, silent place, but as the years dragged on, I came to believe the boy without a voice belonged in a place where words weren't necessary. Since that day, I've often wondered if I took Billy's voice. When I open my mouth to sing, maybe it's really Billy's voice that comes off my tongue. Regardless of where his voice went for the decades that passed, he never spoke again until the day he took his own life in the monastery on the banks of the Cooper River.

Billy said, "I'm sorry, Jimmy. I'm sorry for not being able to protect you and Momma from him."

Those were the first words he'd spoken in two decades—and the last words he'd ever speak. He left his simple room to go to the bathroom and never came back. The thunder I should've heard inside our trailer a quarter century before pounded in my head behind the silence of that monastery when I found him a few minutes later in a puddle of his own blood.

I'll never be tried inside a courtroom for the lives I've taken in every corner of the world because I took those lives while wearing my country's uniform and while sanctioned by those who believe they hold the moral authority to condone every squeeze of every trigger I've ever made. I am an American sniper because I learned, as a nine-year-old child, that I have the capacity to take human life when I believe doing so will protect the innocent. That is the lesson I learned the night my brother and I became Sons of Thunder. I'm a Christian because there's no other source of true peace in all of Creation.

Chapter 2
So Others May Live

John 15:13 NASB
"Greater love has no one than this,
that one lay down his life for his friends."

* * *

I do the work required of me so others may live. As we stumble through this together, I'll tell you a few stories about me, but please don't think I'm bragging. I borrowed the phrase "so others may live" from one of the finest groups of men I've ever known—the United States Coast Guard rescue swimmers. These courageous young men throw themselves from helicopters into frigid and tumultuous waters, where no sane human would dare enter on purpose. They do that for only one reason—so others may live.

I've never been a rescue swimmer, but my craft bears a few similarities to theirs, and if you'll indulge me awhile, I'll do my best to make you understand why I believe that to be true.

I was seventeen when the preacher and his wife signed an innocuous-looking piece of paper, essentially giving the United States Army full custody of a boy who'd known more pain in his heart than most men four times his age.

I was never any good at schoolwork, except for math. For some reason, numbers made sense to me, and they had a way of explaining the world in something other than words. Almost everything in life could be explained mathematically with one enormous exception—love. Love isn't rational, logical, or maybe even definable. Love is simply a gift that can never be bought, sold, borrowed, or stolen. It can only be given, and perhaps that is precisely what makes it most unique among all human emotion.

Before I tell you more about my first days in the uniform of an American soldier, I'd like to tell you a story about love among an unlikely group of Americans, a long way from home, but not so long ago.

In January of 1968, an American-flagged Banner-class environmental research ship christened the USS *Pueblo*, fell into enemy hands, depositing her crew into hell on Earth. Although technically classified as an environmental research vessel, the *Pueblo*'s real identity was that of a spy ship. She was patrolling the Sea of Japan, collecting electronic and signals intelligence from North Korea as part of the U.S. Navy's intelligence-gathering program. The qualifications of the crew and the readiness of the ship for combat have long been debated and discussed, but for the purposes of this story, none of that matters. Ultimately, on the afternoon of January 23rd, the USS *Pueblo* and her crew became prisoners of war after an overwhelming show of force by the North Korean Navy, including killing a young sailor named Duane Hodges in a shelling attack just outside North Korean territorial waters, when the captain of the *Pueblo* made one final attempt to delay capture so classified material on board could be destroyed.

Everything I've told you about the *Pueblo* incident up to this point is historically accurate. What follows exists only as hearsay, but is, in my opinion, the most powerful part of the whole story.

When the crew of the *Pueblo* were taken ashore and imprisoned in a POW camp, thirteen of the eighty-two remaining crewmen were forced to sit rigidly around a table in hardback chairs for days on end. On the first day of their captivity, the door to the room where the thirteen crewmen sat with their backs as stiff as boards, flew open, leaving each man startled and trembling at the thought of what was to come. No one could know the horror that was to be unleashed on at least one of their shipmates. The imprisoners forcefully yanked the sailor from the first chair and beat him savagely until he lost consciousness on the floor.

When the guards left the room, the remaining sailors quickly came to the aid of the beaten man. He regained consciousness, and finally, they helped him back onto his chair.

With no way to mark the passage of time, the prisoners sat stoically in their chairs in fear of what might happen the next time the door swung inward. After what the captives believed to be twenty-four hours, again, the door exploded inward, and two Korean guards forcefully jerked the man in the first chair from the seat and beat him even more savagely than the day before, until once again, the man lay unconscious. Just as they'd done the day before, the remaining sailors helped the beaten man back onto a chair, but one selfless sailor stepped forward and said, "Put him in my chair, and I'll take his seat. He can't survive another beating like that."

Humbled, the remaining men rearranged their places at the table and situated the injured sailor as far from the door as possible. Again, at the imagined twenty-four-hour mark, the door was forced inward, and the sailor in chair number one braced for the savagery he knew would soon be unleashed upon him. As expected, the guards pulled him from the first chair and beat him without mercy, just as they'd done to the previous occupant of the chair.

As the days wore on, each man, knowing full well what awaited him, volunteered for his turn in the first chair to take the place of the man who'd been so brutally beaten the day before. This continued until the love each man had for every other sailor in the room finally defeated the efforts of the guards to wear down the resolve of the prisoners. No one from the room of thirteen ever surrendered any classified information or aided the enemy in any way. Instead, they demonstrated their patriotism, humanity, and most of all, their love for their fellow captives by sacrificing themselves until they were finally released.

Perhaps there aren't words to adequately define love, but those thirteen men of the USS *Pueblo* became the epitome of selfless love in that room, under conditions most people can hardly imagine.

Now, some five decades later, it's easy for us to claim we would've done the same under similar conditions, but few of us will ever be asked to make such sacrifices. I want to believe I would willingly stand up in the place of one of my brothers-in-arms and take his punishment so he wouldn't have to endure the torture. I pray I never have to make that decision, but I'll never let myself forget the terrible sacrifice Jesus Himself made when He stepped from Paradise and into this cruel world specifically to be tortured, beaten, tried, and ultimately crucified to pay the price for billions of people who'd yet to be born. He bore the shame, the guilt, and the agony I deserved. He paid a price unlike any other, knowing full well every stroke of the whip He would take to His back; every piercing from the crown of thorns He would wear; every unimaginable agonizing impact of the Roman soldier's hammer as the spikes would be driven through His wrists and ankles; every labored torturous breath He would gasp on the cross; and finally, the catastrophic tear of flesh from the centurion's spear as His side would be pierced and the life would finally drain from his human shell. He willingly and obediently took my place and the places of countless other sinners who deserve the agony He endured, but because of Christ's unselfish love for me and all who believe, we don't have to get what we deserve. Instead, we will be rewarded beyond measure. And all of this is because He loves us with the purest of all love—a kind of love we could never comprehend in our weak, mortal minds.

Chapter 3
To Become More than I Am

Judges 11:1 NASB
"Now Jephthah the Gileadite was a valiant warrior, but he was the son of a harlot. And Gilead was the father of Jephthah."

* * *

In the United States Army, I found something I didn't know I was seeking: I found a purpose beyond myself. That's not to say that my faith and devotion to a loving God wasn't a greater purpose than all others, but the Army made me feel like part of some enormous family made up of people from the kid down the street, to people from places I never knew were real. Of all the selfless, devoted warriors I was fortunate to serve alongside, it's Willy Williams who I'll never forget.

I already told you how the preacher and his wife signed the papers so I could join the Army at seventeen, so let's pick up the story from there. My first day in the service began at four thirty in the morning at the Military Entrance Processing Station at Fort Jackson in Columbia, South Carolina. The recruiter who told me how the Army would give me the whole world, if I'd just sign up, was there at MEPS that morning to get me started down the assembly line, but he wasn't there for long. His job was done. I was committed, and he had other hopeless boys to lead into the ranks of the Army. My scores on the Armed Services Vocational Aptitude Battery weren't terrible, but they weren't stellar. A sergeant showed me a list of military operational specialties I was qualified for based on my scores. The list wasn't long, but as he talked through each of the MOSs, a magic phrase fell from his lips right after he pointed at 11-Bravo.

He said, "Your scores are good enough for the Army to guarantee you a chance to become a Ranger if you select Infantryman as your MOS."

I was a poor, Southern, barely educated black kid from nowhere, with little hope of becoming anything meaningful. But when he said the word *Ranger*, a chill ran down my spine that I couldn't understand.

I asked, "What's a Ranger?"

He looked up at me as if I'd asked him for the meaning of life. "Come on, kid. You've got to be messing with me. Do you seriously not know what a Ranger is?"

I shrugged. "No, sir. I don't know what a Ranger is, but it sounds exciting."

He grinned and stood from his chair. "How many push-ups can you do, kid?"

I shrugged again. "I don't know. Maybe two or three hundred, but I'd have to stop to catch my breath after that."

He slapped me on the shoulder. "Come with me, son. I'm going to change your life."

I followed him down a long corridor and into an office where two more soldiers sat behind a pair of desks with plaques, pictures, and framed certificates covering the walls. The first soldier's uniform was decorated with tabs and insignia I didn't understand, but I was impressed.

The soldier who led me into the office said, "Sergeant Tate, I believe I've got you a Ranger here."

The man I assumed was Sergeant Tate looked into my eyes as if staring through my skull, and he slowly stood. As he stepped toward me, he eyed every inch of me, from toes to nose, and then he did the strangest thing. With both hands, he shoved me in the center of my chest.

I staggered backward and recovered my balance. "Why did you do that?"

Instead of answering me, he turned to the man who'd delivered me. "Thanks, Mac. I've got it from here."

Mac—I assume that was his name—nodded and vanished, leaving me in the hands of shoving Sergeant Tate.

He scowled. "Why didn't you shove me back, son?"

I bowed my head, but the words of the preacher echoed inside my head. *Look a man in the eye when you talk to him, Jimmy. He ain't no better than you, no matter how big he is or what color he is. Look him in the eye like a man.*

I raised my head and returned his gaze. "Because I was trying to figure out why you shoved me first. Maybe you had a good reason, and shoving you back wouldn't have done any good if you had a reason."

Sergeant Tate threw an arm around me. "Thinking before striking. I like it. What's your name, son?"

"Jimmy Grossmann, sir."

"Don't call me sir, kid. I'm Sergeant First Class Rodney Tate." He pointed toward a tab on his uniform that read RANGER. "Do you want one of these?"

I stared at the tab. "Not without earning it, sir . . . I mean, Sergeant."

He slid a VHS tape into the VCR. "Park yourself in that chair and watch this movie, kid."

The next twelve minutes of my life were spent with my mouth agape and my eyelids refusing to blink. Men in camouflaged uniforms, with their faces painted green and black, did everything my seventeen-year-old brain wanted to do. They shot weapons I never knew existed, jumped out of airplanes, rappelled from towers and cliffs, crept through swamps, and fought like animals in hand-to-hand combat. The movie ended with a group of those same men all cleaned up, wearing some kind of dress uniform, and positioned in formation. Every one of them wore a black beret and stood like a mighty oak tree.

I turned back to Sergeant Tate. "Are those Rangers?"

By way of an answer, he threw his black beret through the air like a frisbee, and I caught it in midair.

He said, "Go ahead. Try it on, and check yourself out in that mirror."

I tugged the beret onto my head and tried to shape it like the men in the movie. Something about it felt wrong. I felt like I was getting something I hadn't earned, and I almost yanked it from my head, but Sergeant Tate motioned toward the mirror.

"Take a look, kid. What do you think?"

I lifted my eyes to the glass, and I didn't recognize the man looking back at me. The feeling I experienced when I first pulled on the beret flooded back, and I jerked it from my head. I gently laid the black felt crown on the desk and nodded at the sergeant.

For the first time in my life, I believed it didn't matter that I was the orphaned son of a battered wife and alcoholic father. In that moment, I knew I could become whatever God intended me to be. "I want to be a Ranger, sir."

He pulled the beret from his desk and tossed it onto his credenza. "And I want you to be a Ranger, Jimmy Grossmann. Now, shuffle your butt back down to Sergeant McKenzie's office, and sign whatever he puts in front of you. Next time I see you, I expect you to have one of those black berets of your own."

I didn't have a watch back then. The truth is, I didn't have much of anything in those days, so I didn't know what time it was when they herded us into the curtain-lined room that had a row of flags on a podium.

When people call America a melting pot, they must be talking about the collection of us in that room. No two of us looked alike. Every race, color, size, and hometown seemed to be represented in that crowd. I didn't know what was about to happen to us, but whatever it was, it felt important. And it didn't take long for our purpose in that room to become crystal clear. An Air Force officer in his dress blue uniform, with shiny gold bars on his shoulder, stepped in front of the flags, and with his presence alone, demanded our attention. Everyone stared intently at him when he spoke.

"Ladies and gentlemen . . . Raise your right hands, and repeat after me."

The pledge we made for the first time that day almost brought tears to my eyes, and I suddenly felt like the lieutenant and I were the only two people on Earth.

I, Jimmy Grossmann, do solemnly swear that I will support and defend the Constitution of the United States against all enemies, foreign and domestic; that I will bear true faith and allegiance to the same; and that I will obey the orders of the President of the United States and the orders of the officers appointed over me, according to regulations and the Uniform Code of Military Justice. So help me God.

I gave that same oath every time I reenlisted in the Army, but there was something about saying it for the first time that was unforgettable and life-changing. I guess I knew the president was real, but I'd never thought of him as anything other than an abstract concept. He became a real part of my life that day, and somehow, that made an ignorant, seventeen-year-old orphan from South Carolina feel like he was important enough for the president to care about.

So help me God.

I don't know what those words meant to anyone else in that room, but for me, they were, and remain, the ultimate force. And from the moment I finished that first oath, I never gave my country anything less than every ounce of strength I possessed.

Immediately after being sworn in, they wrangled us onto four different buses. The Air Force bus looked more like a private motorcoach, and the Marines' bus made me wonder if it would make it all the way to wherever they were going. My bus was mostly white with "United States Army" stenciled in black on each side.

I learned later that the Air Force and Navy buses went to the airport, and the Marines went to Paris Island, but I went to Fort Benning, Georgia, where I would spend a lot of time in the coming years.

"Welcome to the infantry, ladies! My name is Drill Sergeant Donovan, and for the next ten weeks of your life, I'm your momma, your daddy, your teacher, and your worst nightmare. If it comes out of my mouth, you better memorize it, love it, and live it, or you're gonna be dragging your sorry butts back to Kansas with your tail between your legs."

A tall, gangly kid beside me said, "But I ain't from Kansas."

Sergeant Donovan's face looked like it was going to explode. The Smokey-the-Bear hat perched on his head vibrated as if it were experiencing its own personal earthquake.

The drill sergeant ran with short, choppy strides until the brim of his hat was pressed against the poor guy's nose. He yelled, "Who told you it was okay to speak, you maggot? When I'm talking, the only part of your body that needs to do anything is your ears. Have you got me, String Bean?"

The terrified recruit swallowed hard. "Yes, sir. I just thought you thought I was from—"

Drill Sergeant Donovan growled. "You *thought* that I thought? What kind of slop did your momma pour inside your head where your brain is supposed to be? When it's time for you to think, I'll order you to think. Is that clear?"

"Yes, sir."

"And don't ever call me sir again, Private Brain-dump. I work for a living. Have you got that?"

The poor boy trembled in his shoes. "Yes, sir. I mean . . . yes, Drill Sergeant."

Sergeant Donovan kept yelling the rest of the evening, and I wondered if he'd teach *us* to yell like that for hours on end.

When he finally let us go to bed, I climbed onto the top bunk, above the recruit who'd been the drill sergeant's target most of the night. I whispered, "I'm Jimmy."

He looked around as if Sergeant Donovan was going to pop out of one of our wall lockers at any minute. "I'm Willy Williams, and I'm from Rock Hill."

I hung over the edge of the upper bunk and extended my hand, just like the preacher had taught me. "Nice to meet you, Willy. Jimmy Grossmann from Sumter."

Chapter 4

Gird Your Loins

Ephesians 6:13–17 NASB
"Therefore, take up the full armor of God, so that you will be able to resist in the evil day, and having done everything, to stand firm. Stand firm therefore, having girded your loins with truth, and having put on the breastplate of righteousness, and having shod your feet with the preparation of the gospel of peace; in addition to all, taking up the shield of faith with which you will be able to extinguish all the flaming arrows of the evil one. And take the helmet of salvation, and the sword of the Spirit, which is the Word of God."

* * *

The next morning of my life began one of the busiest days I'd ever experience. We showered, shaved, ate breakfast, got our heads buzzed, and got yelled at—all in the first two hours. What happened next was unforgettable.

We marched about a mile to a warehouse, where we stood in line and received what the Army called our "initial issue." Prior to that day, I'd never worn new clothes. Before going to live with the preacher, I'd worn only hand-me-downs from my brother, Billy. While I was living with the preacher, I wore clothes donated by members of the church. I guess the Army had plenty of money for new clothes because I was issued four camouflage uniforms, six pairs of socks and underwear, two hats, and two pairs of brand-new boots.

When they asked me what size shoes I wore, I just shrugged, and that earned me five minutes of yelling, but I didn't care. I kept my mouth shut and took the verbal beating. Five minutes later, for the first time in my life, my feet slid into a pair of boots nobody else had ever worn, and I couldn't stop smiling.

While we were there, they measured us for what would become our Class A dress uniform, and gave every one of us a brand-new pair of the shiniest black shoes I'd ever seen. I remember thinking I'd never have to buy clothes of my own as long as I stayed in the Army, and for a kid like me, I couldn't think of any reason I'd ever leave the Army. They fed and housed me, cut my hair, gave me clothes, and paid me, all at the same time.

We shoved our new clothes into a green duffle bag and marched back to the barracks, where Sergeant Donovan taught us how to fold, roll, hang, and situate everything in our wall lockers. He only yelled at us a couple of times during the whole thing, and to me, that was a victory. Throughout the whole ordeal, my buddy, Willy, never left my side, and he didn't say a word.

After everything was put away into its rightful place, the drill sergeant stood erect and scanned the barracks with a disapproving eye. Then, he lost his mind. For five minutes, he flipped over bunks and wall lockers, filled trashcans with water from the shower, and threw them down what had been the well-organized squad bays. When he was finished, the place looked like a hurricane had blown through, and I didn't have any idea what made him do that.

As he stomped out the door, he yelled, "You bunch of un-grateful little girls better have this squad bay squared away and your butts downstairs and in formation, looking like soldiers in ten minutes, or I'm going to throw every one of you out those windows and see how high you bounce!"

Willy looked down at me and put on half a grin. "I guess he wanted us to thank him for the new duds, huh?"

I said, "I guess so."

The platoon learned a valuable lesson that day: It's impossible to clean a demolished squad bay, put on a uniform, and be downstairs in ten minutes. I may not have aced the ASVAB, but I was smart enough to know that lesson in time management wouldn't be our last.

After a good yelling and a few hundred push-ups, we marched back to the supply warehouse for round two of our initial issue. The yelling ceased during the time they handed out our gear, and I received my first helmet, rucksack, poncho, canteen, entrenching tool, shelter half, and everything else a brand-new soldier would need for boot camp. I'll never know how many thousands of dollars' worth of gear the Army would eventually issue me or how much they'd spend training me to become the warrior I am now, but I pray the American taxpayers got their money's worth out of me.

When I think back on that first official day of Army training, I can hardly imagine how green I once was. Sergeant Donovan taught us how to use, clean, and maintain every piece of gear they issued us as if we were his own children. The yelling got our attention, but his obviously sincere desire to turn us into soldiers shone through, even when we thought he hated every one of us.

That gear the Army issued to Willy and me never saw actual combat, but the same wasn't true for the two of us. We'd see more than our share, and neither of us would ever forget the lessons Drill Sergeant Donovan taught us back there at Fort Benning. I often think about that day when we were given the tools we needed to become soldiers, and it reminds me of the incredible gifts God lays at our feet without us being smart enough to thank him for them. God doesn't storm out of the room and yell at us, even though we deserve it sometimes. He gently nudges us toward our destiny, slowly equipping us with everything we'll need along the way.

I'm thankful for everything the Army gave and taught me, but when I sit alone on a quiet evening, staring out over a river or the ocean, I sometimes feel a little tear fall from my eye when I try to thank God for every gift I didn't understand and took for granted along the way. He gives us everything we need, but not everything we think we need. I've learned the same lesson Willy Williams learned that first night at boot camp: shut up, listen, and be thankful.

Willy and I fought a lot of battles together in those early Army days. Most of the hardships we endured were self-induced, and just like God teaches us every day, we learned to rely on each other when the guns pointed at us outnumbered the ones pointed back at our enemies.

This part is going to sound boastful, but please don't take it that way. I'm telling you about the rifle range because an enormous part of my identity would be forged behind a rifle, and those early days on the range bear a mention. I'd shot squirrels and rabbits with the preacher, but that was done so we'd have something to eat when I was growing up. When Sergeant Donovan marched us to the range for our first day of live-fire training, Willy and I put a little metaphorical distance between ourselves and the rest of the pack. The orphan boys from South Carolina could shoot. The M16 felt like an extension of my own body when I pulled it to my shoulder for the first time, and there was little doubt that I could do things with a rifle that most people thought impossible. It wasn't because of any particular ability I brought to the party that made me a marksman of the highest order. I've always believed it was one of God's gifts I happened to receive, and I took that gift to mean I was doing exactly what I'd been put on the planet to do.

When we finished basic training and advanced individual training, eighteen of the fifty soldiers in our platoon packed up everything we owned and moved across the base to the 1st Battalion, 507th Parachute Infantry Regiment, to begin the Basic Airborne Course, commonly referred to as Jump School. It took three weeks for us to shed the awful moniker of "Leg" and become parachute-qualified airborne soldiers.

Ground week consisted of a lot of running, push-ups, sit-ups, mountain climbers, and every other physical exercise the cadre could dream up. We practiced jumping out of a mock-up of an airplane door from a 10-meter platform and learned to deal with slamming our bodies into the earth a lot faster than most people think. We trained on the lateral drift apparatus to learn what to do when the wind had creative ideas about what to do with a bunch of soldiers falling from the sky.

Tower week was a little more fun, but they still pushed us pretty hard. We learned and mastered the mass-exit concept on the 10-meter tower, had a blast on the swing landing trainer, and felt like kids at the carnival when they hauled us up the 76-meter free tower. With that training in the books, Willy and I were ready to take the first airplane ride of our lives.

I wasn't scared. I'd found my home, and I loved everything about the Army. I'd done more in five months in the Army than I'd done in the seventeen years before reaching Fort Benning combined. Our first jump was called a "Hollywood Jump," meaning we didn't carry anything except two parachutes. We were jumping the old T-10 round chutes back then, and we thought they were state-of-the-art, but airborne equipment has come a long way since those days. The jump was exhilarating and absolutely the best thing I'd ever done. I hit the ground like a sack of potatoes, and Willy thudded in right beside me. Four jumps later, Willy and I were airborne-qualified Infantrymen.

Just like the equipment and uniforms the Army issued us, the skills we added to our résumés were piling up for the two of us. Both Willy and I would soon learn we'd completed the easiest training we'd ever receive as American soldiers. What lay ahead of us would turn two poor boys from way down yonder in the land of cotton, into hardened men of action, heated in the fires of training and hammered on the anvils of combat, until we were the razor's edge, the tip of the spear in America's battle to preserve freedom and defend the way of life our countrymen and women had come to love.

Chapter 5

RIP Doesn't Always Mean Rest in Peace

Galatians 5:22–23 NASB

"But the fruit of the Spirit is love, joy, peace, patience, kindness, goodness, faithfulness, gentleness, self-control;"

* * *

I can't honestly say I knew what a Ranger was the day I graduated Jump School, but that was only days away from changing forever. Forty-eight hours after I earned my jump wings, the Army moved me back across Fort Benning to the Ranger Indoctrination Program. Since then, that program has become the Ranger Assessment and Selection Program, but when I attended the course, it was still RIP.

Becoming a Ranger was less about my physical fitness or competency of my skills required of my MOS, but far more about the Ranger mindset. No one made it to RIP without being in the best shape of his life and having mastered the required skills of his job in the Army. That doesn't mean we weren't pushed beyond our physical limits and tested to extremes in our ability to soldier, but most of all, I learned to think like a Ranger—like a professional member of the Special Operations Community during my time at RIP. I ran countless miles, fired seemingly endless rounds of ammunition, and got less sleep than any other period of my life. But the thing that will forever be ingrained inside my psyche is the Ranger Creed.

Recognizing that I volunteered as a Ranger, fully knowing the hazards of my chosen profession, I will always endeavor to uphold the prestige, honor, and high esprit-de-corps of the Rangers.

Acknowledging the fact that a Ranger is a more elite soldier who arrives at the cutting edge of battle by land, sea, or air, I accept the fact that as a Ranger my country expects me to move further, faster, and fight harder than any other soldier.

Never shall I fail my comrades. I will always keep myself mentally alert, physically strong, and morally straight, and I will shoulder more than my share of the task, whatever it may be, one hundred percent and then some.

Gallantly will I show the world that I am a specially selected and well-trained soldier. My courtesy to superior officers, neatness of dress, and care of equipment shall set the example for others to follow.

Energetically will I meet the enemies of my country. I shall defeat them on the field of battle for I am better trained and will fight with all my might. Surrender is not a Ranger word. I will never leave a fallen comrade to fall into the hands of the enemy and under no circumstances will I ever embarrass my country.

Readily will I display the intestinal fortitude required to fight on to the Ranger objective and complete the mission, though I be the lone survivor.

Rangers lead the way!

Sometimes, words are just words and nothing more, but there are times in life when we devote ourselves to something noble, something truly meaningful, that can make mere words take on a life and a depth of their own. For me, the Ranger Creed fell solidly into that category of words. They weren't just a memorization exercise. They were a foundation for the warrior I would become. They made me accountable to the thousands of men who'd worn the beret before me, and especially to those who would follow in my footsteps.

The devotion to the Ranger way reminded me of the commitment the Trappist monks made to their God, their brothers, and their monastery. Their whole lives were spent in service to God above and their fellow man. Such devotion is rare, and is often the punchline of jokes made by men who rarely accomplish anything meaningful and whose minds are too blind to see and respect true dedication and self-sacrifice.

I would never take an oath that conflicted with my Christian faith, but I came to believe that living by the Ranger Creed was an extension of my faith and responsibility to both God and my brothers.

* * *

Willy broke a few of the small bones in the top of his foot during RIP, so I graduated without him, but our time together was far from over. He recycled back two classes and finally completed Ranger Indoctrination two months after me. Other than the color of our skin, Willy and I didn't look much alike until we donned those black berets. In uniform, we could stare at each other as if we were looking into a mirror. Although neither of us had tasted the sting of combat yet, both of us knew we could put our lives in each other's hands without hesitation.

Little did we know that we would do exactly that too many times to count.

Having a two-month head start in the 3rd Battalion, 75th Ranger Regiment, gave me time to get a taste of what the real Army was like outside of a formal training environment, and I couldn't wait to see my old friend again.

The day Willy arrived at the 3rd Battalion, my platoon sergeant ordered me to take the new kid for a five-mile run and push him as hard as I could.

"Your run time better impress the crap out of me, Grossmann."

Impressing Sergeant Spellman wasn't possible, but I was determined to avoid disappointing him. I got Willy settled in the barracks and broke the news about the run.

"Let's go," he said. "And Jimmy . . . try to keep up."

His long legs left me pumping four strides to his three, but I didn't hold him back.

When we got back to the squad room, I told Sergeant Spellman, "Thirty-three oh eight, Sergeant."

He raised an eyebrow. "Not bad. Now, go see how fast you can do it in tennis shoes."

Willy and I deflated as we looked down at our running shoes.

I sighed. "That *was* in tennis shoes, Sergeant."

Sergeant Spellman shook his head. "I guess that means you're wearing running shoes when we go to war. Is that right, Private Grossmann?"

We ran the five-miler again, this time in our combat boots, and our time wasn't nearly as impressive.

I introduced Willy around, and for the first time since we'd been sworn in together at Fort Jackson, he and I had time to relax and swap stories.

"I guess you know it already," he began, "but my dad's in

prison, and I don't know where my mom is. She left when I was a kid. I ain't never had no real parents, and nobody wanted to adopt a kid like me. I done most of my growin' up in an orphanage, when I wasn't in some foster home where the folks were just using me to get a check."

I twisted a rag around my finger and dipped it into the can of black polish before making tiny circles on the hard leather of my boot. "Yeah, I knew about the orphanages, but I didn't know about your dad. Sorry 'bout that, man. It must've been tough."

He shrugged and slugged my arm. "It don't much matter now. We're in the Rangers, boy. Who would've ever believed two kids like us would end up as Rangers? Can you believe it?"

I inspected the emerging shine on my boot. "It's what God wants us to be. He made it happen."

Willy threw up his hands. "What? God wasn't the one running his ass off and doing push-ups 'til the ground caved in. That was us, man. We did this. And we've got a lot to be proud of."

I gave him a smile and smeared a stripe of polish down the laces of his boot.

He jerked it away. "Hey, man. That ain't cool. Now I'm going get that stuff all over my hands every time I tie my boot."

I chuckled. "I don't think anybody's going to notice."

We polished and talked for most of an hour until Willy asked, "When do you think we'll get a deployment?"

I buffed the toe of my boot. "Who knows? We've still got a lot to learn before we're ready to fight."

"Not me," he said. "I'm ready now."

"We'll see about that. We're spending all of next week on the range. What do you say we make it interesting? Whoever shoots the worst has to shine the other one's boots all month."

He stuck out his hand. "You're on, Jimmy. Get ready to polish, loser."

I leaned back in my chair and unconsciously began humming an old Southern Baptist hymn, and Willy perked up. "Hey, I know that one. One of the foster families I lived with for a while was real religious and made me go to church all the time. The only part I liked was the singing. Can you sing, Jimmy?"

"Everybody can sing," I said. "But most people sing like you polish boots . . . nasty and ugly."

"I'll show you nasty and ugly," he said. "Go ahead. Kick it off, and I'll fall in with you."

I tapped my foot and cleared my throat. As promised, Willy jumped in, and it wasn't long before seven or eight more Rangers jumped on the gospel music train with us.

We sang until Willy stood up and waved a hand toward the group. "That's enough of that church stuff for me. Y'all go ahead. I'm out."

I was torn. Willy was my best friend in the Army and in the world. I didn't like seeing him run away from God. We'd been through a lot of training to get us ready to go someplace and fight, and although I didn't know much about anything back then, I was smart enough to know some of us wouldn't always come home from combat. The thought of Willy's soul not spending eternity in Heaven made me feel like I'd been kicked in the gut.

I couldn't drag my best friend to Heaven with me. He had to make that decision on his own, but just like I'd vowed to fight for my country and live up to my responsibilities to the Army, I made the same vow to God. It wasn't my place to judge Willy or anybody else, but it was my ultimate responsibility to show him how powerful God's love could be. There was only one way to do that. I had to let him see how my relationship with God made my life so much fuller than a life without Him could ever be.

Chapter 6
A Higher Calling

Mark 1:3–7 NASB

"The voice of one crying in the wilderness, 'Make ready the way of the Lord, Make His paths straight.' John the Baptist appeared in the wilderness preaching a baptism of repentance for the forgiveness of sins. And all the country of Judea was going out to him, and all the people of Jerusalem; and they were being baptized by him in the Jordan River, confessing their sins. John was clothed with camel's hair and wore a leather belt around his waist, and his diet was locusts and wild honey. And he was preaching, and saying, 'After me, One is coming who is mightier than I, and I am not fit to stoop down and untie the thong of His sandals.'"

* * *

I liked everything about the Army. What's not to like? But that fateful morning showed me the thing I would love the most about being in uniform.

We had PT, but it was light. We only ran two miles and pushed through two cycles of push-ups, sit-ups, and pull-ups. Morning chow was quick but good. During my years in the Army, I never had a bad meal in garrison. There were times when we were down-range in some country nobody can spell and I had to eat whatever I could find. Maybe that's where I came to understand why John the Baptist liked wild honey and locusts, but as long as we were home, the food was excellent.

Willy and I were assigned to a weapons team. That meant we got to shoot everything that goes boom, and I was in Heaven on Earth. I fell in love with every weapon system I touched, and Willy was right there with me.

That particular morning, Sergeant Spellman called us to attention and briefed the plan of the day. "Good morning, ladies. I hope you got plenty of beauty sleep last night because there won't be much of that this week. It's time to break in the new kids on our block and see if any of them can actually shoot without killing their battle buddy."

He described what we'd do on the first day of range week, and I felt like a kid headed to the county fair. As excited as I was about shooting for five days, I discovered that our platoon sergeant knew far more about us than we knew about him.

He gave the order to set the platoon in motion.

"Forward . . . march!"

"Column right . . . march."

"Forward . . . march."

"Double time . . . march."

The command of double time to a Ranger platoon is like gasoline on a fire. Running is engrained in us, and the pace came easily and comfortably.

Sergeant Spellman kept us in time by singing the "C-130 Rolling Down the Strip" cadence as we ran. There was always something about singing cadence that made running in formation a lot more fun.

Just as everyone was settling in for the long run, Sergeant

Spellman yelled, "Private Grossmann! You like to sing, so get out here, Singer."

That's the instant I became Singer, but now that I'm a lot older and not running in formation anymore, everybody thinks I got the nickname because I sing old Southern Baptist hymns when I'm sniping. I suppose there's no harm in folks believing that.

My baritone was at least an octave lower than Sergeant Spellman's voice, but nobody complained, and from that day on, if the platoon was running, I was singing.

It was three miles to the range, but we were having such a good time, I ran that platoon right past our destination and added an extra mile to the trip. After all, Rangers lead the way.

We were still using Vietnam-era M16s back then, and that rifle felt like an old friend. It seemed to love being in my hands as much as I loved cradling it, and I treated it like it was made of pure gold. Precision-shooting was second nature for Willy and me. Something in our heads gave us the ability to turn off the distractions of the world and drive lead through targets as if there were nothing else except bullseyes. I loved the smell, the feel of the recoil against my shoulder, and most of all, I loved the sound. The buffer spring in the stock of an M16 makes a sound like nothing else on Earth, and to me and Willy, that sound meant that a bullet had just cut another hole in the ten-ring.

What I didn't know back then was how I would feel when my targets weren't made of paper, but flesh, bone, blood, and souls. Nobody is prepared for their first kill. Nobody. God knows that I, a nine-year-old boy named Jimmy Grossmann in a trailer in South Carolina, wasn't ready when I had to stop my father from killing my brother. My M16 didn't look or feel like my father's 20-gauge, but every time I pulled the trigger, I thought about Billy living in silence in that monastery on the Cooper River.

We shot thousands of rounds that week, and with every new

challenge, Willy and I rose to the top of the heap. Our scores mirrored each other's every step of the way, and I'll always believe he was rooting for me just as much as I was hoping he'd never miss a shot.

On the 300- to 500-meter pop-up range, we were shooting at torso-sized targets that popped up randomly in a fan of thirty degrees in front of us. They told us we'd get fifty targets, and the minimum standard was thirty hits on target. I guess that was the Army's version of whack-a-mole, and Willy and I won the big teddy bears.

I didn't count the targets. I just kept shooting until I'd burned through four 20-round magazines. I hadn't missed any targets, but I'd fired eighty shots. Math, as you may remember, was my strong suit, so I gave my surroundings a quick check and discovered that Willy and I were the only two Rangers still firing. Everybody else, including the range safety officers and Sergeant Spellman, was gathered around and watching the shoot-off between the two orphan kids from South Carolina.

Realizing I'd taken my eyes off the range for an instant, I rushed to get my head back in the game. I wasn't interested in polishing Willy's boots for a month. The targets kept coming, and we kept shooting. Every time the bolt locked to the rear in my rifle, I thumbed the magazine release, dropping the spent mag to the dirt, and shoved a fresh one into the well. After six magazines and 120 targets, I dropped the empty mag and reached for a fresh one, but my pouch was dry.

I turned to see Willy reaching for his seventh magazine and finding nothing but air. I was relieved he was out also of ammo, but as if they were falling from the heavens, full magazines of 5.56mm ammunition landed all around us. The whole platoon was throwing mags at us as if we were there solely for their entertainment. I grabbed a mag and shoved it home, slapped the bolt release, and stuck my head back in the sights. The target came, and I put it down. When that magazine ran dry, I dropped it and grabbed another, but Sergeant Spellman yelled, "Cease fire! Cease fire! That's enough, ladies."

Willy later admitted he'd expected applause, but that thought never entered my mind. We spent the rest of the week on the range shooting everything from the M60 machine gun to the Beretta M9. We even got an introduction to the Mk 19 grenade launcher, and I fell in love all over again.

When the week was over, we cleaned weapons until we were covered in bore cleaner and gun oil.

Willy sidled up beside me with an M60 in his arms and said, "Hey, Singer. I want you to meet my new girlfriend. I think I'm gonna marry her. She kicks like a mule, but she's fun to dance with."

I chuckled and made room for him on the bench. "She's a lucky girl. I think I'll ask that Mark Nineteen to the prom."

"Good choice," he said. "Do you think the guys in the regular Army get to shoot as much as we do in the Rangers?"

Our squad leader said, "No, not nearly as much. I was in the hundred and first at Fort Campbell for two years before going to Ranger School. You boys shot more this week than those guys'll shoot all year."

"Hundred and first," Willy said. "That's the Screaming Eagles, right?"

"Yeah, that's right. I kept begging and begging to go to Airborne School, but they're air assault guys at Campbell. I had to volunteer for the Ranger Battalion and go to Ranger School before I finally got a slot at Jump School."

"Is it as tough as they say?" I asked.

The squad leader furrowed his brow. "What? Ranger School? Hell yeah, it's hard. You'll see. Indoctrination is a cakewalk compared to Ranger School, but you guys'll make it. You're doing the right stuff. Just don't get distracted. Keep your heads down, listen, and learn everything you can from everybody who's willing to teach. Have either of you thought about putting in for Sniper School?"

Willy and I looked at each other as if the other knew something. Finally, he said, "We both like to shoot, but I figured you guys would pick the soldiers to go to schools like sniper training. I didn't know we could put in for it."

He chuckled and motioned toward the pile of rifle parts scattered on the bench. "Put that thing back together, give it a good function check, and go talk to some of the guys on the sniper team. They'll tell you about it. If you want to go, come tell me, and I'll send it up the chain."

Willy's eyes nearly popped out of his head. "Are you serious?"

Before our squad leader could answer, I said, "I want to go. In fact, I want to go to every school you'll send me to."

He pointed at me. "And that's why you're going to be a Ranger for life, Grossmann. Keep it up, and you'll be a squad leader before you know it."

I reassembled the rifle I'd cleaned, and Willy and I ambled over to the tree line, where the sniper team was gathered around a staff sergeant I didn't know. He was teaching some kind of class about maps under the shade of a few thousand Georgia pines. Neither Willy nor I said a word. We just stood behind the snipers and listened.

Finally, the sergeant looked up and paused. "Are you two the ones who put on that pop-up-target clinic?"

Willy nodded. "Yes, Sergeant. That's us."

He motioned to his left. "Take a knee, guys. You might learn something."

We followed his instructions and soaked in every word. He

talked about how to pick stalking routes using terrain features for cover and concealment.

When he was finished, he glanced at Willy. "You guys know what stalking is, right?"

Willy nodded vigorously. "Oh, yeah. Of course."

I shook my head in silence.

The sergeant said, "That's what I thought. Why don't the two of you go with Mitchell and Franklin? They'll show you a few things."

We spent the rest of the afternoon with Corporal Mitchell and Specialist Franklin, drinking in every word that came out of their mouths. As the sun dipped over Alabama and Fort Benning turned dark, I knew without a doubt I'd do everything possible to get into Sniper School.

Chapter 7
Soldier of the Year

Judges 7:5–7 NASB

"So he brought the people down to the water. And the Lord said to Gideon, 'You shall separate everyone who laps the water with his tongue as a dog laps, as well as everyone who kneels to drink.' Now the number of those who lapped, putting their hand to their mouth, was 300 men; but all the rest of the people kneeled to drink water. The Lord said to Gideon, 'I will deliver you with the 300 men who lapped and will give the Midianites into your hands; so let all the other people go, each man to his home.'"

* * *

Well-adjusted, popular, lovingly nurtured kids don't often thrive in the Ranger Battalion, but those aren't qualities I had to worry about overcoming. If I were going to adjust, I would've been forced throughout my teenage years to accept the fact that watching my father kill my mother, mute my brother, and die by my hand were normal scenarios in the life of a nine-year-old boy. Popular would've meant that I played football or basketball for the high school team and that I dated a cheerleader or two along the way. I didn't play much of anything in my formative years. There was little time for such trivial endeavors in the preacher's house. We worked the small, sandy farm that was little more than an over-sized garden and a ramshackle frame house in the flatlands of central South Carolina. If the sun was up, we were working. If the sun was on the other side of the world, we were sleeping or reading the Bible by a coal-oil lamp. There were no cheerleaders in my past, and I didn't see any in my future, either.

The boys who made the cut and found their first real home in the Ranger Regiment had a lot of things in common with Willy and me. Don't get me wrong. We had a few quarterbacks and kids from loving, normal homes, but those of us who made the Rangers our family because we didn't have one of our own, stood out, while the Mr. Popularities faded into the crowd.

I could sing, shoot, and PT with the best Rangers in the regiment. Those were the elements of my character that put me at the position of attention in full-dress uniform in front of three officers and seven senior NCOs on a day that would carve out a niche for me for the rest of my life.

I'd been in the Army just over two years, never failed to max out my PT scores, never shot lower than expert on any weapon system, and I'd been to every school my unit offered when the first full-bird colonel I'd ever met said, "Specialist Grossmann, front and center."

I stepped back and marched my way behind and around the nine other soldiers standing at rigid attention beside me. I locked my heels, saluted, and reported squarely in front of the colonel. He returned my salute and almost grinned, but he fought it off. Instead, he motioned with his head for me to center myself in front of the board of officers and NCOs instead of him. I didn't fully understand the reason, but I obeyed his silent command and repositioned.

In a commanding voice I assumed the Army issued him at the

U.S. Military Academy at West Point, he said, "Congratulations, Specialist Jimmy Grossmann. You're the Seventy-Fifth Ranger Regiment Soldier of the Year."

In a rare demonstration of breaking military bearing, the men on the board, including the colonel, clapped their hands before they wore smiles of pride and appreciation. I didn't want their round of applause. I remember wishing it could've been Willy standing there instead of me. He wanted and needed that applause. I just wanted to be the best soldier I could be for my country and for my God.

They took pictures of me shaking hands and smiling, but none of that made me better prepared for combat. They put my name in the base newspaper and posted one of the pictures on the wall in regimental headquarters, but the real reward, at least in my opinion, came inside the small, humble office of my company commander later that day.

The captain slid a stapled stack of papers across his desk. "Congratulations, Singer. You made us look good, and that goes a long way in today's Army."

I nodded. "Thank you, sir."

"No, son. Thank you. Now, take those orders and hand them out. The one at the bottom of the stack is yours."

I scooped up the stack and thumbed through the orders until I found my name beneath a stripe of yellow highlighter and followed by the words: " . . . is ordered to report to the United States Army Sniper Course."

As excited as I was, I frantically scanned the list of names until my eyes fell on the one name I wanted to see more than my own— Specialist Willy Williams.

I closed my eyes and silently thanked God for giving me *and* Willy the one thing we wanted more than anything else in the world.

The captain leaned back in his chair. "I know you're a deeply religious man, Grossmann, but God didn't sign those orders. The colonel did, and you earned them. You should be proud of yourself."

I smiled without meaning to. "Pride gets a lot of good soldiers killed, sir. I'm just honored to have the opportunity and blessed to be in a position to use the gifts God gave me to serve my country."

The captain laughed. "How many times did you practice that response?"

Recognizing the moment of levity, I said, "There was no practice, sir. I just shot from the hip in a very un-sniperly fashion."

"Un-sniperly," he said. "Now, that's funny. Get out of here, Corporal. You've got a lot of school ahead of you and a bunch of packing to do."

I frowned at my commanding officer. "I'm not a corporal, sir."

He pulled another stapled stack from his desk. "Sure you are. Otherwise, I couldn't send you to Ranger School. You're going to Sniper School, PLDC, and then Ranger School. If you survive all of that, you'll come back to us as a tabbed, Ranger-qualified sniper with sergeant stripes in your near future. Now, get out of here. I've got work to do."

My platoon sergeant and I came to attention, performed an about-face, and marched from the commander's office.

In the hallway, I said, "Thank you for this, Sergeant. It means a lot to me."

He threw an arm around me. "Don't thank me, Singer. The Army didn't give you anything except an opportunity. You earned everything else. If you're half the soldier under fire as you are in peacetime, I'd be proud to have you in my foxhole any day."

I froze where I stood, almost trembling in disbelief. My platoon sergeant—a battle-hardened, highly decorated, no-nonsense

Ranger of the highest order—had just given me the greatest compliment any Ranger could receive, and I was dumbfounded.

For some reason—I'll always believe it was God's will—I was chosen to become more than an orphaned son raised by a poor country preacher and his gentle wife, more than the sibling of a damaged, mute older brother, more than what I could make of myself alone. I was chosen to become a warrior—a protector and harvester of human lives. I was chosen to be a quiet, sometimes-silent professional with the ability to pluck souls from their mortal shells on the battlefield. Only God knows why, but I would go on to become a sniper revered by my colleagues and feared by my enemies, but no matter what I became by my own actions or the actions of others, I would never be worthy of the love God pours out on me daily, and I would certainly never deserve the loving forgiveness Christ gave me when his life's blood poured from his torn and tattered earthly body on the cross at Golgotha.

* * *

The captain hadn't been exactly right. PLDC, the Army Primary Leadership Development Course, came first, so I went to Sniper School with corporal's stripes on my uniform instead of specialist rank. There was no additional pay, but being a non-commissioned officer—an NCO—somehow made me feel like a more meaningful part of the Army.

Six soldiers from my company loaded up our gear and rode in the back of a two-and-a-half-ton truck, called a deuce-and-a-half, across the base to reception at the Sniper Course. The next seven weeks of our lives would be spent learning more about rifles, scopes, and ballistics than our brains could hold, but that was only one small part of the course. We learned to build hides, move silently without being seen, and identify targets other's eyes would never pick up.

The Bible tells us to be constantly in prayer, and although that isn't humanly possible, since I was around fourteen, I've done my best to stay in a conversation with God as much as I could. We all have to sleep, but the quiet, peaceful moments just before dozing off have always been precious to me. It was inside those moments when I felt closest to God. The worries and concerns of the world fade away, and my mind and body slow down until communion with God feels truly intimate. I've come to love those moments, but Sniper School robbed me of those treasured times, and I struggled with that fact.

We trained so hard, and the instructors flooded our minds with more information than was possible to digest. For the first time in my Army career, I felt truly challenged. Everything had come so easily to me in those first two years of service. Sure, the schools were physically demanding, but at eighteen, our bodies are almost bulletproof. I had the intestinal fortitude to grind my way through the physicality, but the concepts and philosophy of sniping were more complex than anything I'd ever experienced. Instead of talking with God, I spent every night with my eyes drinking in every word of the training manuals, ballistic data, and techniques of master snipers who'd come before me, and those long, challenging nights of study ended with my mind's need for rest, consuming my body and forcing me into sleep—often with a training manual lying across my chest.

I worried about losing touch with God. I still prayed, of course, but not like I had in years past. When we go without food for hours or days on end, our bodies cry out with hunger, and fatigue tries to overcome us. That's how my spirit felt as I replaced the time I'd usually spent with God with time spent learning my new craft. When a soldier's body breaks, he goes to the medic, but when his soul breaks, the only physician he can turn to is God. I would've gone to the chaplain if there had been time, but every moment of my life was consumed by Sniper School. Spiritual healing came from the most unlikely place.

A ghillie suit is a strange thing. It's a kind of loose-fitting mesh outer garment with strips of burlap, twine, and local foliage designed to make a sniper blend seamlessly into his environment. The morning we were issued our ghillie suits, an instructor named Sergeant First Class Clark Johnson stood in front of the class with his ghillie draped across the lectern. As he lectured about the merits and proper use of the suit, it was as if he were speaking directly to me.

"When you get in theater, you *must*—get that—I said *must* take the time to climatize your ghillie suit. That doesn't mean leaving it outside to get used to the temperature. It means ignoring everything else that distracts you while you focus on the one thing that will make you invisible. The one thing that will keep you alive. The one thing that will allow you to complete your mission and save the lives of your teammates. I don't care if the rest of your team is smoking and joking, playing cards, calling home, whatever. You *will* be in the mud and the rain and the trees and grass, and you *will* make your ghillie look like the environment you'll be operating in. It's worth ignoring all the other important stuff to temporarily focus on blending into your environment. That other stuff will be there when you get back, but this suit . . ." He held up his worn, ugly ghillie. "This suit will make your higher purpose possible, so listen to me when I tell you this. *Make* the time to climatize your ghillie."

I would come to know Sergeant Clark Johnson and work alongside him on more missions than I could count, but in that first meeting, that baby-faced, hardcore Ranger made me understand that priorities have to change from time to time, and the really important things will always be there when you get back.

Suddenly, my soul sighed. God had a plan for my life. He knew what He needed from me, and He knew I had a lot of work to do in preparation for His higher purpose. My faith remained solid. My resolve remained unbreakable. And my purpose remained steadfast. I was temporarily in an environment that required my mortal attention so I could develop the knowledge and skill to become the best I could be, and God was unwavering. I believe He understood that I had to study and devote myself to learning to become what He needed me to be. God is Faithful—with a capital F—but not like people are faithful. I've had friends and fellow soldiers who were faithful and loyal enough to put themselves in harm's way to protect me. That's love and a conscious choice. I've been injured to the point of accepting that my life on Earth had reached its mortal end, but men I fought beside, trusted, and loved fought against unimaginable, perilous resistance to get to me and carry me out of the fight. Those people were brave, strong, and faithful because they cared about me. We were on the same team. We were men of valor, brothers-in-arms, and I deeply value their friendship and loyalty, but that selfless devotion to a brother, to a friend, to a fellow fighter, is empty and hollow when held up next to what Christ did for every soul who will ever live.

He sacrificed himself in a way none of us could withstand, in a manner of death so horrible that even the men who loved Him most—the disciples who'd walked beside Him as He preached, taught, healed, and performed countless miracles—turned their backs on Him, denied knowing Him, and one even sold Him out for thirty pieces of silver. Christ came as a mortal man and made the ultimate sacrifice for billions of people who would despise Him, mock Him, and even those who'd claim He never existed. He paid a price none of us could, and He did it because He loved everyone who'd ever lived and who would ever draw a breath. It's easy to love people who love us, but how many of us are willing to endure ultimate torture and agonizing death for those who hate, loathe, and deny us? That's what Christ did. That's what true love does.

So, I sacrificed some precious time I should've spent with God, but in those hours, I built a foundation on which my career would stand. As the final exercise of the class unfolded before us, I crawled over half a mile through rattlesnake-infested piney fields, at a painfully slow pace, until I was within a hundred yards of eight instructors, including SFC Johnson, and made a killing shot on a target without any of the instructors seeing me. Willy and I were the only two of the six soldiers from our company who completed the course, but I was fortunate to be the honor graduate. In those seven weeks, I learned that shooting was not instinctual. It was scientific. I learned I could move undetected in the environment of my choosing. And I learned God would be waiting patiently for me when I came out the other side.

Chapter 8
Roman Lions

Matthew 11:28–30 NASB
*"Come to Me, all who are weary and heavy-laden, and I will give
you rest. Take My yoke upon you and learn from Me, for I am
gentle and humble in heart, and you will find rest for your souls.
For My yoke is easy and My burden is light."*

* * *

Immediately following graduation from Sniper School, Sergeant
First Class Clark Johnson caught me in the hallway and shoved me
against the wall. My initial reaction was to fight back, but an instant later, the realization that I was about to learn something
more important than everything I'd learned in the past seven
weeks hit me a lot harder than Sergeant Johnson had.

"Look at me," he demanded.

I followed his order.

He pecked the tip of his index finger against my temple. "I
don't know everything that's going on in there, Grossmann, but I
need you to look me in the eye and answer one simple question."

I swallowed hard. "Okay, Sergeant."

If possible, he leaned even closer to my face. "You're one of the best natural shooters I've ever seen, but you've never shot at any-body who's shooting back. You've never looked through your scope and put a man down to keep him from spraying your pla-toon with AK-forty-seven rounds. You've not done that yet."

He paused as if I were supposed to speak, so I said, "None of that is a question, Sergeant."

"No, it's not, but here's the question that you have to answer. I've watched you closer than I've ever watched a student before. There's something different—something special—about you, but you do something most of us don't. You spend a lot of time with your eyes closed and your lips moving. I suspect you're talking to somebody when you do that."

"I'm talking to God when I do that."

"Good. We could all use more of that kind of conversation. But you've got to look me and yourself in the eye and tell me you can press that trigger when the time comes and there's another human being in those crosshairs. I have to know you're not going to go off quoting the Ten Commandments and freeze up when you get to the one about 'thou shall not kill.'"

I drew a long, deep breath. "I don't think that verse means 'thou shall not kill.' If we took that verse literally, we wouldn't be allowed to kill bugs, spiders, snakes, or even germs without com-mitting a sin. I don't think that's what God meant. I think it means commit no murder. The Bible is full of justified killing. David killed Goliath, and the Bible says he was a man after God's own heart. So, yes, Sergeant, I believe I will squeeze the trigger to protect my brothers and stop evil."

He took a step back. "Do you know why I'm here, Corporal Grossmann?"

"To teach me to be a sniper."

He huffed and pulled off his shirt, revealing a massive wound to his left bicep. "No, Grossmann, I'm not here to teach you to be a sniper. I'm here because I got shot in the arm and I'm undeployable until it heals. I'm here killing time while my body heals up enough so I can get back out there and put more bullets in more bad guys."

"I'm sorry about your arm. I'll pray for you."

He grinned, but only with half of his mouth. It was the strangest grin I'd ever seen. "We should all be so lucky to have you praying for us. Where's your Ranger tab?"

"I've not been to Ranger School yet. I only did RIP, but I'm headed there next. I'll get my tab, Sergeant. You can bet on that."

"I know you will." He pulled out his beret from his pocket. "When you get a couple of deployments under your belt and a few notches in your stock, give me a call, and I'll help you trade in the black beret for a green one like mine."

"Special Forces?" I asked with more awe in my voice than I intended.

"Yeah, kid. Special Forces. If you've got the same grit in combat as you've got in training, you've got the goods. Being a Ranger is an honorable thing, but SF is where it's at."

Everybody's heard of the Green Berets, but to me, that path was so far out of reach that I couldn't imagine ever making it to such lofty heights.

Willy pulled me out of my fantasy. "Hey, man. Can you believe it? We're snipers."

I gave him a smile, subconsciously trying to imitate the half-grin SFC Johnson pulled off. "No, dude. We're not snipers yet. We're just sniper qualified. We'll see what the Army does with us now that we've got the school behind us."

"Don't burst my bubble, man."

I shrugged. "Sorry, but have you seen that course list?" I pointed toward a glass-enclosed case, and Willy stepped over to take a look.

He said, "Oh, man. I had no idea there were so many sniper courses. I guess maybe you're right. We've still got a lot to learn."

"I'd say we're going to learn more than we thought possible in Ranger School. We've got four days before we report over there."

Willy let out a sigh. "Do you think it's going to be as tough as they say?"

"We'll see. It's only sixty-one days. We can take anything for sixty-one days."

It wouldn't take long for me to change my opinion.

Phase one of Ranger School took place at Fort Benning, where Willy and I had spent our whole enlistment, and I was starting to wonder if other Army bases really existed. For a Ranger, though, Benning is the center of the universe and the mother of us all. Our first morning there began just like the first day of most schools we'd been through, with one exception . . . I'd never heard an in-structor quote Scripture before.

A stone-faced instructor in a black T-shirt, camouflaged pants, and green jungle boots stood in front of the formation and glared at each of us as if he were going to chew us up and spit us out. After several minutes of posturing and intimidation, he said, "Come to Me, all who are weary and heavy-laden, and I will give you rest. Take My yoke upon you and learn from Me, for I am gentle and humble in heart, and you will find rest for your souls. For My yoke is easy and My burden is light." When he finished, he eyed the formation and spoke barely above a whisper. "Who knows where that's from?"

Several soldiers mumbled, "The Bible."

But I said, "Matthew, chapter eleven, sir."

"Oh, look!" he growled as he ran toward me. "We've got a chaplain in our midst."

He grabbed me by my collar and dragged me to the front of the formation, then he stared down at my name tape. "So, Corporal Grossmann . . . Why don't you tell us what that passage means."

I licked my lips and swallowed the lump in my throat. *Does this guy really want me to explain the verses?*

The instructor held his hands palms up. "Well, Chaplain? Are you going to teach us or not?"

Everything about the situation felt wrong, but I'd never let an opportunity to tell three hundred people about Jesus pass me by.

I cleared my throat. "These are the words of Jesus after He condemns the cities where he taught and performed miracles, but the cities didn't repent."

The instructor took a step back. "You really are a chaplain."

I shook him off. "No, sir. I'm just a Christian."

"Just a Christian?" he roared. "What does that mean? The lions ate a lot of 'just Christians' in the Colosseum."

I was torn. *Should I continue, or stop to join him in the banter?*

I acknowledged his comment, but I didn't respond. Instead, I continued. "The passage you quoted is Jesus's broad invitation to come to him and find comfort and rest."

"Is that what you want, Chaplain Grossmann? Comfort and rest?"

"No, sir. I already have those things with Christ."

He stepped in front of me and whispered, "You can consider me to be one of those Roman lions. Now, get back in formation where you belong, Ranger."

I'll never know what came over me in that moment, but I said, "But I'm not finished teaching from Matthew."

Before that moment, I didn't think it was possible for that instructor to smile, but he did, and apparently, that's exactly what he was hoping I'd say. He took two steps back and pointed at me with both hands. "Our chaplain seems to think his Bible study is more important than Ranger School, so please, regale us with your New Testament wisdom while the rest of us do a few push-ups."

He turned to the formation and yelled, "Get down! Get down and push until Chaplain Grossmann finishes his Sunday school lesson."

No one in the formation believed they wouldn't have to do push-ups at Ranger School, but I never thought I'd be the reason for the first grueling set.

I ripped through the three verses as quickly as I could. "That's all, sir."

As if yelling to the moon, the instructor belted out, "Oh, no, you don't! Keep pushing. I've got questions for our chaplain."

The push-ups continued as I stood there wishing I was anywhere other than that spot while my classmates pushed.

"So, Chaplain, do you think Ranger School is a place all should come for rest?"

"No, sir."

He yelled. "You're right! There's no rest here. I don't care if you're weary or heavy-laden. In fact, you can trust me when I say you're going to know exactly how it feels to be weary and heavy-laden every day for the next two months of your life."

He turned back to the class. "Keep pushing, Rangers. I've got a lot of questions for Grossmann."

He stepped to within inches of my face and yelled, "How about my yoke, Grossmann? Does my yoke look easy to you?"

"No, sir."

"I can't hear you, Grossmann."

"No, sir! It doesn't look easy."

He said, "Take my yoke upon you and learn from me. How about that, Chaplain? How do you feel about that?"

"We're learning from you already," I said.

He grinned and whispered, "You certainly are, but I don't

know about the rest of your Ranger-wannabe buddies whose arms are falling off. What do you think they're learning?"

I bowed my head. "I'm sorry, sir. I didn't—"

"You didn't what, Grossmann? Think? You didn't think before volunteering all your buddies to do push-ups all day?" I shook my head, and he yelled. "Recover! Get on your feet. I'm going to tell you about my burden *and* my yoke." He gave me a shove. "Get back in formation."

When everyone was on their feet again and I was back in my position beside Willy, the instructor said, "Here's my burden, boys and girls. My burden is to turn you into tabbed Rangers, modern warfighting machines, and I take my burden just as seriously as Corporal Grossmann takes his Bible. I'm going to do my job. I'm going to push you harder than you've ever imagined being pushed. I'm going to expect more of you than you've ever expected of yourself, and when this class is over, I'll have my pound of flesh, and I will have turned half of you into real Rangers. The other half will have to spend the rest of their lives dealing with the fact that they're not good enough, hard enough, devoted enough to become Rangers. That's the attrition rate, ladies. Fifty percent. That means the guy beside you ain't gonna be beside you when this is over."

I couldn't help casting my eyes to Willy, and I discovered him looking right back at me.

In unison, we whispered, "I'll be here."

The following five days saw Rangers dropping like flies. Nearly a third of our class was gone at the end of the first week, but Willy and I were still there, still standing right beside each other.

The first phase of training was conducted by the 4th Ranger Training Battalion at Camp Rogers and Camp Darby at Fort Benning. After everyone passed the PT test, we moved on to the water confidence test where we worked through our fear of heights and water—if we had such fears. While remaining calm, we had to walk across a log suspended thirty-five feet above the Victory Pond. Then we transitioned to a rope-crawl before plunging into the water. We then had to jump into the pond and ditch our rifle and load-bearing equipment while submerged. Finally, we climbed a ladder to the top of a seventy-foot tower and slid down to the water on a pulley attached to a suspended cable. At the bottom, we let go and plunged into the pond. A few of us couldn't do it. The fear was just too much. But about ninety percent of us made it through the ordeal, and Willy and I loved every minute of it. For us, it was like a day on the playground.

Next was day and night land navigation. We'd been in the Ranger Regiment for two years, so reading a map and compass was second nature. A few people struggled, but they got a little refresher training from some fellow students, and we proved we could navigate.

We did a two-mile buddy run, and Willy and I finished before everyone else. As a reward for finishing first, the instructors made us do push-ups until every team had crossed the finish line. I'm not sure what we were supposed to learn from that, but I figured I owed the other students a few push-ups after the day-one Bible-study debacle.

Everyone in the class was already airborne qualified, so we did a little airborne refresher training and spent quite a bit of time on explosive demolition. We worked on combatives a lot, and we ended the Benning phase with a twelve-mile forced march in full gear, carrying ninety pounds of equipment. The pace was fast, but for the most part, I loved the action.

I was sore, a little tired, and a lot motivated after the first phase. For the first time since joining the Army, I got to see someplace other than Southwest Georgia. They trucked us to Camp Merrill near Dahlonega, Georgia, and we became the responsibility of the 5th Ranger Training Battalion.

In the Mountain Phase, we learned how to soldier in mountainous terrain. We ran combat control missions while we were tired, hungry, and sleep deprived. We took turns leading the platoon, and I learned more about small-unit tactics than I ever thought I'd know. They pushed us hard, but it was obvious that the instructors wanted to see us succeed in overcoming self-imposed limitations and the mental and physical hardships of operating on less than three hours of sleep every night. It was grueling, but I learned that most of my limitations were psychological and not physical. My body would keep working as long as I had the mental toughness to stay in the fight.

As the mountain training came to a close, we conducted a five-day exercise that included a combat mission against a conventionally equipped force. Just like the rest of the training, the exercise con-tinued around the clock at a relentless pace.

When we'd completed the second phase, they bussed us to an airfield and loaded us onto a C-130 Hercules, and we parachuted into phase three: the Swamp Phase.

Swamp Phase was no fun at all. We stayed wet for days on end, dealing with gators, water moccasins, mosquitoes, and fatigue that felt like it would never end. I begged God for the strength to survive and complete the course. By the final exercise, most of us had lost track of the number of days we'd been in training. In fact, I didn't know anyone who knew for sure what day of the week it was.

I remember finding a piece of earth beside a cypress tree that was almost dry. It felt like a tiny corner of Heaven just for me, and I collapsed with my back against the tree and my helmet, feeling like it weighed a thousand pounds. I don't remember drifting off to sleep, but I'll never forget waking up with one particularly unforgiving Ranger instructor with his foot on my chin.

He scowled down at me as I opened my eyes one at a time. "If I were an Atropian, you'd be a POW or dead."

I closed my eyes and breathed, "Atropians aren't real, and I choose dead."

He wasn't amused, and to prove it, he kicked me from my slumber and tried to yank my weapon away. Fortunately, I'd draped the sling across my shoulder before falling asleep, making it impossible to lose my rifle. We wrestled long enough for him to understand that I wasn't going to surrender, and he shoved me away from him.

"Get up, Ranger. You've got a mission."

Please, God, just enough strength to get through this.

I lumbered my way to my feet and followed the RI through chest-deep water to a stand of trees in about eight inches of black muck. Most of the platoon was gathered, and the instructor apparently needed to amuse himself.

He said, "Raise your hand if you're too tired to raise your hand."

No one moved, so he said, "Good. That means you've got enough left in the tank for one final mission. Listen up, Rangers. Tonight is a small-boat operation. It's a raid on the Atropian Liberation Front's island stronghold. If you make it through this one, the easy part will be over, and we can really start putting the screws to you."

I was right. The Atropians weren't real, but that would've been hard to prove in the next few hours of my life. I was so tired that I didn't remember the last time I'd seen Willy. I didn't even know if he was still in the course. My concerns were squelched when the RI assigned Willy and me as small-boat captains for the exercise.

Willy grabbed my shirt and leaned against me. "Are we still in Georgia?"

"I don't think so," I said. "I think we're in Hell."

"There's too much water for this to be Hell. And besides, you're here, so I know this ain't Hell."

I threw an exhausted arm around my friend and brother, and somehow, we gave each other the last nudge we needed to survive the final exercise.

Finally, we were dry, clean, and finished with Ranger School. All that remained was graduation, a bus ride back to Benning, and enough time for our bodies and minds to heal from the torture we'd been through.

At the graduation ceremony, wives, girlfriends, mothers, and fathers pinned the Ranger tab on the left shoulders of most of the class, but Willy and I didn't have anybody except each other. So, we tabbed each other, and that's a moment I'll never forget. I wish my momma had lived to see me with a Ranger tab on my arm. I think she would've been proud of her boy. I wished Billy could've been there. Maybe it would've been enough to get him to say something—anything—but in the end, it was just Willy and me, and for the two poor boys from South Carolina, we were enough.

Chapter 9
Atheists in a Foxhole

Judges 2:1 NASB
*"Now the angel of the LORD came up from Gilgal to Bochim. And
he said, 'I brought you up out of Egypt and led you into the land
which I have sworn to your fathers;' and I said, 'I will never break
My covenant with you.'"*

* * *

The bus ride back to Fort Benning looked like sixty dead bodies
scattered randomly inside an old bus that had been white at some
point in its life but now resembled some combination of Georgia
red clay dust and diesel exhaust. We slept as if we'd never slept before. In the few moments I spent awake, I listened with unabashed
amusement at the growling stomachs around me. We'd survived
for two months on less than twenty-five hundred calories and
three hours of sleep per day. Our bodies were ravaged by fatigue,
injury, hunger, and unadulterated exhaustion. I'd lost twenty-five
pounds during the ordeal, and Willy looked like a refugee. He'd
been skinny before Ranger School, but I could almost see through
him when it was over.

Was it worth it? I kept asking myself this, and every time, without fail, the answer came back as a resounding yes. We'd accomplished something most people could never survive and would never dare try. We earned something no one could ever take away from us. We were Rangers—not just members of the Ranger Regiment who'd been through the Ranger Indoctrination Program, but full-blown, tabbed, Ranger-qualified elite warriors. But we'd never been tested. We'd never been dipped in the fire of mortal combat where souls teetered on the razor's edge between life and death. We were trained, qualified, and eager, but no matter how much we wanted to believe we were ready to wear the face of war, neither of us knew if we'd rise to the calling or if we'd cower like frightened children in the face of an enemy bent on ending us. No, we didn't know, but we believed, and that is the very definition of faith.

I laid my forehead on the back of the seat in front of me and talked with God. People claim to actually hear the words of God when they pray. I'm not one of those people, but I've never needed to audibly hear His voice. I experience His love in every breath I take and His mercy every time I fail and He forgives. When I opened my eyes, Willy was staring at me, and I gave him a nod.

He said, "What were you doing? Praying again?"

I smiled and stretched. "Yeah. I was thanking God for bringing us through it all."

He turned away and watched the tall pines pass the windows. "You know, Singer, maybe you should give you and me some credit for getting through that. I didn't notice God carrying my ruck or stomping any rattlesnakes out there. As a matter of fact, I'm not sure I believe He's real."

"What? You don't believe in God at all?"

He shrugged. "I don't know. I mean, maybe . . . but He sure ain't never done much for me. I'm just not sure that a god who claims to love us would let stuff happen to us like . . . well, think about it. Why would God let your dad kill your mother and leave your brother in the shape he's in? Stuff like that's why I'm pretty sure He's not real."

I bowed my head and prayed for the wisdom and words to come. When I opened my eyes, Willy was still staring at me.

"So, what did He say?"

I sighed. "It doesn't work like that, Willy. God doesn't talk directly to us anymore. He talks to our hearts."

He chuckled. "Okay, then. What did He say to your heart?"

I smiled back at my friend. "I think He wants me to tell you about the Rocky Mountains."

He scowled. "The Rocky Mountains? What's that got to do with anything?"

"Have you ever seen them?"

"The Rockies? Sure, I've seen them on TV and pictures and stuff."

"But you've never seen them for real, right?"

He said, "You know I've never been anywhere the Army didn't take me."

"But you *believe* the Rockies are real, don't you?"

"What kind of question is that? Of course they're real."

"And you have no doubt whatsoever about that?"

He cocked his head. "Where are you going with this? My brain is still scrambled from Ranger School."

"I'm proving to you that things exist, even though you've never seen them. Just because you've never acknowledged God, or you've never felt Him for yourself, that doesn't mean He isn't real. Just like the Rockies. They're real, whether you believe in them or not."

He waved a dismissive hand. "That's not the same."

"You're right. Those mountains, no matter how pretty they are, can't keep you out of Hell."

He snapped his fingers. "Now, that's something I definitely don't believe is real, for exactly the same reason. How could a God who's supposed to love you send you to Hell?"

I laid a hand on my friend's shoulder. "That's just it. He doesn't send anybody to Hell. People send themselves there. The only way to avoid sending ourselves to Hell is to trust in God."

"It's all too neat and tidy for me. I mean, really, look at the whole evolution thing. There's tons of proof that it all started with the big bang. That's what they taught us in school."

"I'm glad you brought that up," I said. "Help me understand it because they didn't teach it at my school."

Willy straightened himself in the well-worn seat. "So, it started with everything in the universe crammed all together in a ball, and it exploded. That's where all the planets and stars came from, and scientists can prove it."

"They can prove it, huh? That sounds reasonable to me."

He lowered an eyebrow. "Wait a minute. Are you saying you believe in the big bang theory?"

"Sure," I said. "I'll buy it if you can answer one question for me."

"I'm not a scientist or nothing, but I'll try."

I smiled. "Who put that hot, dense ball of everything there so it could explode?" Willy's mouth fell open, and I gave him a break. "You don't have to answer right now. Just let me know when you figure it out."

He shook me off. "No, wait a minute. That's a good question. Maybe that ball was just always there."

"Kind of like God?"

"You know what I mean," he said. "Don't you Christians think the Earth is only like five or six thousand years old?"

"What difference does it make? If I'm right, or you're right, it doesn't matter. We're still just two dudes on a big rock floating around in space. Whether that rock has been here six gazillion years or six minutes, it's still a rock, and we're still on it. There's no consequences for believing anything about how the Earth got here, but that's not true when it comes to Heaven and Hell."

"What do you mean?"

I said, "Let's assume you're right, and there is no Heaven, no Hell, and no God. If I'm wrong, I live my life loving people and trying to make the world a better place to live, then, one day, I'll die, and that'll be the end of me. I'll just be asleep forever."

He raised his head and stared out the window again. When he turned back, he said, "Okay, I've never thought about it like that. I guess that means if you're wrong, it doesn't really matter, but if I'm wrong, and Heaven and Hell are real . . ."

He didn't finish his thought, and I didn't push. I was playing the long game. God and I would win him over. It just might take a while.

* * *

When we got back to Fort Benning, both Willy and I were anxious to move to a sniper team, but instead of turning in our weapons and team gear and picking up our M24 Sniper Weapon System, we arrived home to find our unit gone.

"They're deployed to Northern Africa," said Staff Sergeant Turner from headquarters.

"Then when are we being deployed?" Willy asked.

"You're not," he said. "You're going back to school."

Willy groaned. "Back to school? What school? We just got back from Ranger School, and we're wrecked."

Turner said, "You can rake leaves and cut grass if you don't want to go to the High Angle Course."

Willy almost begged. "Can we at least have a few days to let our feet heal up?"

Turner laughed. "Yeah, I think you've earned a few days off. Do you want to take some leave and go see your families?"

Willy and I shared a look, and I said, "No, we don't want to go anywhere. We just want to sleep, eat, and heal."

Turner said, "I remember that feeling. You're reporting to the High Angle Course a week from Monday, so you better be back in shape by then."

Over the coming months, Willy and I graduated at or near the top of our class, not only at the High Angle Course, but also the Precision Rifle and Extreme Long Range Precision courses. It felt as if Ranger School had been our personal set of keys to any course we wanted to attend.

Once we'd at least tripled our marksmanship knowledge and skill, we headed back to our unit, anxious to get on an airplane to go somewhere and put our skills to work. Our ignorant yearning for combat was quashed once again when Sergeant Turner said, "Sorry, guys. You're still stuck here with us, but there's an instructor from the Sniper Course who wants to come down and do some one-on-one with you."

"Who?" I asked.

"I don't know him, but I think his name is Johnson. Did you have a Sergeant First Class Johnson as an instructor?"

I said, "Yes, he apparently got hurt on a mission, and he's teaching at the school while he's healing up."

"That happens a lot," Turner said.

We met Sergeant First Class Clark Johnson in the sniper platoon's squad room, and he wasted no time getting started.

"It's good to see you guys again. You've been through all the schools, and you probably think you're ready to go downrange and pop some bad guys, but don't get too excited yet. I'm going to take you through some scenarios and teach you a few little tricks of the trade that nobody talks about at the schoolhouse."

We got to see Sergeant Johnson shoot for the first time on day one of his personalized class. He either blew a few shots to make us feel good, or he wasn't a crack shot. But before our time together was over, we learned more about moving silently and stalking our prey than we thought possible. Shooting to unimaginable standards of accuracy, believe it or not, makes up less than five percent of the sniper's toolbox. For me, shooting was the easy part. Stalking was the challenge.

During the Army Sniper Course, we had to stalk without being seen to within a distance we could confidently make a shot on a team of instructors, including Sergeant Johnson. Both Willy and I completed the stalking phase, but unlike my friend, it didn't come easily for me. At the time, I wasn't sure exactly how Sergeant Johnson wound up teaching a private sniper advanced course for Willy and me, but before the class was over, he sat on the ground in front of us while we cleaned our rifles.

"Gentlemen, you need to understand why I'm here."

That got our attention, and we ceased our task of rifle maintenance.

He continued. "This would never happen under normal conditions, but your unit is deployed, and I'm undeployable. Since you haven't had time to acclimate to life on a sniper team after all the training you've been through, I was tasked to get you two up to speed on how combat is going to feel."

Combat? Are we finally being deployed?

Willy cocked his head. "The Army tasked you to come do this just for us?"

Sergeant Johnson looked away. "Yeah, sort of."

"Sort of?" I asked. "You're doing this off the record, aren't you? Why?"

He dragged a finger through the sand between his boots and took the hard line. "You two barely made it through the course. If I'm going downrange with snipers, I want them to be the best they can be. I'm looking out for myself. That's all."

I smiled. "Barely made it, huh? I was the honor grad, and Willy was number three. We've never 'barely made it' through any course the Army sent us to."

He grunted. "Yeah, well, I needed something to do, and you guys needed some extra schooling."

I kept smiling. "It sounds like you're getting warmer, but we still haven't come to the truth."

He leaned in. "All right. Fine. Your unit is getting their teeth kicked in over there in the sandbox, and snipers are few and far between. You guys are going, and my conscience is clear now. You weren't ready three months ago, and the truth is, you're still not ready, but you're as close to ready as I can get you. Don't go over there and come back in coffins. You got me, snipers?"

The excitement boiling inside my chest was almost impossible to contain. My unit was in trouble, and Willy and I were being sent to help. We were young, green, and perhaps overly ambitious out of ignorance, and those are dangerous ingredients in a deadly stew.

I asked, "Do you know when we're leaving?"

He held up two fingers, and I swallowed the lump in my throat.

"Two weeks? That's quick."

Sergeant Johnson shook his head. "No, not two weeks . . . Two days."

He hopped to his feet, and Willy said, "Can I ask you one more thing, Sergeant?"

He took a knee. "Sure. What is it?"

I ran through the list of questions I thought might come out of Willy's mouth. *What's it really like to kill somebody? How many kills do you have? Why aren't you being deployed?* But nothing I guessed turned out to be the question Willy had for our mentor.

My friend looked up and squinted against the sun. "Do you think God is real, Sergeant Johnson?"

The crooked grin I'd first seen on graduation day of Sniper School showed up again, and the seasoned sniper placed a hand on Willy's shoulder. "Specialist Williams, you're about to learn a valuable lesson eight thousand miles from home. There ain't no such thing as an atheist under incoming fire, son. And you can take that to the bank."

Chapter 10
How I Pray

Matthew 6:6 NASB

*"But you, when you pray, go into your inner room, close your door
and pray to your Father who is in secret, and your Father who sees
what is done in secret will reward you."*

* * *

Willy and I were the only snipers being deployed, but we weren't
the only soldiers being sent downrange to rejoin our unit overseas.
Having other butts on the airplane was reassuring. Before
boarding the C-17, we were issued new gear to replace anything we
had that wasn't serviceable and to fill holes in what we'd already
been issued. One particular collection of gear we didn't need replaced was our pair of M24 Sniper Weapon System rifles in .308
caliber, SR-25 select-fire 7.62mm rifles, and spotting scopes. By
the time we boarded the airplane, we believed we had every piece
of hardware we'd need in the sandbox, but what we didn't have
was real-world experience, having the bad guys shooting back at
us. That would soon change, and so would we.

We didn't talk much on the plane. It seemed as if everyone was
a bit lost in their own thoughts. I didn't know everyone on the

plane, but many of the soldiers around us wore unit patches on their right shoulders indicating they'd served in combat with that unit. Those soldiers wore a look that was very different than everyone else's. They seemed to know something the rest of us couldn't know . . . yet.

Somewhere over the North Atlantic, it occurred to me that I'd never been on an airplane when it landed. Every time I'd taken off in an airplane or helicopter, I'd stepped out the door before it touched the ground. In Jump School, it was a parachute that delivered me back to Earth. Helicopter insertions had more options for getting out. I'd rappelled, fast-roped, parachuted, leapt into the water, and stepped from choppers at a hover, but feeling the wheels of the huge C-17 kiss the runway would be an entirely new experience for me.

That thought led me into another stream of fascination as I tried to list every new experience the Army had given me. I chose to step from the world in which I lived with the preacher and his wife and into a realm of unknowns. The Army taught me every critical skill I possessed, and the mindset they instilled in my skull changed the way I looked at the world. I'd never depart from my Christian faith, but Ranger thinking would become my window on the world for years to come.

The landing, as it turned out, was a non-event, and I wondered if every landing was so docile. Maybe landing isn't so bad after all, but a parachute ride is still a lot more fun.

We descended the ramp to find a cadre of Rangers waiting to meet us. Willy's and my reception party was a pair of snipers sitting on the hood of a hardened Humvee called a Peacekeeper. The vehicle wore armor plating and bullet-resistant glass. The turret on top boasted an M2 .50-caliber machine gun we affectionately called the Ma Deuce. Though not a sniper-specific weapon, it was a heavy weapon that could lay down enough fire to change the tide of a gunfight that wasn't necessarily going the good guys' way.

Sergeant Mitchell slid from the hood of the vehicle and stuck out a hand. "Welcome to the sandbox, boys. How was the ride?"

I shrugged and glanced back at the enormous cargo plane. "Long."

Sergeant Mitchell surveyed the interior of the massive beast. "Yep, they all are. Grab your gear, and we'll take you for a little local orientation ride on the way back to the base."

Willy and I shouldered our gear and deposited it into the back of the Peacekeeper. Sergeant Mitchell caught the hatch before I could pull it closed. "You might want to keep your rifles out. Things get dicey around here sometimes, and I wouldn't want to get you killed on your first day—especially unarmed."

I hadn't expected a firefight on our first day in-country, but I'm a Baptist, and there's no sprinkling for Baptists. We're dunkers, and I was about to experience submersion like I'd never imagined.

Willy pulled out his M4, and I gave his choice a long, contemplative stare. "You're going with the five-five-six, huh?"

He held up the rifle and eyed the front seat of the Peacekeeper. "That's what they've got, so I figure they know more about what works in this place than I do."

I couldn't find any flaws in his logic, but something made me pull two rifles from my case—my M24 sniper rifle and an M4 that was identical to Willy's.

Sergeant Mitchell climbed into the front passenger seat, and Specialist Franklin slid in behind the wheel. Our tour began quietly enough.

Mitchell said, "Look how the street narrows past this next intersection. That's their favorite spot to give us a little peck on the cheek. The sun's still up, so they probably won't hit us now, but you never know with these guys. They're not playing with a full deck."

I watched a three-vehicle convoy cross right to left at the intersection. "Are those our guys?"

Mitchell leaned forward. "Those are regular Army. They're infantry from the Eighty-Second Airborne. They never move in singles. Most of the time, you'll see five or six vehicles at a time. You know, the whole strength-in-numbers thing."

Franklin jumped into the conversation. "That's mostly what we do over here—provide overwatch for those guys while they're kicking in doors."

Willy asked, "Why aren't the Rangers the door-kickers?"

Franklin said, "We are, but there are a lot more doors than there are Rangers in-country, so it's nice to have the paratroopers—"

A sound like distant firecrackers silenced our driver, and he shoved the Peacekeeper into reverse. We accelerated backward, and Franklin spun the wheel. Before I realized what was happening, gravel, dirt, and sand boiled from our tires as we roared down the cross street, where the guys from the Eighty-Second had gone.

Sergeant Mitchell thrust himself from his seat and into the turret with the Ma Deuce.

"What's happening?" Willy yelled.

Franklin palm-spun the wheel and sent us sliding through another intersection as the popping grew louder. "The paratroopers are under fire. One of you, get up here!"

I squirmed from my seat and slid into Sergeant Mitchell's seat with my rifle in my arms.

"Keep your eyes on the rooftops and high windows and call targets to Sergeant Mitchell!"

A cloud of dust and smoke filled the air in front of us, and I fought to see anything other than flying debris. As I strained to pick out assailants, the big .50-cal roared to life, and Sergeant

Mitchell laced a line of armor-piercing rounds up the side of a building to the right. Once the .50 started firing, everything in the environment turned into indescribable chaos. Bullets, sand, dust, and the roaring echoes of combat filled the air.

I'd trained for over two years for that moment, but nothing had prepared me for the reality of my first firefight.

I caught a glimpse of a gunman to my left and yelled, "Eleven o'clock high!"

Mitchell didn't hesitate. He cut the gunman down with a short burst from the .50, and the man's rifle fell to the street.

We continued down the block with .50-cal rounds exploding overhead, and AK-47 rounds bouncing off our windshield. A window in the dust cloud opened just enough for me to see orange flames dancing from the belly of an overturned Humvee.

I yelled, "They're on fire!"

We drew ever closer to the atrocious scene, and the horror of the moment burned through my soul.

Franklin yelled, "Do you see our guys?"

I scoured the scene and counted American uniforms. "I see three on their feet and two down."

Franklin roared, "Find an overwatch position!"

I slammed my body forward to search the rooftops. "I can't see!"

Franklin yelled, "Open your door!"

I pulled the lever and swung the heavy door outward. Incoming fire ricocheted off the armor outside my door, but I didn't withdraw. "Found one!"

"Get up there and cover our guys," Franklin ordered.

Neither Willy nor I hesitated. We were clear of the vehicle and inside the building almost before Franklin's order stopped echoing. The building was four stories high with steep stairs along the back wall. We took the steps three at a time as the weight of our weapons and ammo beat down on our shoulders and arms. My heart pounded as if battling to provide the oxygen my body so desperately needed.

When we broke through the door to the roof, it would've been easy to believe we were on a mountaintop with nothing but perfectly blue sky in every direction. If not for the cacophony of small-arms fire from below, it would've been a perfect scene.

We threw ourselves against the low parapet surrounding the roof and laced our barrels across the crest. The scene below was unlike anything I'd ever seen. American soldiers poured rounds into the surrounding buildings, and descending rounds pummeled them from above.

I closed my eyes for an instant and beckoned to the heavens above. "Give me strength."

I reopened my eyes to see with unmatched clarity. The fire belching from the assailants' rifles were flashing neon signs begging for my attention. I raised my M24 and sighted on the closest gunman. My scope gave me a view no one else on Earth had, and I could count the beads of sweat pouring from the gunman's face. I estimated the range, made the elevation and windage adjustments in my mind, and watched my crosshairs paint their deadly prophecy across the man's torso.

I'd pressed the trigger of that rifle tens of thousands of times. I knew precisely how far it would move before breaking, but I felt the mechanical motion like never before. Every millimeter of trigger-pull felt like miles as everything in my world came into crystal, silent focus. I don't remember the recoil of the rifle or the thunderous crack of the bullet leaving the muzzle, but the view through my circular window on the world was something I'll never wash from my mind's eye.

I didn't hate the gunman. I didn't feel anything for him. Every emotion pouring through my flooded mind was the tireless, unyielding need to protect my brothers on the ground and in the overturned vehicle. The man beneath my crosshairs left this world an instant after I felt the trigger reach its stop. His weapon fell silent, and his body dissolved as if his every muscle turned suddenly to useless, willowing gelatin.

The reality of taking a life didn't come in that moment. Instead, the dire necessity of finding and eliminating another target filled my head. Nothing was more important. Nothing else mattered. Nothing else existed.

Raising my barrel to pan the scene, I saw another orange flash dot the landscape, and I put the man down with one shot. I didn't remember calculating anything, and I moved as if programmed to keep my fellow Americans alive.

I don't know how many men I killed on my first day in a country I couldn't find on a globe, but I know how many Americans survived because Willy, Mitchell, Franklin, and I placed precision fire on target, time after time, until the gunfire fell silent and the dust cleared, leaving the scene burned, bullet-riddled, and blood-soaked.

I collapsed to the dirty roof and leaned back against the jagged wall behind me, and Willy wiped sweat from his face with the filthy sleeve of his shirt.

"Are you okay?" I asked, suddenly thirstier than I'd ever been.

Willy slowly shook his head. "I don't know, man. What was that?"

I licked my parched lips. "I don't know, but I think we won."

He then did the last thing any rational human would do in a situation like that. He laughed. His chest heaved, and his throat barked until finally, exhaustion overtook him and he caught his breath.

"What are you laughing at?" I asked.

He pointed a dirty finger at me. "You."

"Me? Why are you laughing at me?"

"You were singing."

"Singing? What do you mean, I was singing?"

He collected himself. "You were singing church music. It was something about a roll being called up yonder. Wherever yonder is."

"No, I wasn't," I insisted.

"Oh, yes, you were. And that ain't all. You prayed, too. Right before we started shooting, you closed your eyes and prayed. But I couldn't hear what you were saying."

I replayed the episode in my mind. "I was asking for strength."

Willy traced his fingertip through the dirt and grime on the roof. "Maybe next time you could ask for some of that strength for me, too."

Chapter 11

Blessed with a Curse

Psalms 40:1–3 NASB
"I waited patiently for the Lord; And He inclined to me and heard my cry. He brought me up out of the pit of destruction, out of the miry clay, And He set my feet upon a rock making my footsteps firm. He put a new song in my mouth, a song of praise to our God; Many will see and fear and will trust in the Lord."

* * *

Sitting on that rooftop, it occurred to me that the fight may not really be over. Just because the shooting had temporarily stopped didn't mean there wouldn't be more, and through the years, I came to believe the shooting would never end by man's hand. Only Christ could bring true peace by His triumphant return.

I rolled over and peered across the parapet to see the street occupied by American soldiers. Without a radio, Willy and I had no means of communication with Mitchell and Franklin, and for the first time, I realized I had no idea where either of them was. I suddenly felt as if we were alone and a long way from what we should've considered our home.

"What are you doing?" Willy asked.

"I'm trying to figure out what to do next."

He said, "According to Sergeant Johnson, we're supposed to stay in the fight until we're certain it's over or that we're dead."

"I'm pretty sure I'm not dead, and I think it's over, but I can't be sure."

"What do you see?"

I scanned the street. "The Humvee isn't on fire anymore. And it looks like they're loading the wounded into the first two trucks."

"Can you see Sergeant Mitchell?"

I pored over the windows and rooftops on the opposite side of the street, and Willy stuck his head over the low wall.

"There they are," he said as he pointed toward the street.

Sergeant Mitchell looked up to see us looking back at him. He gave the hand signal for us to remain in place while they cleaned up the street. We kept watch over the movement below, as well as anything or anyone who showed up in a window or on a rooftop.

The silence was eerie and made the sound of my breathing appear amplified. As I got my respiration under control, I heard an engine approaching from the north, and I pulled my rifle to my shoulder. Through the lens of my scope, a plume of dust rose on the heels of a Toyota pickup truck with a massive gun mounted in the bed.

I turned to Willy. "Put eyes on that truck. Does he look like a friendly to you?"

Willy spun to see the approaching vehicle. "No, he's definitely not a friendly. That's a technical, and I'm pretty sure it's a Dushka."

I yelled over the parapet. "Sergeant Mitchell!"

He glanced up, and I pointed down the street. "Technical moving in from the north."

He spun to face the direction of the approaching threat and then back up at me. "Kill it!"

I had a .308, and Willy had a 5.56. Killing a truck from a mile away was well outside our capability, but that .50-cal on the vehicle spelled nothing short of destruction for the Americans on the street.

Pulling my eyes from the technical for a brief scan of the street revealed the scene to be free of injured American soldiers, but the overturned Humvee blocked the road to the south, leaving no clear egress corridor. Taking out the Toyota suddenly became more than an order. It became a vital necessity for the survival of the soldiers under our overwatch.

I scoped the oncoming truck. "What do you estimate the range to be?"

Willy groaned. "Twelve hundred yards, at least."

I sighed. "We might as well throw rocks at him at that range. There's no way I can get a round to puncture the skin at that distance."

Willy shrugged. "I guess that means we wait until he's within range."

Sergeant Mitchell yelled up at us. "Get some lead on that thing! We need five minutes down here."

I yelled down, "He's twelve hundred yards out."

Mitchell shook his head. "I don't care if he's ten miles away. Hold over and put some bullets in the air!"

The .308 is a great bullet, but it's little more than a pesky annoyance at three quarters of a mile. Even if I hit the truck, the round would be traveling so slow it would have very little energy and no chance of penetrating the windshield or hood. I kept the Toyota in my crosshairs until I believed it to be within a thousand yards. I pressed the trigger and watched for my bullet's vapor trail as it flew northward toward the threat.

Willy said, "It went right ten feet."

"Ten feet? Are you sure?"

"Yeah, three meters. I saw the impact."

I held left of the technical and sent another round downrange. Willy's call had been spot-on. The center of the windshield exploded, and I brought my aim back to the right, just enough to center on the driver. As the echo of my third shot sounded through the canyon of buildings, the vehicle swerved left before correcting and coming to a stop in the center of the street.

"You got him!" Willy yelled as if we were a mile apart.

Everything inside me wanted to celebrate with my spotter, but something made me keep my focus on the vehicle through my scope.

Willy slugged my shoulder. "You got him, man! Nice shooting."

I still didn't move, and my persistence was rewarded. I calmly said, "Get back on the scope."

Willy obeyed and stuck his eye back to the spotter's scope. As soon as he brought the scene into focus, he said, "He's going for the gun. Put him down, Jimmy."

Hitting a truck at a thousand yards is a lot different than hitting a moving man. I believed I'd killed the driver, but the passenger was clearly determined to get on the gun and return fire. The chances of him hitting us were minuscule, but he was going to wreak havoc on everything and everyone in our vicinity if he got his hands on that Dushka.

I kept my cool and performed the range calculation in my head by using the average height of a man measured by the mil-dots in my scope. If my math was correct, there were 860 yards between my scope and the gunner's chest. The official effective range of the .308 cartridge in my rifle was 800 yards, but I'd proven it could still do enough damage to destroy a windshield and probably kill a driver at nearly 1,000 yards. That gave me confidence in both my rifle and the cartridge.

Willy pulled me from my trance. "Shoot him, Jimmy! Send the round. Send it!"

I drew in a full breath, let half of it out, and stopped breathing. I could see the results of my heart beating in the crosshairs of my scope. Even though each thump moved my rifle only fractions of a mil, the variation was enough to miss the small target at such a range. I'd heard of snipers and Olympic shooters being able to fire a round between heartbeats, but I'd never mastered the technique.

Forcing my body and mind to relax, I watched the bouncing crosshairs and counted the rhythm. Through my scope, I saw the gunner bound across the closed tailgate and position himself behind the Duskha. The muzzle of the heavy weapon bounced as it belched fire and lead into the air. The rounds could've been headed directly for Willy and me, but I didn't care. My job was to stop that weapon at any cost.

With my heart rate measured and my mind completely at ease, I pressed the trigger. A bullet traveling through warm air at supersonic speed leaves a ghostly trail behind it that's easy to see through a good scope. I watched the vapor trail as the bullet arced through the sky between me and my target. I should've trusted Willy to watch the flight and impact while I racked another round into the chamber, but I kept my eye focused on the wispy trail. To my delight and near disbelief, my round flew in a delicate arc until it struck the Dushka's mount, sending the gunner leaping backward and temporarily silencing the weapon.

The man felt himself with both hands and discovered he'd not been shot, so he threw himself back to the weapon and opened fire again.

Willy said, "Send it again. You're on target."

In my mind, I wasn't on target. I'd hit the gun and not the gunner, so I raised my crosshairs almost imperceptibly and pressed the trigger again. I didn't watch the second round. As long as the wind hadn't changed, I was confident of my bullet's destination.

As I cycled the bolt of my rifle to feed another round, the impact of the Dushka's .50-caliber rounds slapping into buildings around me echoed through my head. As I settled back into my sight picture, the technical was still mounted in the Toyota, but its barrel was silent, and its gunner was nowhere to be seen.

Willy slapped the parapet wall. "You did it! You blew him right out of the truck."

I stayed in the gun. "Get back in that scope, Willy. He might not be down for good."

"Are you serious, man? There's no way that dude survived that."

"Just keep watching. Those guys on the ground are counting on us."

"Whatever, man, but I'm telling you, you nailed that dude."

I scoured the ground around the truck, hoping to see the spreading pool of crimson that should be covering the ground beneath the Toyota, but it didn't come.

Willy gasped. "He's crawling away."

I watched for the motion my spotter saw, and I didn't have to wait long. The gunner was dragging himself across the sand-covered road, and I held the same sight picture I'd used for the standing shot. My trigger felt like nothing more than a breath of wind as I pressed through the break and the bullet left the muzzle. Just less than two seconds later, the gunner's body bucked and came to rest on its side with the blood I'd expected finally covering the ground around him.

Willy said, "Are you happy now? That guy's not getting back up."

I considered Willy's question and felt the weight of my soul. Nothing about what I'd done in the previous minutes of my life made me happy. Taking a human life is never to be taken lightly. I'll forever believe I saved lives by taking others, but celebrating would never become part of my post-mission routine. Back then, I wondered if I'd ever grow out of the agony I felt every time I played a role in a soul leaving its body. Now, all these years later, I still wonder if I'll ever reach that level. Part of me hopes I never find it easy to end a human life. The humanity within me has been on the edge of extinction since the first time I pulled a trigger and stopped evil from prevailing.

My father had been my first target, and with him went a piece of me that can never be restored. I've often questioned what would've been the result if I had found another way to stop his rage. Would my mother still be alive? Would Billy have been able to live a life without the trauma of the night's horror robbing him of his voice, his mind, and ultimately, his very life? Would I have survived if I'd let my father live, or would he have killed all of us?

Willy's questions about a loving God allowing such horrific things to happen rang in my head like endless rolling thunder. Had the events of that night turned me into something less than a man and closer to an animal capable of collecting souls from a distance? Innocent people are alive today because I was blessed with a curse to do my terrible work and coexist in society with men and women of honor and boundless morality. My curse, I've come to believe, is one thing that gives my life meaning and defines my purpose on Earth. I would serve my God and my country as long as breath filled my chest, but to many in far-off corners of the world, I would become a harvester of men, an assassin, a cold, distant, invisible murderer . . . and nothing more.

Chapter 12

Were You Scared?

2 Timothy 1:7 NASB
*"For God has not given us a spirit of timidity,
but of power and love and discipline."*

* * *

"They're all alive, and they want to buy you two a beer!"

That's how Staff Sergeant McMillan, the sniper platoon sergeant, opened the after-action report. "If you don't know our new arrivals yet, they're right back there, hiding in the corner like good little snipers. Guys, meet Corporal Jimmy "Singer" Grossmann and Specialist Willy Williams. The two of them bagged eight confirmed kills on their first day in-country. Stand up, boys. Take a bow."

I ducked my head, but Willy hopped to his feet. "That's right. We announced our presence on the street."

Whoops and jeers rose from the eighteen other men in the room, and I grabbed Willy's wrist and dragged him back into his chair. "Cut it out. That's not what we're here to do."

Sergeant McMillan knocked on the wooden table. "It looks like Singer already has his head in the right place. Hell of a job out there today, all of you. We brought everybody home without any body bags."

He briefed the details of what happened and said, "Get some rest, gentlemen. You'll be back outside the wire in less than twenty-four hours to support another door-kicking mission with the Eighty-Second Airborne. This time, though, we're sending a pair of Rangers with every entry team. We know how to stay alive and roll up the bad guys without excessive collateral damage, so we're trying to pass some of that wisdom along to the paratroopers. They're good at killing people and breaking things, but it's not always the *right* people and things. Any questions?"

A sergeant from the left edge of the group said, "Yeah, I've got one. Why do you call the new guy Singer?"

Sergeant McMillan said, "Because he's got the voice of an angel. If you've not run PT with him calling cadence, you ain't lived."

"Sing something for us!" came an anonymous voice in the room.

Cheers and coaxing filled the air, but I shook it off. "Not tonight. Maybe tomorrow if we don't have to kill anybody."

Willy jumped in. "If you really want to hear him sing, just spot for him. He can't stop singing when he's pulling the trigger. And you'll never believe what he sings out there. He sings church music, and it'll make you cry like a baby."

I survived the embarrassment of my first after-action report and the good-natured jeering from the platoon, but by the time it was over, exhaustion wrapped her relentless arms around me and dragged me toward sleep. Our quarters were far from luxurious, but they were dry and spacious enough to store most of our gear and still have room to sleep. The platoon sergeant put Willy and me together, so I pointed toward my corporal stripes and claimed the top bunk.

Willy rolled his eyes. "Come on, man. We're both E-4s. Let's flip for it."

I curled my middle finger into my palm and flipped him on the back of his hand. "There, we flipped. I'm on top."

He gave in, and we crawled into our racks, ready to pass out. An instant before my body and mind were rewarded with the rest they so badly needed, Willy said, "Hey, man. Are there pictures up there by your rack?"

I pried my eyes open and examined the wall. "No, there's nothing up here except some leftover pieces of tape. Why?"

"There's a picture of a girl down here, and she's all right. Here, check her out."

I watched his hand rise beside my bunk, and I took the picture from between his fingers. The woman was sitting on a porch swing with a baby beside her, and Willy was right. She was beautiful. I flipped over the print and read the back.

Your girls miss you, and we can't wait for you to come home to us.

I tossed the picture back down to Willy. "I wonder who they are."

"I don't know, but I wouldn't mind going home to those two. Do you want babies, Jimmy?"

"I haven't thought about it. But if you don't shut up and let me go to sleep, you're not going to live long enough to have any of your own."

To my surprise, he didn't say a word, and I drifted back toward slumber. I'd almost fallen asleep when I heard Willy say, "Hey, man. Were you scared out there today?"

I kept my eyes closed and let the battle play out on my mind's movie screen. Every minute of the fight came back in striking detail. I could see the dark eyes of the men I killed. I could smell the smoke and fire. Every sound echoed as if trapped in a canyon it couldn't escape.

"No, I wasn't scared. Were you?"

I could almost see him shrugging his skinny shoulders. "No . . . of course not. We're Rangers, man. We're made for this stuff."

I made a mental note to explore Willy's question with him in the days to come, but little did I know that he'd have far more to say about the topic before I could launch my probe.

Sleep came, and so did the morning. I wanted far more of one and less of the other, but I would have to adjust to the cycles I was given, and sleep seemed to be low on the priority list for my unit.

Our platoon sergeant did something I neither understood nor liked at the time, but in the end, it made sense. He said, "Specialist Williams, you're going with Sergeant Gonzalez, and Singer, you're with me. You both did a fine job yesterday, but you've got a lot to learn, and somebody's gotta teach you."

We had no choice in the matter, and neither Willy nor I liked the split, but the Army didn't care what we liked. It cared about winning wars and keeping Americans alive.

Sergeant McMillan said, "Let's take a walk, Singer. You don't mind me calling you Singer, do you?"

I fell in step with him. "No, Sergeant, I don't mind. In fact, I kinda like the nickname."

"Good. I wasn't going to stop, but it's nice to know you're okay with it. What do you think about your rifle?"

"My rifle, Sergeant?"

"Cut out the sergeant crap when it's just the two of us unless I'm chewing you out for something. In fact, pull your rank insignia off your gear. If we get rolled up and taken prisoner when we're outside the wire, we don't need our captors knowing who's in charge. It's also a bit of a countersniper measure. We don't want other gunners knowing who outranks who. They tend to shoot the ones with the most stripes or wearing officer's rank. I assume you don't want to get shot. Am I right?"

"No, I don't want to get shot, and to be honest, after yesterday, I don't really want to shoot anybody, either."

He stopped in his tracks, turned, and grabbed a handful of my shirt. Through gritted teeth, he growled. "Are you going soft, Ranger? Are you showing me your weakness right now? Is that what's going on?"

I spoke barely loud enough for him to hear. "No, Sergeant. I'm not soft. I'm a well-trained, lethally dangerous man, but I prefer being a man of peace. I will kill, Sergeant, but never because it pleases me. Only because it's necessary."

He gave me a shake and shoved me away. As I stood there trying to guess what would happen next, he bounced a pointed index finger off my chest. "And that's precisely why you're going to be one of the best snipers in this platoon. That's why you're my shooter, and I'm your spotter. I'm going to teach you everything I know about staying alive, and you're going make sure those soldiers out there kicking in those doors don't have to worry about looking up. They're going to know that a deadly, dangerous man has their backs."

Without another word, he returned to his measured gait, and I followed. He lifted a combination lock on the hasp of an enormous Conex box and spun the dial. Seconds later, we were inside the metal container with a pair of bulbs hanging overhead, illuminating the space. Six feet inside the door was a wall of steel bars with another locked door, and Sergeant McMillan dialed in the combination on a second lock. Without looking over his shoulder at me, he asked, "Have you ever shot a three-three-eight Lapua?"

"Not yet."

He chuckled. "You're just full of good answers today, aren't you, Singer?"

"Just the truth, Sergeant."

"I'm not chewing you out, so drop the Sergeant. I'm Chris when we're alone. Got it?"

"Got it," I said.

He pulled a rifle that looked nearly identical to my M24 and stuck it in my hands. With the exception of the weight, it felt just like my .308, but it had a much bigger scope.

"Sling that rifle and grab two cans of ammo."

One hundred shots later, with consistent hits at 2200 yards, I had made a new friend.

Chris talked me through the ballistics of every shot, and I recorded the DOPE on every shot. DOPE is Data on Previous Engagements. It's the only information a sniper needs to know about his weapon and ammo to set up any future shot. Knowing exactly how far a bullet will drop during its flight to a target at any given distance is absolutely crucial, and that is the primary information provided by DOPE. Barometric pressure, temperature, altitude, wind, muzzle velocity, and flight time are all important, but knowing exactly how hard the Earth will pull on a bullet is the greatest piece of data a sniper has when it comes to selecting elevation and holdover for long shots—shots like the ones I took at 2200 yards.

Chris asked, "Do you remember the combination to the armory?"

"Of course. I watched you open both locks, and a sniper's primary purpose is to watch, record, and remember."

Back came the stiffened finger on the center of my chest. "That's my boy." He paused as if on the verge of saying something of vital importance, and maybe what he said was even more important than I could understand at the time. "Since you know the combinations, I expect you to lock up that rifle if the day ever comes when you don't deserve it anymore. Got me, Ranger?"

I'm sure I looked like a goofy kid at Christmas behind the grin I couldn't suppress.

He said, "Don't get happy on me yet, my man. We've still got a fifty-cal to dance with, so I hope you like big girls."

It wasn't my first time on the M82A1 Special Applications Scoped Rifle, but it would be my first time stretching the weapon beyond what Ronnie Barrett—the weapon's designer—intended to be its effective firing range of 1800 meters. I put a hundred rounds through the beast that day, and my shoulder never let me forget it. The weapon was heavy, awkward to carry, and looked like a rugged old warrior who'd been around longer than anybody else. That's what made me name the old warhorse Methuselah, even though I wanted to call it The Old Mule for the way it kicked every time I pulled the trigger.

Sergeant McMillan said, "I know what you can do with a three-oh-eight under fire, so let's see what kind of show you can put on tonight with a real bullet."

He checked his watch and then the sun. "Take your new best friends and get some rest. We're moving out an hour before sunset. If your boyfriend wakes you up, kick him out. I need your A game tonight, sniper."

I hefted the two rifles into my arms. "Roger that, Sergeant. See you tonight."

My sore shoulder and I nestled into the top bunk, and I tried to imagine what the coming night would bring.

Would it be more of the same fighting we'd seen the day before? Would everything change in the dark? Would I, once again, have to take the lives of men to protect my brothers? Would every night be more of the same?

Perhaps my mind knew how much my body needed rest because I didn't ponder the endless questions for more than a few minutes before I was engulfed in silent darkness and peaceful sleep.

When I opened my eyes, I checked my watch and found Willy sitting on the floor with my .50-cal between his legs.

He looked up and shook his head. "Will you have to carry this thing?"

I stretched and slipped from the bunk. "Nope. I don't *have* to carry it. I *get* to carry it. With that thing, we'll never have to wonder if we can reach out and touch a bad guy with a technical at two thousand yards."

He slid the rifle away. "You hungry?"

"Starving," I said.

He tossed me an MRE—a meal ready to eat—the Army's version of fast food. Mine was a ham loaf—or at least that's what the package said. There was a square orange brick in the bag that was supposed to be dehydrated peaches, but it tasted more like cardboard than any fruit I could think of. In the bottom of the pouch was a small packet containing matches, two pieces of gum, a tiny bottle of hot sauce, and a folded length of toilet paper. At least a couple of those items looked like they might come in handy before the night's mission.

With our fine-dining experience behind us, Willy leaned back against the wall and tapped the toes of his boots together.

"What is it?" I asked.

He dragged a heel across the plywood floor and retied his laces.

I bounced my tiny hot sauce off his chest. "What's up, man? You can talk to me. We've been through all the Army could throw at us for almost three years together. Don't clam up on me now."

He twisted his mouth and finally said, "That's kinda what I'm thinking about. I mean, we've been together through everything, from the time that lieutenant swore us in at Fort Jackson, all the way through to whatever that was yesterday. And now, here we are getting split up. It just ain't gonna be the same, you know? We're kinda like brothers or whatever, and now I'm going out with

Sergeant Gonzalez, and you're hooked up with the platoon sergeant."

I drew my knife and picked at a sliver of ham loaf from between my teeth. "Yeah, I get you, but those guys know the score over here. They've been doing it while we've been shooting at paper targets. We've got a lot to learn from them."

He stared at his boots. "Yeah, I know. Gonzalez is cool, and I'm sure Sergeant McMillan is all right, but it just ain't gonna be the same."

I gave his boot a nudge. "You and me know all the same stuff, Willy. We got nothing to teach each other. When we get schooled up, they'll probably put us back together. You know how it is. The needs of the Army come first."

"Yeah, I know. It's just . . . Well, remember last night when I asked if you were scared out there?"

"Sure, I remember."

He groaned and twisted, curling his legs beneath him. "Remember when I told you I wasn't scared?"

I nodded, but I didn't say a word.

He said, "I know you said you weren't scared, either, but I need you to know something. That was the first and only lie I've ever told you, Jimmy. I *was* scared. I ain't never been shot at before. Sure, we trained 'til we was too tired to train anymore, and then we kept training, but it ain't the same, man. It ain't the same as the real thing. You know?"

I was a twenty-year-old kid who barely made it through high school, and my best friend on Earth needed me to pour some wisdom on him. I didn't have any, so I turned to God, and He made my mouth move.

"It's all right to be scared, Willy. Everybody gets scared. The difference between men like us and the boys who haven't been through what we have is that we're held to a higher standard.

We've got a responsibility those losers don't have . . . and probably won't ever have. We volunteered for this thing, and now, we're in it. Those people back where we grew up, and a couple hundred million more just like them, need us."

He looked up and made eye contact for the first time. "Yeah, but that don't mean we ain't scared just because we volunteered for some stuff we didn't understand. I mean, tell me that you knew this is what you were signing up for."

"I can't tell you that. I just knew there wasn't anything for me in Sumter County, South Carolina. Look at us, Willy. We're Ranger snipers. Three years ago, we weren't nothing, and now, we're somebody. Somebody with skills and responsibility and the guts to do stuff most people can't. It's okay to be scared, man, but you can't let that fear cripple you. There's too many people depending on us."

I watched him swallow the lump in his throat, and he pulled the picture he'd found the night before from his pocket. He spun it through the air, and it landed at my feet. I stared down at the picture of the beautiful woman and baby on the porch swing.

Willy said, "That's Beth and Torri Gilley, Jimmy. She's a widow, and that baby ain't got no daddy no more. Tommy Gilley used to sleep in that bunk right there—the same bunk I'm sleeping in—and he got blown up in a mortar attack . . . last week." Willy slapped his hand against the bunk. "Right here, Jimmy. This is where he slept, and now he's dead. There probably wasn't enough of him to send home. He probably got blown apart out there, and now that little girl has to grow up without no daddy. And for what, Jimmy?"

I slid closer to my friend. "I don't have answers to questions like that. Nobody does. But what we're doing is important. Yeah, it's dangerous, but everything worth doing comes with a price. We can't change that."

He kicked my boot. "Then why ain't you scared, Jimmy? Huh? Why? Is it that Jesus stuff, or have you got some kind of death wish or something? Why am I scared, and you ain't?"

I draped a hand across the toe of his boot. "It's not that I'm not scared. It's just that I know God has a plan for me, and for you, too. We may get killed over here. I don't know. But what I do know is that when I die—and I will die sooner or later—I know the life I get after this one is gonna be in a place where nobody will ever hit my momma again, and my brother Billy will be able to talk again. And there won't be any more tears or pain or need to shoot anybody ever again."

He wiped a tear from his eye he hoped I didn't see and leapt to his feet. "It must be nice to be so sure about something like that."

I stood. "It is nice. In fact, it's the nicest feeling there could ever be, and you can have it, too, Willy. All you have to do is ask for it."

He kicked open the door to our tiny room. "Oh, yeah? That's it, huh? Just ask for it. Nothing's that easy, Jimmy. Nothing."

I took a step toward him. "It really is that simple. I'll pray with you."

He shook his head and wiped away another tear. "God ain't got time to hear prayers from nobody like me. Maybe He'd listen to you if you prayed for me, though."

Chapter 13
Learning Without End

Proverbs 20:18 NASB
"Prepare plans by consultation and make war by wise guidance."

* * *

Staff Sergeant Chris McMillan, the sniper platoon sergeant, circled his gloved hand above his head. "Mount up, and don't forget to come home, boys."

I slid onto the back seat of the Peacekeeper behind the driver.

Chris took the front passenger seat and asked, "Ready for this one, Singer?"

"Always ready, Sergeant."

The driver shot a look over his shoulder. "Wait a minute. Are you the singing sniper?"

I expected Chris to field the question, but he left me dangling in the wind. "I've been singing a lot longer than I've been shooting, so I may be the sniping singer."

"Sing something, man. Everybody's talking about you."

"What do you want me to sing?"

"Whatever you want, dude. I've been over here so long I think I forgot what music sounds like. I'm Jerry Rivers, by the way."

"Nice to meet you, Rivers. Did you go to Vacation Bible School when you were a kid?"

He seemed to play back a childhood memory. "Yeah, one time. I went with some cousins in North Carolina when I was like ten or eleven."

I let my foot keep time against the metal floor of the Peace-keeper. "Good, then you'll know this one. I'll start it, but you have to sing with me, okay?"

While being rattled around in that hot, uncomfortable, noisy machine, Rivers and I sang "Onward Christian Soldiers" until Sergeant McMillan finally learned all the words and joined in.

When it came to an end, Chris said, "I've done a lot of stuff on the ride out to a mission, but I've never done that."

I asked, "Are we going to the same place we got ambushed yes-terday?"

Chris said, "Same city, different location. Do you know Sergeant Ballenger from weapons platoon?"

"I know him," I said. "He was my squad leader. Solid dude."

"Yeah, he's as solid as they come. We're covering him and a new kid named Adams or Adderly or something like that. They're leading a squad from the Eighty-Second. We'll set up and call them in."

He tossed a folded map into the back seat, and I pored over it.

"We're the red X," he said. "And Ballenger's team will hit the buildings on the north side of the street. We're covering the east end, and Gonzales and your buddy, Williams, got the west end. They're two vehicles ahead of us."

"I bet they're not singing," Rivers said.

Chris chuckled. "Yeah, probably not. So, anyway, back to the set-up. You're digging us in, Singer. If I don't like what you're doing, I'll get involved, but it's your show 'til you screw up. Got it?"

"I got it, Sergeant."

Rivers brought us to a stop two blocks from our overwatch site. "Is this close enough?"

Chris gave me an eye, and I looked down at the hundred-and-fifty-pound load I would carry two blocks and up at least four flights of stairs. Nothing about that sounded enjoyable to me, but I was concerned my platoon sergeant might think less of me if I shied away from the physical demands of such a task. On the other hand, maybe he'd think I was an idiot for working harder than necessary.

I could've talked myself into either decision, so I let my mind forget that anyone else was involved, and I made the call. "Get us closer, Rivers."

He pulled the Peacekeeper back into gear and stepped on the throttle. "All right. I'll get you a little closer, but I'm not going all the way to Rodeo Drive, even with two snipers in the vehicle."

He removed one of the city blocks from our trek and dumped us a thousand feet closer to our objective. Chris and I poured ourselves from the Peacekeeper, shouldered our gear, and moved as quickly as our feet would carry us under the burden of three rifles, two hundred pounds of ammunition, a spotting scope, and enough gear, food, and water to keep us alive for two days.

I was wrong about having to climb four flights of stairs. Our selected building had six. The added elevation would give us a much better view of the street that would become a battlefield, but it also added an element of complexity to the DOPE. I'd been through the High Angle sniper's course, so I was up to the task. I just hadn't anticipated the new variable.

When we reached the roof, Chris waved a hand across the scene. "What do you think?"

I grounded my gear and cautiously approached the two-foot parapet on the street side of the building, then scanned the street below while keeping myself as low as possible. "It's good visibility, but if we have to engage any target directly in front of us on the street, we're going to be hanging over the wall and shooting straight down."

He nodded. "Good. Keep looking, but don't get shot."

I lowered my head and inspected the roof surface and the low wall. To my delight, there was a three-inch hole ten to twelve inches above the roof deck. It was the perfect size to slide the barrel of my rifle through and do my deadly work. Dropping into the prone position, I sighted through the hole and was rewarded with a flawless and unobstructed view of the street below and enough angle to provide a lateral fan of fire of at least ninety degrees.

I rolled onto my back, looked up at Chris, and pointed toward the hole. "And this is nothing short of a gift from God."

"Sometimes these things happen. Most of us strike it up to snipers' luck, but you obviously think of them as being a little more divine. No matter what you call them, you've still got a nest to build, so get to it."

I moved my gear into place while he set up his spotter's scope to my left. As I was positioning my mat, backpack, ammo, and water, Chris used a pair of sticks and a piece of brown burlap to provide a layer of concealment for himself and his scope. My barrel hole wasn't big enough for his scope, so he was forced to work slightly above the top of the knee wall.

With everything arranged, I nestled in behind my .338 Lapua Magnum and pulled the lens caps from my scope. As always, I closed my eyes, asked for strength, and gave thanks for the gift of the perfect sniper hide. When I opened my eyes, I sighed in disappointed disbelief at the scene through my scope.

I rolled onto my side and stared up at my platoon sergeant. "You knew, didn't you?"

He gave me a knowing smile. "Yep. That hole you thought was a godsend is only big enough for your barrel. When you look through that scope that's an inch above the barrel, you can't see anything except dirty, rotten concrete."

I lay there, shaking my head, and he gave me a solid kick to my hip.

"Don't just lay there, sniper. Fix it!"

I pulled my rifle from the hole and studied the problem with my heart rate climbing by the second.

Chris gave me another kick. "This ain't training, Ranger. This is real-world stuff. We've got a platoon of paratroopers waiting for us to tell them we're ready to keep them alive, and you're staring at a hole in a wall. Improvise, adapt, overcome!"

I snagged a piece of burlap from my pack, laid it across the top of the wall, and rested the forearm of my rifle on the strip of cloth.

Chris rolled his eyes. "Is that the best solution you could come up with? You're willing to put your head over that wall so any countersniper with a slingshot could put you down. You've got to do better."

Everything in my world was a test, and what I was enduring in that moment was no exception. The difference was the lives of the paratroopers who were relying on me for overwatch. My brain turned cartwheels inside my skull as I studied everything in my environment.

There has to be another way. What am I missing? Think, Jimmy, think.

Every time I looked up, Chris was checking his watch and growing more anxious with every passing second. As I focused on the hole, an idea came. I lowered my rifle back to the roof and snatched my tool pouch from my pack, then pulled a pair of screwdrivers from the pouch and chiseled away at the hole. If I could make it one inch bigger, I could slide my barrel through and still have room to see through my scope. I swung the screwdrivers as if my life depended on enlarging that hole. My life, or the lives of the soldiers beneath me, may have been hanging in the balance.

Chris tapped the face of his watch. "Tick . . . tock . . . tick . . . tock."

The concrete was breaking away, but not quickly enough. I was running out of time, options, and ideas.

Finally, Chris said, "Wouldn't it be cool if you weren't all by yourself and you had, oh, I don't know . . . maybe a teammate or a spotter who could help you?"

"That would be cool," I said. "Hey, teammate. Have you got any ideas that might make this easier?"

He dragged his tool pouch from his pack and kicked it toward me. I pulled it open and poured out the contents. Right on top of the heap was a beautiful black hammer with a pick on one end and a hammerhead on the other. I snatched up the tool and dove back into my task of chipping away the concrete. The more I swung that hammer, the more sweat poured from my face. That's when something heavy and solid landed beside my left foot. I turned to see a brick lying harmlessly on the roof about six inches away. Not understanding what I was supposed to learn from the brick, I looked up at my spotter.

He pointed toward the brick. "What if that had been a mortar round or a hand grenade? You were so focused on your losing battle with that hole that you forgot you were in a hostile warzone, where ninety percent of the people in this town would love to watch a grenade splatter-paint your sniper butt all over that wall. You're not thinking like a sniper—or even a Ranger, for that matter. You're trying to muscle your way through a problem that isn't a problem." He took a knee beside me and whispered, "Don't get tunnel vision."

I didn't know for sure what he was talking about, but I was smart enough to know I was missing something obvious by focusing on a tiny hole in a wall. I scampered backward and scanned the environment. On my third visual pass around the rooftop, I paid more attention to a hodgepodge pile of timbers, rocks, and half of a metal barrel. Keeping myself low, I duckwalked to the pile and pulled it apart, piece by piece, until a jagged break in the low wall appeared behind the debris.

I sighed and repositioned the timbers and rocks until I had a beautiful loophole through the wall. Shaking my head at my own ignorance, I meticulously moved my nest behind the new hide and positioned myself behind my rifle. "Tell the paratroopers we're in position."

Chris made the radio call four minutes after the sun sank beneath the western horizon, and one of the longest nights of my life began on that dilapidated, dust-covered rooftop.

I learned two distinct things in that first hour of my second day on the battlefield. First, I learned the easy answer is rarely the right answer. And second, I learned not to pray for things I don't understand. I spent thirty seconds thanking God for the wrong hole when the perfect sniper position existed only feet away.

Often, the life of a sniper is a lonely existence, but I had the decided advantage of a real relationship with God. He put the people in my life I needed to learn from and grow with. He gave me the intellect to understand the complex mathematics of technical marksmanship and blessed me with strength of both body and mind. Most of all, though, He loves me in ways I can never fully fathom, and that gift alone is the one thing that sustains me when I'm silent, far from home, and invisible to the rest of the world.

Chapter 14
Rules of Engagement

John 14:30–31 NASB
(The Words of Jesus) "I will not speak much more with you, for the ruler of the world is coming, and he has nothing in Me; but so that the world may know that I love the Father, I do exactly as the Father commanded Me. Get up, let us go from here."

* * *

Peering to the east, especially through my scope, the ominous black sky felt like an evil wave determined to consume the coming night and everyone in it. Believing that evil can't touch the soul of a Christian is like believing you can survive alone in the middle of the ocean simply because you know how to swim. In this world, evil abounds. It's everywhere. Until Christ returns and claims what is His, Satan rules the world. Christ Himself told his disciples this truth before he was arrested, tried, and ultimately crucified. The enemy of God—the purveyor of confusion and the architect of sin—perhaps believes himself to be God's worthy adversary and antithetical equal, but nothing could be further from spiritual truth. God *will* win. Of this, I am certain. But until the greatest of all battles is fought at Armageddon, I can't allow myself to forget this truth. As much as I trust and love my God, believing I can't be touched or even killed by men driven by ultimate evil while living in the world is a fool's belief. Evil would touch me. It would show its face in the deeds of men who would slice and pierce and batter my human body and mortal mind for the entirety of my life on Earth. But my faith and God's promise would never let me surrender to those forces of evil, regardless of the ravages of their relentless attacks.

The coming night would teach me more about myself than any other night of my life, and I'll always wonder if everyone has such a night in their life. I pray they do not.

The tiny speaker pressed inside my ear and connected to the radio at my side crackled to life. "Sierra One, Delta One, commencing mission."

Sergeant McMillan keyed his mic. "Delta One, Sierra One, Roger. All Sierra elements are operational. Happy hunting, guys. We've got your backs."

I swallowed hard as the sidewalks below filled with columns of American Infantryman from the 82nd Airborne Division, led by the warriors of the 75th Ranger Battalion—my brothers, my responsibilities. The mission was to grab as many high-value targets as possible and bring every American home safely. The city was filled with loyalists to the warlord we wanted, and grabbing his lieutenants was the best method to get to the man who'd intercepted tons of humanitarian aid in the form of food, medicine, and of course, cash meant for the starving and dying under his nose.

I watched as the first team pressed through the first door of the night. It wouldn't be the last, but it would be the dawning of my new reality for weeks to come. Silence ruled the night inside the first building. Radio chatter bounced in my head, but no shots were fired, and the team emerged empty-handed but not discouraged. The first three doors produced identical results. I couldn't be certain what was happening behind the walls between the team's entry and exit, but so far, no Americans were down. But that all changed in the blink of an eye.

The soldiers hit door number four with the same force they'd pressed through the first three, but it wasn't sufficient. When the Ranger stepped back six feet, the night was about to come alive. His heel impacted the door halfway up the jamb, and it collapsed inward. Two soldiers followed the door, covering the man who'd kicked it in. A pulse of explosive orange flame huffed through the opening, and I turned the zoom on my scope until the smoking doorway filled my circular world through the black aluminum tube. My mouth instantly went dry, and my pulse quickened.

An American came tumbling backward out of the doorway, and I slid my finger from the guard and onto the curved trigger. The range was less than two hundred yards, so missing the shot wasn't a concern. Killing the first human through the door who wasn't in a U.S. Army uniform was my only thought until a child of no more than eight or nine stumbled through the door and across the soldier. The child spat on the American and kicked at his ribs. One of the paratroopers grabbed the boy, hauling him from his feet and pressing him to the wall of the house. I watched as the soldier patted down the boy in search of weapons or explosives while the rest of his team stormed the open doorway. Running toward an explosion is the last thing a man's mind and body want to do, but the brave warriors on the ground in front of me did exactly that, with utter disregard for their own safety, wanting only to fight alongside their brothers and refusing to leave them inside that house alone.

I pulled my attention from my scope just long enough to see Sergeant McMillan lay his SR-25 .308 rifle across the low wall in front of him. He'd abandoned his spotter's scope and readied himself for the coming firefight.

As he nestled into the weapon, he said, "I've got odds. You've got evens."

"Roger, Sergeant."

Target number one, odd, stepped through the door and onto the street. He raised a rifle toward the soldier who was still detaining the boy, and the first round from McMillan's muzzle sent the gunman to the ground, stopping his heart before he came to rest.

Number two, even, was next, but he wasn't alone. An American had him by a twisted arm, frog-marching him onto the street. My right index finger twitched, but killing a man in custody wouldn't be one of the sins I'd commit that night.

I closed my eyes for an instant, thankful I hadn't taken the shot, and when I reopened them, something to the right caught my attention. My night vision captured the flash and illuminated the white smoke trail snaking its way through the air directly at us.

I yelled, "RPG!"

The rocket-propelled grenade flew as if in slow motion toward our hide, and I watched it come, fearing I would die in the first minutes of the night's battle, leaving my brothers-in-arms alone and without overwatch.

Sergeant McMillan ordered, "Shoot him!"

I sent a .338 round through the grenadier's chest, nearly cutting him in half.

Although the man would never fire another weapon in anger, his final pull of the trigger could spell my doom. Instinctually, I turned my face away and covered my head. The seconds ticked by like hours until the hissing whistle of the RPG soared over our heads and impacted the building behind us. The explosion was massive, sending debris in every direction. Had the RPG hit our position, neither of us would've survived. Instantly, the night turned to a hell of its own making.

Back on my scope, I watched the boy yank himself away from the paratrooper and pull off his shirt. He ran down the center of the street, twirling the shirt over his head like a signal flag and stopping every dozen strides to point directly toward my position.

"What's he doing?"

I thought I'd asked the question silently inside my head, but Sergeant McMillan answered, "He's telling everyone where we are. Shoot him!"

I raised my crosshairs until his small frame lay in the center of my scope, and I pressed the trigger, taking up the slack until the boy's body turned to a ragdoll and he melted to the ground—the life inside him extinguished.

I eased my finger from the trigger, having never fired the round. "Somebody else shot him," I said.

"It doesn't matter. Get back on that doorway!"

I spun my rifle until my crosshairs fell on the open door still belching smoke. Faint muzzle flashes from inside the house told the sickening story of what was happening in there. Americans were dying or killing—likely both—and although neither is the stuff of sweet dreams, I silently prayed for the safety of my brothers. The overwhelming feeling of helplessness consumed me as I continued to watch without any ability to help the men I was charged with protecting. I wanted to be inside that house, dispensing fire with my brothers, but holding my position was my order and my responsibility. I would destroy anyone determined to harm them on the streets, but inside the houses, they were on their own.

The sharp crack of a single rifle shot from a rooftop across the street drew my attention to Willy's position. A second round came, followed by a third, and I leaned to my left in a wasted effort to see who or what he was shooting.

McMillan growled, "Stay on the door, Ranger!"

I shook off my almost-irresistible urge to see Willy's target and returned my attention to my team.

A winded voice poured through my earpiece. "Sierra One, Delta One is secure. We're coming out."

Sergeant McMillan said, "Roger, Delta One. Your man on the street is three meters right of the doorway. Do not engage him."

The adrenaline of combat tends to lead warriors to believe everyone in the environment is their enemy. As horrible as it is to be killed by a foe, every soldier would willingly die a thousand deaths at the enemy's hand rather than fading into eternity with his brother's bullet in his chest.

Our team moved through the door and onto the street with four prisoners, flex-cuffed and hooded, at the same instant a Peacekeeper rounded the corner at breakneck speed. The vehicle slid to a stop in front of the team, and as quickly as the initial flash had appeared, the prisoners were inside the vehicle, and the assault team was back against the wall.

"Delta One, Sierra One, say status."

The Delta leader looked up as if speaking directly to Sergeant McMillan. "It was a flashbang. No shrapnel. We're Charlie Mike."

McMillan sighed. "Roger, Delta One, continuing mission. You all right over there, Singer?"

"I'm all right," I breathed as I pressed the stock of my rifle back into my shoulder.

The team moved across an intersection and to the first door on the block. The lead Ranger turned the knob, but nothing moved. He shouldered the slab of wood, but it continued resisting, and he motioned for the breacher. The heavy-booted door-kicker launched himself toward his objective with impressive speed and force, but the door refused to surrender.

He knelt and pulled his pack from his back. Seconds later he pressed an explosive breaching charge to the door and ordered the rest of the team to press themselves against the wall.

When the charge blew, the door's resistance came to an end. Through the smoke, dust, and debris, the Ranger-led squad stormed the house as if they were one creature with a dozen legs. The small amount of light that had been escaping the hole where the door had been turned to the absence of light. Through my scope, it felt as if I were peering into the depths of Hell.

Only fifteen seconds after the team stormed the structure, a massive explosion echoed from inside the house. I swung my muzzle to every window and crack in the wall, desperately trying to see the Americans still on their feet, but smoke and debris were all I could see. Pieces of the building crumbled and fell to the street in testament to the force of the blast, and I prayed the team was still alive.

For the first time, I saw a crack in Sergeant McMillan's composure. He crushed his push-to-talk button and almost yelled into the mic. "All Charlie and Delta elements, this is Sierra One. Stand down . . . stand down!"

One by one, most of the Delta and Charlie teams reported standing down, but every team leader wanted to know why. Sergeant McMillan had a more important call to make rather than try and explain what we'd just seen. He said, "Delta One, Sierra One, over." He waited an eternity and tried again. "Any Delta One Team, Sierra One, report!"

Everything inside me wanted to tear myself from my rifle and charge down the concrete stairs to find the Delta team, but my training forced me to stay in the gun. I never pulled my eye from the scope as I scanned incessantly for any signs of life in the building.

As I strained and begged to see survivors, two more explosions rocked the suddenly quiet darkness, and I felt the tremor in my bones. Without looking away, I said, "They're blowing up this building. We've got to move."

Sergeant McMillan said, "Stand fast, sniper. They're not after us, they're gunning for the ground teams."

His reassurance did little to ease my fear that we'd soon be falling six stories into a pile of concrete rubble and bodies, but I stood my ground and worked the target.

As the echoes of the latest explosions drifted into the night and softened, a smaller, more concentrated blast sounded from perhaps a quarter mile away, and I listened closely in an effort to identify the difference between the charges in the houses and the newest sound. "What was that, Sergeant?"

"That was an RPG. Find the smoke."

I raised my muzzle and scanned the horizon in search of a rising plume of white smoke, but there was none to be found.

Sergeant McMillan said, "All Sierra Elements, Sierra One. Report that RPG."

A voice rang in my ear. "Sierra One, Sierra Five. Contact on Sierra Three's position. No movement."

Sergeant McMillan keyed up. "Sierra Three, report!" Only silence came, and he shook his head. "Delta Command, Sierra One. We lost Sierra Three, and—"

Another round of explosions roared from the street level, and I caught a glimpse of movement at the intersection. As I spun my rifle to focus on the movement, six targets filled my scope. I said, "Six military-age males, all armed, five hundred yards. Permission to engage."

"Kill 'em," came McMillan's cold, singular order.

I pressed the trigger and cycled the bolt six times, delivering half a dozen souls to eternal judgment. The first died with an RPG tube on his shoulder. The second left this world looking up as if confused by the sound of my rifle. Number three perished while pulling the trigger on his AK-47. He got off a few rounds that flew harmlessly over my head. The remaining three paid the ultimate price while running like frightened mice. With every press of the trigger, part of me died as well. It wasn't regret that immediately haunted me for the deed I'd done. It was anguish that such a deed was required, regardless of whose trigger finger sent the six rounds downrange.

With the immediate danger quelled, I spun back to the house. "Did anybody come out?"

McMillan said, "Not yet. I've got the house. You scan for targets."

"Sierra One, Delta Command, QRF is en route to Sierra Three's location. Continue mission."

The Quick Reaction Force was made up entirely of Rangers, including some of the best medics and riflemen in the battalion. I didn't know who the snipers were on Sierra Three, but no matter how badly I wanted to help them, the QRF was their best hope of survival.

I dialed back the magnification on my scope to allow a wider angle of view and began slowly examining every inch of the battlefield beneath me.

I listened to the comms as the ground elements worked toward the house where Delta One Team had experienced the explosion. At least four teams moved in practiced coordination down the street, and they became my primary responsibility. I scanned above and around them as they moved.

A man with an RPG leaned out from a third-story window, and I placed a .338 Lapua Magnum round between his shoulder blades, sending his body tumbling from the window and onto the street below. One of the ground teams stepped around the corpse as if he were a piece of rubble.

An unidentified American voice spoke over the radio. "Nice shooting, whoever you are."

I didn't want credit for the kill. I only wanted to keep Americans alive as long as I was on that rooftop, but McMillan keyed up. "Chalk seven more up to Singer."

"Was I singing?" I asked.

McMillan chuckled. "What do you think?"

"I'm sorry."

He grunted. "Don't be sorry, Jimmy. As long as the bodies are dropping, you keep right on singing."

When the ground teams reached the house, most of the soldiers fanned out and established perimeter defense. The remaining paratroopers formed an entry team and pressed toward the door. I recognized four Rangers at the head of the element as men from my former weapons platoon, and they were leading the entry.

"Stay on the hunt," McMillan said. "I've got the door."

A sniper's eyes and ears are his greatest weapons. First and foremost, a sniper is an intelligence-gathering machine. The act of pulling the trigger is a minuscule portion of a sniper's life. No matter how badly I wanted to be pushing through that door with my former teammates, I had a new mission. Rather than kicking in doors beside those brave men, I was charged with watching their backs so nobody could prevent them from fulfilling their mission, and step one of my reason for living was to locate and identify potential targets.

I'd been scanning the same street for over an hour, so I had a perfect snapshot in my head of how the area should look. If anything changed in the environment, I should be able to immediately identify the change and classify it as friend, foe, or indifferent. The first change in the world around me wasn't visible to my eyes, but my ears picked it up loud and clear.

I tilted my head so Sergeant McMillan could hear. "Vehicles approaching from the east and north."

Without hesitation, he said, "It could be the QRF."

I closed my eyes and listened intently. "They don't sound like friendlies."

McMillan said, "Oh, so now you can tell the good guys from the bad guys based on the way their trucks sound?"

"Not exactly how they sound, but how they're being driven."

He said, "You've got young ears, and mine are old and battered. If those vehicles aren't the Quick Reaction Force, you put them down. Got it?"

"Got it, Sergeant."

The approaching vehicles were definitely not the QRF. They were the gasoline that was about to be poured on the kindling fire before me.

Chapter 15

The Taste of War

* * *

When the convoy of vehicles came into sight, I called out, "One technical in sight . . . and followers."

"Stop 'em."

I withdrew my Lapua—Samson—and replaced it with Methuselah, my .50-cal. Measuring the range to the first vehicle using the reticle inside my scope, I held the windage and elevation instead of making the adjustments in my scope, and pulled the heavy rifle tight against my shoulder.

"One shot, one kill" is a common phrase tossed around when people who aren't snipers talk about snipers, but it doesn't represent the reality of what we do. As much as we'd love to have the ability to precisely place every first shot, regardless of distance, it just doesn't work that way. There are too many environmental and physical variables to consider for every shot to be a kill shot every time. Fortunately, at six hundred yards, the engine compartment of a pickup truck isn't a challenging target. The only significant factor complicating the calculation was the speed at which the vehicle was approaching, but the muzzle velocity of the .50-cal gave me the freedom to miss by a foot or more and still kill the truck.

As I pressed the trigger, the part of my brain that understands math changed my plan. I adjusted my point of aim and pressed the trigger until the mammoth rifle bucked and thrust itself into my shoulder. It took part of a second to refocus through the scope after absorbing the punishing recoil, but to my relief, my plan had worked perfectly. My armor-piercing, incendiary round struck the right front wheel of the truck, sending the vehicle into a violent turn to the right. At the speed he was traveling, the turn was un-controllable for the driver, and the truck rolled, tumbling sideways through three quarters of a full roll, leaving the underside com-pletely exposed. Without hesitation, I sent a second round directly into the gas tank, turning the vehicle into an inferno and blocking the road for the following convoy.

The car immediately behind the truck couldn't arrest its mo-mentum in time to avoid a collision with the overturned burning truck, and by that stroke of luck for the good guys, the roadblock's effectiveness instantly doubled.

Sergeant McMillan said, "Nice shooting, sniper. You know any hymns about hellfire, 'cause you just delivered a dose."

The convoy scattered into a disorganized hodgepodge of trucks occupied by confused drivers. It wouldn't take long for them to find an alternate route into the fight in front of me, but I bought our ground teams at least a couple of minutes.

The attack turned out to be far more concerted than I antici-pated. The convoy I delayed made up less than a quarter of the total ground force pouring itself onto the street below. Four other vehicle teams rolled onto the street and opened fire with everything they had. Men leaned from windows with Kalashnikov rifles firing full-auto into the night. The fire belching from their muzzles made them easy targets, but the incoming fire from every direction made it difficult to focus on one target at a time. Everything about the fight had become chaos of the highest order.

The consolidated force surrounding the house where the initial explosion occurred was in the firefight of its life, and I was determined to keep as many Americans alive as possible. Methuselah, my .50-caliber Barrett, was the wrong weapon for the direct-fire support mission, and Samson, the Lapua, wasn't much better. The SR-25 in Sergeant McMillan's hands was the perfect weapon for the mission into which we'd plunged, but I hadn't brought my .308. Before dismounting the .50, I put rounds through the hoods and grills of every vehicle I could see. The ragtag fighting force might deliver an uppercut we'd never forget, but I wouldn't give them the opportunity to retreat in their vehicles. If they ran, they'd do so on foot and under heavy American fire.

I heard a brief, shrill whistle, followed in rapid succession by three more, and the sound pulled me from the intensity of the gunfight long enough to wonder what the sound could be. When it happened twice more, and the concrete of the wall behind me exploded into crumbling shrapnel, there was no doubt left in my head about the origin of the sound. It was supersonic, incoming, 7.62mm Kalashnikov rounds aimed at my head. There are two ways to get my attention, and incoming fire only inches from my skull are both of those ways.

I suppose most normal people would retreat or duck for cover, but my first instinct was to scan for the flashing muzzle pointed most directly at me. There was no shortage of possible gunmen, but my night vision gave me a tool to ease that task. I settled on a muzzle flash at four hundred yards from the rifle of a fighter who'd taken cover behind the corner of one of the useless vehicles stranded on the street. His head appeared just long enough to point the front sight of his rifle roughly in my direction and squeeze off a volley of view. He ducked back behind the vehicle after spending just under two seconds exposed. I watched the cycle three times. Two seconds exposed, followed by four seconds behind cover. An instant before the fourth appearance of his head, I pressed my trigger, and he moved directly into my bullet's path, turning his skull into mist. He was the first man I'd ever killed—who wasn't inside a vehicle—with Methuselah. Why that held a place of significance in my mind is something I'll never understand, but putting a .50-caliber round through the body of a man never stopped haunting me.

The short-lived celebration of my temporary victory came to an end, and I was back in the midst of the fight. I gave one more pass of the street and the buildings lining the sidewalks before exchanging my .50-cal for Samson. Just as I slid the barrel through my loophole, a pair of explosions rocked everything in my world. From where I lay, the explosions could've been inches or yards away, but an earthquake of noise, shock wave, and flying debris rattled my soul as if the end of time had come.

The horrific sound that followed turned my stomach as I checked my nine o'clock to see the first floor of the building, where Willy and Sergeant Gonzalez were, burst into flames. As the dust cloud rose, the sound of the explosion faded to silence, punctuated by the staccato of automatic rifle fire.

Sergeant McMillan made the radio call time after time, but an answer never came, so he reported the situation to the Tactical Operation Center. He glanced at me and yelled, "The fight is in front of you, Ranger! Keep *your* head in *your* fight! You can't worry about Willy right now."

I tasted the bitterness of the bile rising in my throat as I imagined the horrific death Willy and Gonzalez were on the verge of suffering as their building continued to burn with ever-climbing flames lapping at the exterior. There was nothing I could do for them, but I could make the combatants on the street pay for putting my closest friend and brother-in-arms into such peril.

Samson bucked and delivered crushing blows to the fighters below. I wasn't sniping at that point. I was killing targets of opportunity with no range or windage calculations. The weapon in my hands had just become a hammer, and every enemy fighter on the ground, a nail.

Lost in the fury of battle, with ammunition stores waning, I poured lead onto the street and swore if I survived the night, I'd never leave my SR-25 behind on any mission that had the possibility of turning into a direct-fire event. Even though I had far superior ability to kill with one shot using Samson, the speed and agility of the smaller, lighter .308 would've more than made up for the loss of the heft of the Lapua.

I continued engaging targets until I heard a whistle, followed by a thud, followed by a groan from deep within Sergeant McMillan's gut. I spun my head, but the move felt like slow motion as the reality of the moment consumed me. My platoon sergeant, teacher, and spotter lay sprawled across the roof with his left hand pawing at his right shoulder and his eyes widening with every breath.

I grabbed my med bag and thrust myself toward him. I prayed he'd been shot low enough on the arm for me to get a tourniquet above the wound, but the bullet struck the right edge of his rifle stock, ripping dense plastic from the rifle and embedding it into his wound.

I slid my hand behind his shoulder to feel for the exit wound and felt a gaping hole with blood pouring from his body. Forcing him onto his stomach, I poured QuikClot into the wound and shoved it full of gauze. Rolling him back over, I gave the entrance wound the same treatment and lowered my face to within inches of his. "You're not going to die, Sergeant. I won't let you die. I need you to stay on your back and keep pressure on this wound as long as you can. Do you understand?"

He shoved his SR-25 toward me, and through gritted teeth, he growled, "Mow 'em down, kid."

I pressed his left hand into his wound and gave him a pat on the chest. "Don't you worry, Sergeant. I'll get us through this."

Low-crawling back to my fighting position, I pulled Samson out of the way and pressed the shorter barrel of the .308 through the crevice in the knee wall. Although the bullets were smaller, the rifle was faster and far more maneuverable than either of my heavy guns.

Dividing my attention between Sergeant McMillan and the street full of gunmen below, I poured lead from the sky, eliminating the most threatening targets first. The teams on the ground carried less ammo than me, but they weren't making any effort to conserve their stores. The more gunmen who fell, the less ambitious the remaining fighters seemed to be. I believed there was no way for the ground teams to see that phenomenon, but from my vantage point, it was obvious.

Several of the aggressors from the rear of the oncoming throngs broke ranks and drifted into the night. For some reason, the cowardice and lack of resolve of those men sickened me. None of the Americans beneath me were looking for an escape. They dug in and fought like honorable men driven by valor, determination, and devotion to the mission of freeing that war-torn country from the talons of an evil warlord bent on the accumulation of wealth for himself at the expense of the innocent, starving families beneath his feet.

As if watching it play out on a movie screen, the soldiers beneath me broke off into squads and small teams and moved between buildings, slowly and methodically flanking the aggressors. Determined to cover their maneuver, I scanned the street in search of the deadliest threats and eliminated them, one by one. I caught a glimpse of a man kneeling in the street with an RPG tube on his shoulder. Placing the crosshairs on his chest, I pressed my trigger, but instead of the sound of the crack and the recoil of the rifle, I heard and felt the sickening click of the firing pin falling on an empty chamber.

The rifle fired and expelled the spent shell casing, but the bolt failed to lock to the rear on the empty magazine, so I dropped the magazine from my rifle, inserted a full one in its place, pulled the charging handle, and heard the telltale sound of the RPG leaving the tube. My heart sank to my boots as I helplessly watched the trail of the RPG as the grenade flew directly toward the rooftop where Willy and Gonzalez had been nestled before the explosion that started the fire. If they were still alive and on that roof, my failure to change magazines had just cost them their lives.

I didn't have the stomach to watch the grenade's impact. Instead, I committed one of the darkest sins of my life. I didn't kill the grenadier out of duty to my country or in the name of freedom. I put two rounds in his chest out of anger and vengeance. When his body collapsed to the street, I roared like a wounded animal and poured three more rounds into his corpse.

Chapter 16

Hold On

1 Peter 3:13–16 NASB

"Who is there to harm you if you prove zealous for what is good? But even if you should suffer for the sake of righteousness, you are blessed. And do not fear their intimidation, and do not be troubled, but sanctify Christ as Lord in your hearts, always being ready to make a defense to everyone who asks you to give an account for the hope that is in you, yet with gentleness and reverence; and keep a good conscience so that in the thing in which you are slandered, those who revile your good behavior in Christ will be put to shame."

* * *

Terrified by my failure to both my teammates and my God, I shrank behind my rifle and turned to Sergeant McMillan. He was still conscious, but the look on his face said he wouldn't be much longer. I crawled to his side. "Stay with me, Chris. Do you think you can walk?"

Through clenched teeth, he said, "We'll see. Get me to the hatch."

Unwilling to expose my head and shoulders above the knee wall, I lay on my back, holding my platoon sergeant between my legs, and crawled backward. As we inched across the roof, he mumbled something, and I stopped.

"What did you say?"

He took a long, deep breath. "I asked if you were hit."

"Me? No, I'm not hit."

"Are you sure?"

"I'm pretty sure I'd know if I'd been shot."

He took another breath as if it could be his last. "You lost it a little bit. You really need to make sure you're not bleeding."

I assumed he was delusional from the blood loss, so I went through the motions of checking myself for wounds. "I'm good, Sergeant. We've gotta keep moving."

I shouldered open the hatch and dragged him through the opening as the waning gunfire reassured me that we were on the verge of ending the fight. I pulled the radio from Sergeant McMillan's side and called in a situation report.

The radio operator in the TOC said, "Roger, sitrep. Evac is en route to rally point Foxtrot."

I closed my eyes, pictured the map in my head, and keyed the mic. "Unable, Foxtrot. Request Echo."

"Stand by, Sierra One."

The QuikClot powder had done its job to the extent possible, but the gaping exit wound behind McMillan's shoulder was still oozing blood. I opened my kit and stacked more gauze on top of the blood-soaked pile already stuck to the wound, then I drew a roll of duct tape from my pack and leaned toward my patient's ear. "This is going to hurt, but I need you to stay with me. I'm going to move your arm away from your side, tape the wound, and then tape your arm to your body."

He swallowed hard and nodded. When I lifted his right arm away from his side, he gasped and bellowed as if I'd ripped it from his body. The tape went on quickly, and I wrapped the entire roll around his shoulder and body. I needed the gauze to stay in place until a real medic showed up.

Sergeant McMillan panted like an exhausted dog when I finally leaned him against the wall. While he was catching his breath, I said, "Stay here. I'm going back up to check the street, but I'll be back, and I'll get you down those stairs. The medics will be a block away when we get to the ground. Stay awake!"

He nodded and kept panting.

Back behind my gun, I surveyed the street and welcomed the sight of the tide of war shifting. The warlord's men were on the run in disorganized, frantic retreat. The paratroopers of the 82nd continued the barrage of aggressive fire, and I took advantage of our new situation to stand and stare toward Willy's hide. Even through my night-vision goggles, I couldn't see any evidence of Willy or Gonzalez on the now-burning rooftop.

Focus, Jimmy. Get Sergeant McMillan out safely. That has to be the priority. The QRF is coming for Willy. They're coming. Just do your job, Ranger.

The thoughts roared inside my head, but my heart was breaking for Willy. Was he still alive? Had he burned to death? Is it possible he made it down the stairs and out of the building?

I put two dozen rounds downrange to add insult to injury before packing up everything I could carry or drag out of the building. I tied Methuselah and Samson together and fashioned a bridle to wear them like a rucksack. With a fresh magazine in the SR-25 and six spares in my pouches, I abandoned the rest of the equipment and ammo on the rooftop.

As I slid through the hatch, Sergeant McMillan slid himself up the wall with enormous effort and steadied himself against my shoulder. "I can walk a little."

I cupped him with my left arm and cradled the SR-25 in my right. Getting him to the street would be the easy part. I had gravity on my side for that portion of the exfiltration, but the horizontal portion was going to feel like a fifty-mile forced march.

We rounded the first landing and heard footsteps echoing up the stairs.

"Put my pistol in my hand," he said.

I drew his sidearm and slid the 9mm into his palm. He gripped it with his left hand, and we continued down the stairs. The footsteps kept coming, and I tried to come up with a reason why they might be friendly boots, but nothing could be further from that possibility. They wouldn't come for us. The TOC knew we were coming down, and—

AK-47 full-auto fire filled the stairwell, and bullets bounced in every direction off the concrete walls. Any thought I had of friendlies climbing to meet us shattered like broken glass. I laid Chris against the wall and moved in front of him, determined to protect him from the impact of another bullet. I raised the .308 and set my jaw. They weren't taking us alive. We might become casualties, but we would not become prisoners.

My ears discerned two unique reports from at least two different rifles. I was outgunned, but I had the high ground. Fire bloomed twenty feet below me, and I was suddenly blind, disoriented, and on my back.

Did I take a round in my chest? Why can't I see? Am I still alive?

The world around me was pitch-black except for random orange bursts of muzzle flashes. Still confused and dazed, I rained fire down on the belching muzzles until the bolt locked open. I dropped the empty magazine and shoved a fresh one in its place. Even though the incoming fire seemed to stop, I continued dispensing killing-fire down the stairs.

Pausing only long enough to convince myself that at least the lead element of the climbing enemy had fallen, I returned to Chris and hefted him to his feet. I continued our descent in the dark, feeling my way as we went. Aside from being blind in the dark, it felt as if someone were pouring warm syrup over the left side of my face. I reached up to mop away what had to be sweat and discovered the reason my world had gone dark. My night-vision goggles were gone, and jagged edges of plastic and glass protruded from the flesh of my forehead. I'd been shot in the nods, and the syrup was obviously my own blood.

I yanked Chris's nods from his head and pulled the webbing over my skull. When I dropped the nods into position, half of the world returned in grainy, green mist in front of me. I believed my left eye was gone, but I prayed I could keep enough blood inside my body to get Chris to the medics.

I probably said the prayer inside my head, but it sounded as if I were yelling into the heavens and beseeching God to get us out of that building. I'll always believe the prayer was answered, but I don't remember stepping through the ground-level doorway and into the night. I must've done it, though, because I remember the medic catching Sergeant McMillan as he fell from my arms behind the medical vehicle. In reality, it looked like an ambulance crossed with a Humvee, but to me, it was a gleaming chariot of hope.

A second medic hefted the ropes from my shoulders and laid my two heavy weapons inside the vehicle just before shoving me onto the bumper. He yanked the nods from my head and shined a light into my left eye. I could see the light, so I wasn't completely blind, but the light felt like a thousand needles being driven into my brain.

"Am I going to die?" I asked.

The last answer I could've expected came out of the medic's mouth: He laughed. And kept laughing. "No, man. You're not going to die, but you're the luckiest dude I've ever seen. You've got pieces of your nods stuck in your head. It's gonna take hours to get you cleaned up."

"What about Sergeant McMillan?"

The medic looked over my shoulder. "It looks like you saved his life, Ranger. You're a hero. Get in. We've got to get you two out of here."

I shoved him away. "No! Take him and those two weapons. I'm going back for Willy."

He grabbed my shoulder and pushed me toward the vehicle. "No way, man. We ain't leaving you out here. Get in the bus."

I cupped a hand around the back of his neck and drew him past me and into the waiting truck. The SR-25 and I headed back into the night to keep the vow I made when I learned the Ranger Creed.

I will never leave a fallen comrade to fall into the hands of the enemy.

I raked broken pieces of nods from my hair and flesh as I ran the block to get back to Willy and Gonzalez. After descending the stairs with Chris and almost a hundred extra pounds of weapons slung across my back, the run with only the .308 felt like I was gliding across the ground. As I rounded the corner of the building and onto the street that had been the center ring of the night's circus, two Rangers raised M4s into my face, and I threw up both hands. "I'm Corporal Grossmann from sniper platoon."

The Ranger on the left laid his hand on top of the other man's rifle and pushed the muzzle downward. "Singer! What are you doing down here? Where's McMillan?"

I caught my breath. "He got hit in the shoulder. He's alive and on the medevac. Willy and Gonzalez were on top of that building behind you."

Both Rangers turned and stared into the rising flames, and the first said, "Are they . . ."

I said, "We lost comms with them after the series of explosions, and they took an RPG directly on their position, so I don't know, but I'm going in after them."

One of the men grabbed my arm. "No! You can't go in there. That's crazy. You'd never make it through the door."

I pulled my arm away from him. "I don't have a choice. I'm going in. I'm not leaving them behind."

The two Rangers stared at each other for only seconds before they pulled open their magazine pouches and withdrew their loaded mags.

"What are you doing?" I asked.

The second man said, "You can't run into a fire with live ammo hanging on you. If it cooks off, we'll be corpses when—if—they find us."

I followed suit and emptied my ammo while the two men called over a paratrooper. "What's your name?"

The soldier said, "Specialist Turner, Sergeant."

"Good. Now, listen close, Turner. Get one of your squad mates and guard this gear. We've got two Rangers stuck in that building, and we're going in after them. You and this gear better be right here when we come out. You got me, Turner?"

The paratrooper turned and eyed the burning building. "You're going in there?"

"Yeah, and if it were you stuck in there, we'd come in after you, too. Do you have a radio?"

Turner pulled a mic from his shoulder. "Yeah, I got one."

"Get on it, and get us a Blackhawk or a Chinook over this building. If we come out, we'll do it through the roof."

Wasting no more time, the three of us hurled ourselves through the opening where a window may have been sometime in years past, but that day, it just happened to be the opening with the fewest flames lapping at it.

The building was an oven of scattered flames and boiling smoke. The building itself was concrete, so it wouldn't burn, but everything inside was on fire and in complete disarray. The flames made it impossible for us to keep our nods in place, but fortunately, the fires lit the area as if it were daylight.

Finding the stairs was simple since the stairwell was acting as a chimney for the black rolling smoke. Even if we could survive the climb, our lungs would look like black boot polish by the time we reached the roof.

I didn't know the two Rangers, but both appeared older and more experienced than me, so as badly as I wanted to find Willy, my brain's desire to survive made me turn to them for ideas.

The man who'd led the charge through the window drew his canteen and lifted the bottom of his uniform shirt. He drenched the material with the water from the canteen and pulled the dripping-wet cloth over his nose and mouth. The younger Ranger and I followed his lead and copied him. With water-soaked filters over our noses and mouths, we could breathe relatively cool, filtered air as we sprinted up the stairs. The heat and smoke were horrific, but our lungs and legs were still pumping. We searched every floor on our way to the top, but there was no sign of anyone, especially snipers.

As we left the fourth floor on our way to the roof, the air freshened, and the smoke cleared enough for us to see the hatch leading to the roof. The blown-out windows served as vents for the smoke, but what I saw at the hatch made my blood run cold.

One leg protruded through the narrow opening with columns of blood pouring from the flesh. The American boot attached to the foot was twisted into an impossible position, and the howling wind of the furnace that was the building waved across the leg, causing it to swing in arcing trails like the pendulum of a clock.

I hit the hatch with my shoulder as if bursting from the gates of

Hell, but the heavy grate never budged. I staggered back and hit it again with the same result. It was pinned from the outside, but three determined Americans were driven by an unseen force to find or make a way through the obstacle. It was impossible to tell who the leg belonged to, but selfishness overcame me, and I prayed it wasn't Willy's.

The three of us pressed our backs to the hatch and dug our heels into the floor. With groans and growls, the metal door moved an inch, then two, and finally swung open enough for the rest of Sergeant Gonzalez's body to wilt through the opening and pour itself onto the floor. A pair of fingers that weren't mine landed on the dead man's neck, probing for a pulse they would never find.

With the opening cleared, I forced my way through and onto the roof that was nearly identical to the hide where Sergeant McMillan and I had been only minutes before. I pulled my nods back into position and pieced together the scene with my one clear eye.

"Willy! Willy! Where are you?"

I listened as if begging all of creation to whisper a breath of hope, but my pounding heart filled my ears and left me with only sight to locate my brother. On my second pass over the disheveled scene, I caught a glimpse of movement near a pile of smoldering rubble and dived toward the motion with my arm stretched to its limit.

I was rewarded by the gloved hand of Specialist Willy Williams. I gripped his hand, and he squeezed mine.

"Willy! Hold on! I'll get you out of there."

Refusing to release his hand, I went to work moving bits of rock, lumber, and every imaginable piece of junk from atop my friend. The other two Rangers joined the task, and soon we had enough rubble moved to see Willy's face and most of his upper body.

I slapped the nods from in front of my eyes and laid a hand against Willy's face. "Hold on, Willy. We've got you."

With our faces only inches apart, my friend's eyes looked like pools of muddy water draining into lifelessness.

He whispered, "I can't feel my legs, Jimmy."

"It's okay. We're here to get you out. A chopper's on the way."

Willy tried to take a breath. "I'm not going to make it, Jimmy."

"You're going to be fine," I said, but the scene before me was driven to make me a liar.

As we worked to slowly remove more debris from around Willy's body, the older Ranger bowed his head when we slid a section of timber from across Willy's chest and a hiss of air escaped his body.

"It's a sucking chest wound," the seasoned warrior whispered.

I squeezed my friend's hand. "Does it hurt, Willy?"

The tiny movements of him trying to shake his head looked like the death throes of man who'd reached his end.

With the tip of my trigger finger, I scratched a tiny cross in the dust and debris on the roof, then I lay beside my friend and held his face in my hands. "Listen to me, Willy. We're going to do our best to get you out of here, but you've got to listen to me. Blink for me if you understand."

He blinked his dying eyes, and I said, "When they crucified Jesus, He wasn't alone. There were two thieves being crucified at the same time, and one of them asked Jesus to remember him when he entered into His kingdom, and Jesus told the thief that He would be in Paradise with him that very day. All the thief had to do was believe, and when his human suffering ended, his soul would ascend into Heaven to never hurt again. That's all you have to do, Willy. Just believe that Jesus is God and He died to pay for your sins. Tell Him you believe, Willy. Even if you can't say it out loud, He hears your thoughts. Tell Him you know you're a sinner and you're sorry, and *know* He will save you. Tell Him, Willy. Tell Him, and just like the thief on the other cross, today you'll be with Jesus in Paradise."

Emptiness consumed me, and I clutched Willy's hand for the very last time as I watched my dearest friend form the words "I'm sorry" with his trembling, bloody lips, and then the dim, narrow light drained from his eyes.

Chapter 17

The Roaring Silence

Proverbs 10:21–22 NASB
"The lips of the righteous feed many, but fools die for lack of understanding. It is the blessing of the Lord that makes rich, And He adds no sorrow to it."

* * *

I lay on that pile of rubble for what could've been minutes, or perhaps eons, holding onto Willy's hand. His pulse was silent. His eyes were empty. He was gone, and I was once again alone in the world . . . or so I believed.

The riotous sound of a CH-47 Chinook helicopter coming to a hover over our heads dragged me from my stupor, and I looked up to see the rear ramp open on the massive flying machine. The pilots expertly maneuvered the chopper into position over the parapet of the building, and the wind from the pair of massive rotors of the Chinook turned the rooftop into a brownout. Dust and debris flew in every direction, leaving the three of us to cover our faces and wait out the torrent.

When the filth from the rooftop finally surrendered, leaving the air over the building breathable again, the two Rangers and I pulled the rubble from Willy's body and loaded him aboard the helicopter. We pulled Sergeant Gonzalez from the hatch in the roof and hefted his corpse up to the waiting soldiers inside the helicopter. The two Rangers stepped aboard with the help of a hand from two crewmen on the Chinook, but I couldn't pull myself from the battlefield.

I stood with my arms folded above my eyes in a wasted effort to block the wind from above and stared out over the darkened city where so much blood had been shed and so many souls had left their earthly bodies. Everything about the night felt wrong. Everything about my life felt wrong.

A pair of strong hands grabbed my plate carrier and yanked me aboard the waiting Chinook. The crewman dragged me to a webbed seat along the right side of the massive bay and shoved me into the netting. The instant I hit the seat, the pilots flew the chopper away from the burning building and landed a few seconds later in a clearing two blocks from where the firefight had begun. I couldn't count the soldiers who ran, limped, and crawled up the ramp, but by the time we were airborne again, there must've been fifty bodies, both living and dead, in the bay of the Chinook.

I leaned forward, landing my face in my palms with my elbows planted solidly on my knees. Warm liquid flowed over my left hand and down my arm, but I couldn't feel the wounds dispensing the blood. I closed my eyes and let the previous two years of my life play out like a movie on the screen of my mind. Every memory I saw was of Willy. I watched the two of us slowly morph from poor orphaned kids from South Carolina into warriors under the firm hands of men who'd been through countless fights like the one I'd just survived. Just like the one that had taken Willy's life.

Willy's determined refusal to believe slowly melted away as my words sank in, little by little. I relived the first conversation I'd had with him about the love of God and how He wants the best for His children, all of His children, even the ones who don't believe yet.

I heard the words of my testimony to Willy and relived the hours I spent working to bring Christ to my friend and my friend to Christ. Part one was easy. Christ wanted nothing more than to climb into Willy's heart. But part two was a little more challenging.

I'd said, "It's all about the love, Willy. He wants to give you everything—peace, joy, comfort, security, forgiveness . . . All of it. He came to Earth in the form of His only son and paid a price for our sins that only He could pay. We could never do enough to deserve His forgiveness and His love, but that's the best part. We don't have to do anything to deserve it or earn it. All we have to do is believe, which involves repenting, acknowledging, and accepting Jesus as our Lord and Savior. That's the first step in shrugging off the old man and taking Jesus into our hearts."

The words thundered inside my head, and I wanted to trade places with my friend lying lifeless on the floor of that helicopter.

Why can't I be the one who didn't survive? Why can't Willy still be alive? Why?

I was empty and alone on that chopper, with fifty other men packed in like sardines.

A massive soldier—bigger than anybody I'd ever seen—took a knee between my boots and grabbed the fabric of my shirt. "Pick your head up, Ranger. You're still alive, and you've still got work to do."

Did he say Ranger or Christian?

"There's nothing you can do for those guys now. They're gone, but you're not. You've still got responsibilities to yourself and to the rest of us who are still alive. We're your brothers, man, and we're still in the fight together. You got me, Ranger?"

I wanted to let his wisdom seep in, but I couldn't stop thinking that Willy wasn't just another dead soldier. He was my friend—a living soul I wanted to draw into God's kingdom with me. He'd become a brother-in-arms, and I believed in the seconds before his final breath, he'd also become a brother in Christ.

I lifted my face to stare into his. "It's my first time."

"Your first time for what?" he yelled.

"It's my first real gunfight, and the first time I've ever lost a real friend."

He gave me a shake. "It won't be the last. You can bet on that. And the fights never get easier. We just grow more calloused and harder. There will be more, and who knows? One hot night, half a world away from home, you and me might be in the pile of bodies, but until that night comes, we've got to keep fighting and remembering the ones who didn't come home. Don't ever forget them. Their memory is one of the things that keeps us soldiering on."

He reached up and probed at what must've been a gash over my left eye. "That's a nasty hole in your head, kid. Give me your kit."

I shook my head. "I don't have a kit, Sergeant. I used it up trying to keep my platoon sergeant from bleeding out."

He shoved several soldiers around like rag dolls until he found a med kit on somebody's belt. He wrapped my head with gauze and tape and then shined a light in my face, examining my left eye. "Whatever you do, don't tell the docs you can't see out of that eye. Do you understand?"

I didn't, but I nodded anyway.

He said, "It's full of glass and blood, but I don't think it's gone. I think the vision will come back once they get you cleaned up."

I leaned toward him, closing the already short distance between us. "What's your name, Sergeant?"

"Just call me Mongo. Were you the shooter with Sierra One?"

I nodded. "Yeah, Sierra One is my platoon sergeant. He took a round in the right shoulder, but I put him in the hands of some medics who showed up in a hardened ambulance. He was alive when I left him."

"Why didn't you go with him? You're in pretty bad shape yourself."

"I had to find Willy."

"Who's Willy?"

I motioned toward the corpse a few feet behind him, but he didn't turn. Instead, he shook his head. "I'm sorry, man. What's your name, Ranger?"

I took a long breath. "I'm Jimmy Grossmann, but everybody seems to think my name's Singer."

He gave me a slap on the shoulder. "All right, then, Singer. Where's your rifle?"

I shrugged. "Who knows?"

I thought I heard him laugh, but I couldn't be sure. He pressed an island-sized hand against my chest and pushed me back against the netting. "Keep your head up, Singer. You're a Ranger, and we don't let nobody see us with our heads hung down. When we land, stay on the bird. You probably don't know it yet, but you're shot up pretty good. Your legs probably won't work real well when you try to stand up. The adrenaline will be worn off, and you're gonna crash. It's gonna be a mess when everybody piles off this thing. You just stay in that seat, and I'll carry you off if you can't walk. You're gonna need a real doc—and not just a used-to-be combat medic."

"You're a medic?" I asked.

"I was before I came to Ranger Battalion. Now I'm a full-time mortarman and part-time medic."

Mongo was right. When we touched down at the forward operating base, the ramp came down, and soldiers stormed out of the

Chinook like it was on fire. I leaned forward and pushed myself to my feet, but my knees didn't get the memo. My vision from the one good eye I had left was blurry, and I suddenly felt like I'd been dipped in ice water.

A force I couldn't name lifted me from the floor of the Chinook, and I looked up to see Mongo's bloody, dirty face.

"I told you to stay in your seat, you hard-headed mule. Hang on. We'll get you some help."

He half dragged, half carried me from the chopper until a soldier appeared out of the chaos with four rifles slung across his back. "Hey, are you the sniper who ran into that burning building?"

I nodded, and he shoved three of the rifles toward me.

He said, "I couldn't carry the ammo, but these are the rifles you told me to watch before you ran in there. I'm glad you're still alive, man. I was worried about you. I ain't never seen nobody do anything like that."

Mongo took the rifles from the paratrooper and pushed him aside.

I said, "Only one of those is mine. The other two belong to a couple of Rangers who went with me to find Willy."

The paratrooper stepped back toward me. "What are you talking about? There wasn't nobody else with you. You ran into that building by yourself."

Sometime later, I opened my eyes—well, my *eye*—and all I could see was a bright white light. I squirmed and raised an arm to shield myself from the light, and a pair of hands grabbed my arm and forced it back to my side.

"Don't move."

I recoiled. "Where am I?"

"You're in the hospital, and we're pulling shrapnel out of your head. What's your name?"

"Grossmann. Corporal Jimmy Grossmann."

"Well, Corporal Grossmann, I need you to hold still. I'm going to give you something to help you relax while we keep working on your head. Do you understand?"

I nodded, but a strong forearm came down hard across my forehead. "Don't move," a new voice said, and I froze.

When I woke up, my head felt like it was clamped in a vise. I couldn't focus on anything, and my body ached as if I'd been run over by a truck . . . twice.

"Good morning, sleepyhead. How are you feeling?"

I turned my head to face the voice, but she was just a blurry image. "I've been better."

"Yeah, I bet. You were a mess when you came in here last night, but you're going to be okay. I suspect you'll be heading home in a couple of days."

"Home?" I asked. "Is the war over?"

She chuckled. "What war?"

"The one I was in last night."

"That's not a war," she said. "But I guess it felt like one to you. No, it's not over. I'm not sure it'll ever be over, but as far as you're concerned, all you've got to worry about for a while is healing up."

"I can see out of both eyes," I said, remembering what Mongo told me on the Chinook.

The woman laughed. "No, you can't, but nice try. There's a bandage over your left eye, and you're right one is full of blood. The bloody one will be fine in a few days, but we'll have to wait and see about that left one. Are you hungry?"

I heard her question, and I was hungry, but for some reason, all I could say was, "Willy's dead."

Chapter 18

Guest of Honor

James 1:19–20 NASB
"This you know, my beloved brethren. But everyone must be quick to hear, slow to speak and slow to anger; for the anger of man does not achieve the righteousness of God."

* * *

She was right. Whoever she was, she predicted my future as surely as if she'd been the one directing it, but it didn't happen quite as quickly as she thought it would. It took four more days in-country before the Army wrapped me up and sent me back to Fort Benning, the place everybody around me seemed to call home.

My second day in the field hospital began much like every morning of my life—with a prayer of thanksgiving. Before I opened my eye, I thanked God for keeping me alive and for putting me in Willy's life. I'd never forgive myself for running out of ammo at exactly the wrong moment, but I would always be grateful beyond words to have led my friend and brother into the loving arms of God. As important as Willy will always be in my life, he wasn't the only person I cared about. I needed to know about my platoon sergeant.

I opened my eye to see a world washed with white snow. Shapes and shadows moved across my milky window on the world, but focusing was impossible. Maybe it was some sort of coping mechanism, but I did something that morning no one would expect in such a moment. I laughed. The thought of a one-eyed sniper who couldn't see past his eyelids was, somehow, hilarious to me.

"What are you laughing about, Singer? Have you lost your mind already? For God's sake, you've only been in-country for three days. It takes most men three or four months before they completely lose it and turn hysterical."

I caught my breath. "Is that you, Sergeant McMillan?"

He gave my foot a squeeze. "Yeah, Ranger, it's me. I never did get to thank you for what you did out there. I would've bled to death on that roof if you hadn't been there, and I won't forget it."

"Come on, Sergeant," I said. "Anybody in the battalion would've done the same."

He grunted. "Maybe, but I want you to know that I'd wade into Hell with you anytime, sniper."

I didn't know what to say, so I lay there in silence, reliving the hell he and I had endured the previous night.

He interrupted my stroll down Nightmare Lane. "How'd you survive getting shot in the eye, anyway?"

"Those guys were terrible shots," I said. "They hit me in the nods and cut a pretty good gash in my forehead, but it was just a glancing blow."

He huffed. "Glancing blow, my butt. Judging by that bandage, they nearly scalped you, kemosabe."

I shrugged, still unsure of what to say. That's when I felt him settle onto the foot of my bed.

"They tell me you went to get Gonzalez and Williams. Is that right?"

Whatever the damage was to my eyes, I learned in that moment

I could still form tears. "I was too late, Sergeant. They didn't make it."

He sighed. "Yeah, I heard." He paused for a long moment and spoke barely above a whisper. "They told me you thought there were two other Rangers with you when you went in."

"Yeah, I don't know either one of them, and they never told me their names, but we crawled onto the Chinook together after loading Willy—I mean, Specialist Williams and Sergeant Gonzalez —onto the chopper."

"Are you sure they were Rangers?"

I thought back to the moment when the two soldiers confronted me on the street. "I guess I just assumed they were. I don't know for sure. Why does that matter?"

He scooted closer. "When they debrief you, it might be best if you don't mention those guys."

"You want me to lie?"

He said, "No, I'm not telling you to lie. It's just that . . ."

"They were real, Sergeant. I didn't imagine them."

He let out a long breath. "Sometimes, in combat, we see and hear things that aren't exactly in line with reality the way the rest of the world sees it. I'm just saying, maybe those guys weren't officially part of last night's op, and bringing them into the report might not be the best thing."

I furrowed my brow, and it felt like I'd been hit in the face with a sledgehammer. "You mean they might've been Delta or something?"

I couldn't see him, but his breathing told me he was weighing his next words carefully. "You just never know. Whoever they were, they never got on the Chinook, so you're not going to do yourself any favors by telling anybody about them. If they really were there, you don't want the brass thinking you left the two of them on that rooftop. You get what I'm saying?"

I felt a fire burning in my chest. "You're telling me I imagined them. Is that what you're saying?"

"No, hang on a minute. That's not . . . It's just that when we're wounded and running on adrenaline, we don't always—"

I cut in. "How 'bout Mongo, the giant who carried me off the chopper? Did I imagine him, too?"

"Easy, Corporal," he said, reminding me of the rank structure. "Mongo is quite real, and he *was* on the chopper. As you have more time to rest and heal up, it'll all make more sense, and you'll know the right thing to do."

Believing I'd imagined two Rangers who fought their way through a burning building with me wasn't something I was prepared to swallow.

They were real. I know they were. There's no other explanation.

Desperate to change the subject, I asked, "How's the shoulder?"

"Thanks to you, I didn't lose enough blood to kill me, but I'm shot up bad enough to share a cab with you."

"Huh?"

He chuckled. "It was a joke. We're both heading back to Benning. We might as well share a ride."

"I've never been in a cab."

His chuckling turned to full-blown laughter. "You're a strange dude, Singer. But don't ever change."

* * *

By the time we climbed aboard the C-17 Globemaster, I could see out of my right eye well enough to tell the difference between a person and a dump truck, but my newfound sight wasn't my only revelation. I learned I'd taken a round to the outside of my left leg at some point in the night. The doctors called it a through-and-through, meaning the bullet hadn't hit enough meat to expand and start tearing flesh from bone. It just pierced a nice, neat little tunnel through the outside of my leg about halfway between my hip and my knee. Golden bullet is what somebody in the hospital called it, but gold or not, I didn't ever want another bullet in any part of my body.

Back at Fort Benning, the long battle to restore my vision began, and everything about the process made me mad. I could see out of my right eye a little better every day, and I believed my left eye would catch up sooner or later, but all the signs were pointing toward later. Much later.

My body, including my leg, was healthy. I ran five miles every day. I did a thousand push-ups and at least as many sit-ups, but each day I longed a little more to be back downrange with my team. It wasn't the fighting I missed. It was my responsibility to my brothers. They were still kicking down doors and slugging it out with the local warlords every night while I was stuck in garrison doing one-eyed rehab.

One morning, a couple hours after sunrise, I was sitting in the grass outside my barracks, doing some stretches after my morning run, when a major walked up with a folder in one hand and a bottle of Gatorade in the other. He tossed the bottle to me, and I leapt to my feet to salute, but he waved me off.

"As you were, Sergeant Grossmann. Carry on. Stretching is important."

"Thank you, sir, but I'm Corporal Grossmann, not Sergeant."

He opened the folder and handed me a couple of sheets of paper stapled neatly together. "No, you *were* Corporal Grossmann when you woke up this morning, but you'll be Sergeant Grossmann when you fall asleep tonight. Congratulations on the promotion, son. How are you doing?"

I dropped my gaze. "I'm all right, sir."

He cleared his throat. "Look at me, Grossmann. Tell me how you're really doing."

I squinted against the bright morning sun. "Forgive me, sir, but I don't know who you are."

He stuck out his hand. "I'm Major Butterworth, the rear detachment commander."

I stood and shook his hand. "I'm sorry, sir. I didn't know."

"Relax, Grossmann. We're just a couple of Rangers talking about life, so tell me what's going on."

"I don't want to complain, sir, but what am I supposed to do? I'm a sniper, and I haven't fired a shot in weeks." I pointed toward my good eye. "I can see. I can shoot. I'm in great shape. I should be back over there with my platoon, sir. I'll be honest. I'm mad, and every day that passes with me stuck here in garrison makes it worse."

He took a knee beside me. "I'd like to have a thousand more just like you, Grossmann. A lot of soldiers would be beating down the door looking for a medical discharge, and here you are mad as a hornet because you can't deploy with one eye. You're a Ranger to the bone, son. I can't deploy you, and you have to understand that. You need time for that eye to heal, but I need you to tell me what you want—other than a plane ticket back to Northern Africa."

I grimaced. "Are you asking me if I want out of the Army, sir? If you are, the answer is no. The Army, and especially the Rangers, is all I've got. I can't do anything else other than hoe corn and bale hay."

He plucked a piece of grass and stuck it into the corner of his mouth. "I hear you can sing a little."

I huffed. "There ain't much call for a singer in the Army, sir. I'm a sniper."

"You *were* a sniper, Sergeant Grossmann. If you really want to stay in the Army, it may be time to think about something you can do with just one eye."

My blood boiled, but I held it together. "Are you saying I can't be a Ranger anymore?"

He shook his head. "You'll always be a Ranger. Nobody can take that away from you. You earned that tab, son, but the Army can't keep paying you to do PT by yourself every day while you're hoping to regain the sight in your left eye. I need to know what else you might like to do in the Army."

"But I'm a sniper, sir."

He planted himself on the grass beside me. "Let me tell you a story about a Green Beret officer who turned into a rear detachment commander in the Ranger Battalion. I rode a dying C-130 Hercules into the jungle canopy on the Amazon because the National Guard pilots and crew wouldn't survive the jungle without me, even if they lived through the crash. Me and four other Special Forces guys could've stepped through the door the minute the flames came shooting out of the belly of that plane, but we didn't. We stayed with it. Everybody except the co-pilot lived through the crash, and all the pieces of that airplane hadn't stopped moving before two dozen commandos working for some South American drug lord stormed the crash site with every rifle they had bullets for."

He paused and stared into the sky for a moment before continuing. "When the fight was over, there were a bunch of dead bad guys, four Air National Guard crewmen, and four Green Berets standing around with smoking rifles in our hands. We patched up the wounds, stuck the co-pilot in a body bag, and headed for the river. It took us three weeks to get out of that jungle, but we did it."

I stared into the eyes of a man who'd seen more than most men ever imagine possible.

He spat the piece of grass from his mouth. "When we got home, they told me I had a perforated diaphragm and that I'd killed the only two sons of some muckity-muck in Colombia—or some godforsaken place down there. I could take a medical retirement, or I could face charges for murdering a bunch of cocaine cowboys who were trying to murder me. That's how I ended up sitting beside you in the grass this morning, Sergeant. I gave the Army my life, and they gave me a swift kick in the butt for my trouble. Now, I need you to tell me what else you want to do, other than being a sniper."

I couldn't imagine the anguish Major Butterworth had to swallow, but something about his story made the rage in my chest subside just enough to say, "I might like being a combat medic, sir."

He slapped me on the arm and hopped to his feet. "Pack your bags, Sergeant. You're going to Fort Sam Houston to learn to keep Rangers from dying when they think there's no other option."

I stood and offered a salute, and he returned the courtesy. "Oh, I almost forgot. We're having a little ceremony this afternoon. Is your Class A uniform squared away, Ranger?"

I pictured my dress uniform hanging neatly in my wall locker. "It's got corporal stripes on it, sir."

He checked his watch. "Get your butt over to clothing sales and get your rank straightened out, Sergeant. The ceremony is at sixteen hundred, and you're the guest of honor."

Chapter 19
Little Treasures

Matthew 6:19–23 NASB

"Do not store up for yourselves treasures on earth, where moth and rust destroy, and where thieves break in and steal. But store up for yourselves treasures in heaven, where neither moth nor rust destroys, and where thieves do not break in or steal; for where your treasure is, there your heart will be also. The eye is the lamp of the body; so then if your eye is clear, your whole body will be full of light. But if your eye is bad, your whole body will be full of darkness. If then the light that is in you is darkness, how great is the darkness!"

* * *

I suppose the Army has been a big fan of ceremonies since its earliest existence. General Washington probably even ordered a few formal gatherings that few of his soldiers really wanted to attend. Major Butterworth said I was the guest of honor, but I suspected he was just being dramatic to make sure I showed up. There was no reason there would be any ceremony involving a one-eyed sniper who would become a combat medic. I've been wrong more times than I've been right in my life, and my belief about the ceremony that afternoon definitely fell into the category of me being wrong.

The lady behind the counter at Military Clothing Sales said, "I can sell you a new Class A jacket, Sergeant, but there's no way I can have your rank sewn on it by this afternoon." But as she was breaking the bad news, she cocked her head and pursed her lips. "Step back a minute, Sergeant. I may have an idea."

I followed her mysterious command and took two steps backward.

When I froze in place, she said, "Just a little to the left, please."

I shuffled to the left as my curiosity grew by the second.

She slid her glasses down her nose and mumbled. "Mm-hmm. Yep. It just might work."

"What might work, ma'am?"

She rounded the end of the counter and took several determined strides toward me. I sidestepped her charge, and she stopped in front of a mannequin behind me in full Class A uniform with gold sergeant's stripes on his arm. She pulled the jacket from the dummy and handed it to the other dummy in the room, so I slid my arm into the sleeve and pulled the green dress jacket around my shoulders.

She buttoned it for me and stepped back with her glasses still at the tip of her nose. "That'll have to do. Take your ribbons and name tag off your old jacket and leave it with me. Bring back the showroom jacket when you come back to pick up yours. That's the best I can do."

I couldn't resist giving her a hug.

She squirmed away and said, "Take your hands off me. I know all 'bout you Rangers. Ain't none of y'all can be trusted. I oughta know. I done been married to one for twenty-five years, and that man looked just as fine as you when I snagged him."

She helped me position my name tag and ribbons perfectly on the borrowed jacket, and I marched into the ceremony with my pants bloused above my jump boots, with toes that looked like mirrors, thanks to thousands of hours spent learning to polish. To my surprise, Major Butterworth met me at the door, shook my hand, and led me to a table by the podium.

There must've been a hundred Rangers in the place. They were laughing, drinking, nibbling on something from tiny plates, and generally making the best of having been ordered to attend some ceremony in the middle of the afternoon.

A sergeant major I didn't know came to attention in front of the podium with a sharp click of his heels. The rack of medals on his chest looked like they ran all the way across his shoulder.

As I watched the sergeant major, someone laid a hand on my shoulder and said, "Get up. You're singing the 'National Anthem.'"

I looked over my shoulder to see a full-bird colonel standing over me. Suddenly, my purpose at the ceremony became clear, so I pushed back my chair and rose to my feet.

The sergeant major ordered, "Room . . . attention!"

Everyone in the room snapped to attention, facing the podium. The order came, "Present . . . arms!"

An honor guard squad rounded the corner with a collection of flags, the Stars and Stripes standing high and proud at the center of the formation. The other flags were lowered in reverence to the Red, White, and Blue. The colonel gave me a nod, and I cleared my throat. I hadn't sung a word in weeks, so my throat felt like I'd swallowed a thousand razor blades, but I got through the "National Anthem" as the gathered Rangers stood erect with blade-sharp hands touching the outer edge of their right eyebrows in a perfect military salute.

As my vibrato closed on the home of the brave, the sergeant major gave the command, "Order . . . arms!"

The room erupted with cheers and claps. I had to admit it felt pretty good. I'd been down for too long, and I'd forgotten how good singing made me feel.

The colonel stepped to the podium. "Ladies and gentlemen, and all you Rangers, too . . . please have a seat."

His joke was rewarded with the expected amount of laughter and jeers. I pulled my chair from beneath the table and slid back onto it, but the colonel would have nothing of it. "Oh, no, you don't, Sergeant Grossmann. You can stay on your feet."

I self-consciously adjusted the black eyepatch over my left eye and stood at attention.

He said, "You can stand at ease, Sergeant, but don't expect to spend much time sitting down tonight."

I crossed my hands in the small of my back and stood with my feet shoulder-width apart in the traditional at-ease position as the colonel said, "To begin the proceedings, let me introduce the platoon sergeant for sniper platoon, Sergeant First Class Christopher McMillan. Get up here, Chris. I think you've got a few things to say about why I ordered everyone to be here this afternoon."

Sergeant McMillan stepped to the podium and shook the colonel's hand . . . with his left hand.

The colonel said, "That feels a little awkward, Sergeant."

"Not as awkward as getting shot in the right shoulder, sir."

That got a good laugh, and the colonel took his seat.

Chris pushed the microphone away. "I've never needed one of those things. Any of you who went through Ranger School while I was an instructor over there can attest to that."

A round of "Hooah!" and knowing groans filled the room.

"All right. That's enough, you bunch of babies. Somebody had to whip you girls into shape. Okay. It's time to get down to business. The only guy in the room who doesn't know why he's here is the reason we're all here, and if he *had* known it was all about him, there's no way he would've shown up. He's one of the most humble, mild-mannered men I've ever known, but you'd never get anybody who's ever been in his crosshairs to testify to that fact."

A voice from the back of the room yelled out, "That's because they're all dead."

Sergeant McMillan pointed toward the man. "How right you are, Ranger."

The more Sergeant McMillan spoke, the more interested I became. I couldn't wait to find out who he was talking about. I believed I was on the verge of meeting a real American hero, and I couldn't wait to shake his hand.

Chris continued. "Raise your hand if you've ever been deployed with real bullets in your rifle."

Every hand in the place shot up. "Now, keep your hand up if you scored your first enemy kill within an hour of hitting the ground downrange."

Two hands remained in the air.

"Now, keep your hands up if on your second day downrange, you scored twenty-four confirmed kills as a sniper *and* you saved your platoon sergeant's life after he'd been shot in the shoulder."

The remaining hands fell from the air, and Sergeant McMillan turned to me. "Put your hand up, Singer."

Instead, I bowed my head, too embarrassed to look up at the true warriors in the room.

Chris stepped from the podium, hooked his left arm around me, and pulled me against him. I don't know if he said it loud enough for anyone other than me to hear, but I'd never heard more sincerity from any man in my twenty years on the planet.

He said, "I'll return the favor some cold, dark night, somewhere in the world, but right now, all I can do is say thank you, brother."

I had endured heart-wrenching loss, unimaginable pain, and training that would turn most men into corpses, so I wasn't prone to moments of emotion, but nothing had ever touched me the way Sergeant First Class Chris McMillan's sincere expression did that afternoon, so long ago at the center of the universe, for every Ranger who's ever worn the beret and tab. I didn't want the men around me to see the tears, but I couldn't stop them from coming.

I heard Chris sniff as he fought back the tears, as well, but somehow, he mustered the grit to keep talking. He grabbed a fistful of my Class A jacket and shook me. "This man—this Ranger—got my bleeding under control while still gunning like the hardcore direct-action sniper he is. I don't know how many men he put down after those bastards put me down, but I know this . . . That night, in that godforsaken cesspool on the other side of the world, this man made a believer out of more bad guys than most of us put down in our whole careers. Let me tell you something. If you're pinned down or kicking in doors and you hear this man's voice on the radio, you go do your Ranger thing, boys, because Jimmy Grossmann's got your back."

He paused and took a drink before continuing. "Stay on your feet, Singer. The colonel has a couple of things for you."

I pushed my chair back in and turned to face the podium, where the colonel stood with a binder in one hand and a small box in the other. He placed the box in Chris's hand and opened the binder. "On your feet!"

Everyone stood, and the colonel said, "I wish I could spend the rest of my career without ever having to read another citation like this, but unfortunately, it's part of our chosen craft—part of the ugly reality of what we do for those who can't do it for themselves. Many of you in this room have stood in front of me while I read a citation much like this one, and for that, I thank you on behalf of a grateful nation who'll never know your name."

Everyone seemed to understand the weight of what was about to happen, but I was still in the dark until the colonel said, "Attention to orders! The United States of America. To all who shall see these presents, greeting: This is to certify that the President of the United

States of America has awarded the Purple Heart, established by General George Washington at Newburgh, New York, August seven, seventeen eighty-two to Corporal Jimmy Grossmann, United States Army, for wounds received in action in an undisclosed location in Northern Africa, on twenty-seven and twenty-eight August, nineteen ninety-one. Given under my hand at Fort Benning, Georgia, this fifteenth day of October, nineteen ninety-one. Signed by the adjutant general and the secretary of the Army."

Sergeant McMillan pulled the medal from the small, hinged box and pinned it to my borrowed jacket with his one good hand. I watched him fumble with the task, and I whispered, "This should be yours, not mine."

He smirked. "I've got plenty of my own, and if you stick around long enough, you'll have a drawerful, too."

No one clapped, I suppose out of understanding just how close every Purple Heart in the room came to being a flag draped over a casket.

Chris was right. My first Purple Heart felt foreign and heavy, but it wasn't my last. I was awarded two more medals that afternoon, but they're not important. Putting stock in awards and decorations would've meant my eyes were cast in the wrong direction. Instead of looking down at the ever-expanding collection of ribbons on my chest, it was always more important for me to look up and give thanks for the endless bounty of priceless gifts God granted me every day. Every new breath, every new experience, and every opportunity to serve my fellow man were gifts from on high, and I would spend my life looking to Heaven instead of looking at myself. My rewards awaited me at the end of my life on Earth. Until the day when I receive that great reward for a life of faithful service to my God, I would continue to devote myself to Him and to the preservation of godly principles.

Chapter 20

Go Fish

John 9:10–11 NASB

"So they were saying to him, 'How then were your eyes opened?' He answered, 'The man who is called Jesus made clay, and anointed my eyes, and said to me, 'Go to Siloam and wash;' so I went away and washed, and I received sight.'"

* * *

The morning sun climbed into the sky and brushed off the chill the late fall night had brought to Southwest Georgia, and I sat in the parking lot of the armory waiting for the man with the enormous ring of keys. He finally arrived with a steaming cup of coffee in one hand and the key ring and his tool pouch in the other.

"Good morning, Sergeant Adams. Let me help you with that."

The armorer shoved the heavy canvas bag toward me. "Thanks, Singer. What are you doing out here so early? Congrats on the Bronze Star, by the way, and I'm sorry about the Enemy Marksmanship Medal."

I grabbed the tool pouch. "It's not so much their marksmanship that got me. I just happened to step in front of their bullets."

"That was nice of you," he said. "I'm sure it was temporarily good for their egos that they could get a bullet in you."

In a brief moment of arrogance that I should've avoided, I said, "I didn't let them live long enough to enjoy their accomplishment."

Sergeant Adams laughed and pushed through the heavy door of the armory. "Are you shooting this morning?"

I pointed at my eye patch. "One last time."

He frowned. "Are they kicking you out, man?"

"Not out of the Army, but I'm headed to Fort Sam Houston to combat medic school. I report on Monday, but I just had to send a few more rounds downrange one final time."

"That sucks, man. I'm sorry. But look at it this way. They can't ever take your sniper tab away, and you'll be a great doc."

I said, "We'll see. God puts us where He needs us to be, so maybe I'm supposed to be a medic."

"That's a great attitude. Keep your chin up. Say, do you have anybody to spot for you this morning?"

"I'm alone."

He checked his watch. "Miller will be here any minute, so he can mind the shop. I'll go spot for you. It'd be an honor."

He unlocked the armory cage and waved me inside. I ran my hand across the long row of rifles until I came to one particular pair at the end of the rack. "That's Samson and Methuselah."

Adams scowled. "What?"

"These are the two rifles Sergeant McMillan gave me overseas. I named them, but I didn't know they made it home."

Adams laughed. "You snipers are weird dudes, you know that? Go ahead and pull them off the rack. I'll grab some ammo and meet you outside."

* * *

The long-range training facility lay before me with eight man-size targets at varying distances out to a thousand yards.

Adams set up his spotter's scope and called the targets. "With eyes, find the black-and-white range marker on the left."

I looked over my scope and found the marker. "Contact."

Adams said, "Move to three o'clock at fifteen mils to the vertical target."

"Contact."

"Go to glass," he ordered.

I nestled into Samson's stock with my right eye focused through the scope. "Target is white, oriented vertically with brown grass to seven o'clock."

"That is your target," he said. "Check parallax and mil."

I reached across my scope and gripped the parallax turret, carefully dialing the target into crisp focus and reading the mil-dots in my scope. "One point four."

Although I couldn't see him behind me, I knew exactly what Adams was doing. He was running the ranging calculation for distance and reading the wind. My only role in the coming seconds was to slowly exhale until just before the natural pause when my lungs were almost empty. Reaching that point, I said, "Ready."

Adams called, "Hold over two point three and point four left. Check level, and send it."

I made the holdover and windage correction and pressed Samson's trigger. Just over two seconds later, the beautiful sound of copper and lead striking steel rang through the air.

Adams and I continued the practiced ritual for another hour before trading places. I spotted for him and fought the urge to correct a few little flaws in his shooting technique, but after all, he wasn't a sniper, and I wasn't going to turn him into one that morning.

The ritual was exactly what I needed before watching Fort Benning fade away into the distance behind me with Fort Sam Houston and a new military occupational specialty on the horizon. I was losing so much of my identity by driving away from my career as a Ranger sniper, and the selfish, worldly part of my heart was breaking as my truck took on the feel of Jonah's great fish. Maybe it was God's will for me to become a medic, just like it was His will for Jonah to go to Nineveh. Jonah didn't want to go, either, but his will—just like mine—didn't really matter. Learning to submit to His will is what really matters. God's plan was far more important than any short-term selfishness I harbored. The bulk of my drive was consumed by prayers pleading for forgiveness and asking that His will be done in my life, regardless of the direction. I had no way to know where I'd land when that great fish finally spit me out, but no matter what lay ahead, my heart and I came to terms with accepting and embracing the path. It's all about learning to submit my will to God's.

* * *

I checked into temporary lodging and reported for duty at the combat medic course on Monday morning and was immediately ordered to take a PT test and undergo a physical exam. As any Ranger should, I exceeded every maximum standard on the PT test and scored a perfect three hundred. I grabbed a shower and changed into my uniform before heading off to find the hospital for my exam.

A military physical exam is a little different than the ones civilians enjoy. I spent an hour lumped in with a group of new, bright-eyed soldiers fresh out of boot camp and on their way to becoming medics . . . like me. They checked our vitals, tested our hearing, and gave us thorough eye exams. Of course, I failed the eye exam, but I expected to be given a waiver to remain in the

Army, in spite of my lack of vision in the left eye. Other than that, all indicators pointed to me being in perfect physical condition.

When it finally became my turn to see the real doctor, I pulled off my shirt and sat on the stainless-steel table, awaiting the physician's arrival in the exam room. When the door opened, a middle-aged man in a lab coat over camouflaged pants and black boots strolled in with a clipboard in one hand and his head cocked at an odd angle—I assumed to take advantage of his bifocals.

Without looking up from the clipboard, he said, "Sergeant Grossmann, I'm Doctor Filburn. You have an interesting medical record."

I stood and offered my hand. "Yes, sir. I got shot up overseas."

He waved a hand. "Have a seat. I just want to make sure I understand what's going on with you. Are you looking for medical review to separate from the service?"

"No, sir. I'm here for the combat medic course. I don't know if it says it in my medical records, but I'm a . . . well, I mean I *was* a sniper in the Ranger Battalion, but . . ." I pointed to my eye patch.

"I see. Well, let's have a look."

He pulled a tool from a holder on the wall. "Open up and say ah."

I did, and he explored my throat and teeth. After that, he pulled his stethoscope from his pocket and rubbed the bell against his pants. "These things are notoriously cold."

He listened to my chest and then moved to my back. "Take a few deep breaths for me."

I did, and he moved the bell to several spots as he listened to my breathing. He made a few notes on the clipboard. "All right, well, I guess we should take a look at that eye. Go ahead and pull off the patch."

I slid the pirate accessory off my head and looked into the same light he'd used to study my throat. He made a few groaning noises and asked, "When did this happen?"

"Back in August, sir."

"What happened?"

I cleared my throat. "I was carrying my wounded platoon sergeant down the steps in a building in Africa, and a militant shot me in the night-vision device I was wearing. I killed him and three others in the stairwell, but not before I lost my eye."

"So, you're a Ranger?"

"Yes, sir, but I don't know where the Army will put me when I finish the combat medic course."

He took a step back, placed the light in its holder, and laid a hand on my shoulder. "You're not going to believe this, Sergeant Grossmann, but you must be the luckiest guy I've ever met."

I interrupted. "Yes, sir. I was fortunate overseas, but I don't chalk it up to luck. I'm a believer, and I think God has plans for all of us. He wasn't finished with me."

He smiled. "I wasn't talking about being lucky overseas. I was talking about right now. Stay where you are, and I'll be right back. Oh, and you can put your shirt back on."

He reclaimed his clipboard and left the room as I pulled my shirt back on and wondered where he'd gone and why he thought I was so lucky to be there that particular morning.

When he came back into the exam room, he wasn't alone. He motioned to the new man and said, "Sergeant Grossmann, this is Doctor Harland. He's an Army reservist on his two-week, annual active duty."

I stood and stuck out my hand.

He shook it and said, "Have a seat, and let me take a look at that eye of yours."

He produced a small light from his pocket and flipped off the light switch, sending the exam room into total darkness except for his small penlight. He shined the beam into my damaged eye. "Close your right eye and tell me what you see."

I did as he asked and said, "I can see light, but it has a black circle in the center. It's not clear, but I can tell the difference between light and dark. That's about it."

He flipped the room lights back on and sat on the corner of the small desk. After running a finger down a page of my records, he looked up. "Have you spoken with a surgeon about that eye, Sergeant?"

I shrugged. "I don't know if he was a surgeon, but he was a doctor at Fort Benning. He told me it might heal itself a little over time but that I'd never get my vision back."

Dr. Harland said, "That guy doesn't sound like an eye surgeon. I don't know what cosmic forces brought you in here this morning, but I just happen to be an eye surgeon. In fact, I'm a pretty good one, and your doctor at Fort Benning was right."

My heart sank, but he continued. "If nothing is done to treat your eye, it will heal a little over time, but it'll never be usable again. I guess you can thank your lucky stars that you and I stumbled into each other. I'm going to replace your cornea with a donor cornea, and in a few weeks, sniper, you can go back to killing people downrange."

The emotion that overtook me at my Purple Heart ceremony returned, but I fought back the tears. "You mean I'm going to get an eye transplant, and I can go back to the sniper platoon?"

He flipped my chart over and pulled his pen from his pocket. Seconds later, he showed me a drawing of the human eye. "There's no such thing as a complete eye transplant, yet. Maybe someday that'll happen, but we're not there. What we *can* do, and what I *will* do, is replace the cornea with a healthy one from a donor." He pointed with his pen. "This is the cornea, and yours is practically destroyed. We'll get you on the donor list, and as soon as we find a match, I'll schedule an operating room, and you and I will spend a little quality time together."

I looked up in awe and disbelief. "This can't be happening. Can you really do that?"

He pulled a card from his pocket and stuck it in my hand. "I'll only be here three more days, but I'm the only board-certified eye surgeon in the Army system. So, when we find a donor, I'll either come back down here or we'll fly you out to Colorado for the surgery. Unless something out of our control happens, I'll have you back in sniping shape before you know it."

I took his card and stood on trembling knees with joy, disbelief, and praise consuming me. "Thank you, doctor. I have to tell you something, though."

"Sure, what is it?"

It was my turn to smile. "It had nothing to do with lucky stars, Doctor Harland. I believe God put you on the bank precisely at the moment when that whale spit me out."

Chapter 21

Patience, Patients

Colossians 3:12–13 NASB
"So, as those who have been chosen of God, holy and beloved, put on a heart of compassion, kindness, humility, gentleness, and patience; bearing with one another, and forgiving each other, whoever has a complaint against anyone; just as the Lord forgave you, so also should you."

* * *

I stood at parade rest in front of the first sergeant's desk as he flipped through my file. "Sergeant Grossmann, what, under great Heaven, are you doing at my schoolhouse?"

"I'm sort of asking myself that same question right now, First Sergeant. I just got some of the best news of my life over at the hospital."

He looked over his glasses. "Good news from an Army hospital? This should be entertaining. Let's hear it."

I pointed toward my file. "I guess you know my history . . ."

He made a sound that could've been a word, but I wasn't sure. An E-5 sergeant doesn't keep talking when an E-8 first sergeant opens his mouth, so I shut up. He looked up again with expectation on his face, so I took that as an invitation to continue. "Well, First Sergeant, I was in Ranger Battalion and got shot in the face overseas. The Rangers don't like one-eyed snipers, so I told 'em I'd go to the combat medic course, and the next thing I know, I'm down here at Fort Sam."

He grunted. "So, you're a Ranger who could've taken a medical retirement, but instead, you came down here to my school. What's wrong with you, son?"

I withheld the laughter rising in my chest. "As it turns out, First Sergeant, there's nothing wrong with me that the eye surgeon over at the hospital can't fix. I'm apparently getting a corneal transplant so I can go back to sniper platoon."

He slowly shook his head. "I knew this was going to be entertaining. Have a seat, Ranger. I'll get the hospital on the phone, and we'll get some answers. The last thing I need is a disgruntled sniper screwing up my schoolhouse."

I took the offered seat and waited for him to get through the minefield of the hospital telephone system.

When he finally got Doctor Harland on the phone, he said, "Good morning, doctor. This is First Sergeant Pearlman over at the schoolhouse. I've got a young Ranger sniper in my office telling some tale about an eye transplant, and I need to know what to do with this guy."

I couldn't hear Dr. Harland's response, but the first sergeant took some notes and grunted at regular intervals. Finally, he said, "I see. And how long will it be before young Sergeant Grossmann can go back to killing bad guys instead of saving lives with a red cross on his arm?"

I watched and listened intently, hoping to get a hint of the doctor's answer, but the stone-faced senior NCO didn't offer a bit of what he was hearing until he said, "All right, then. I guess that means I've got to teach this knuckle-dragger to read and eat with a fork so he can wash out of CMSTP."

My heart sank, and it was obvious the first sergeant could see it in my face.

He hung up the phone and pulled off his glasses. "The combat medical specialist training program is sixteen weeks long. During those sixteen weeks, some of the best medical professionals in the Army are going to teach you more about how to keep the insides of soldiers on their insides than you ever wanted to know."

He tapped on the cover of my file. "It looks like you've spent the bulk of your career in some kind of school or another, so you're going to feel right at home. You're one of two reclass soldiers in this class. The other is a specialist who decided he didn't like packing parachutes anymore and wanted to be a medic instead. He'll wash out early, but that doesn't matter. You're still going to be the senior man, and the only man in the class with combat experience."

He picked up his glasses and pointed them at me. "Listen to me, Sergeant. Do not screw up my class with war stories and bull crap from Ranger Battalion. You got me?"

I nodded. "Yes, First Sergeant."

"What is it, soldier? What's that look about?"

I swallowed hard and twisted the heel of my boot on the floor beneath my chair. "Nothing, First Sergeant."

He stuck the glasses on top of his head. "Nineteen years, Sergeant. That's how long I've been wearing this uniform. I've got six combat deployments and thirty-four good soldiers who died while my hands were inside holes some bad guy put in their bodies. I've seen some stuff, Sergeant Grossmann, so don't try to tell me that look is nothing."

I played out the coming scene in my head, and no matter which variables I changed, it always ended the same. If I said what I was thinking, First Sergeant Pearlman would kick me out of his school before the first day of training. I accepted the outcome and opened my mouth. "It's just that, I'd like to know what Dr. Harland said about the timeline."

The first sergeant pushed his chair back from his desk and rested his feet on the corner of the fifty-year-old office relic. "Anxious to get back behind a rifle, Sergeant?"

"No, First Sergeant. I mean, yes. But I want to complete this school and go back to sniper platoon, too. I don't want to just be a medic."

"*Just* a medic? Is that what you said, Sergeant?"

I groaned. "I didn't mean it that way. I'm . . ."

"Relax." He flipped open my file and stuck his glasses back on his nose. "Jimmy. That's your name, right? Not James?"

I nodded. "My folks were simple people from South Carolina. Jimmy fits me better than James, First Sergeant."

"You're not a very patient man, are you, Jimmy?"

I shook my head. "I'm working on that. I pray about it a lot, but I get anxious sometimes. I thought my career as a sniper was over until I met Doctor Harland, and I'd made my peace with that. I thought the best way I could serve after that was to become a medic."

I paused and replayed the scene of the firefight that killed Willy and Gonzalez and almost killed Sergeant McMillan. "We need good medics out there, First Sergeant, but I'm a good sniper, and that's where God wants me. Otherwise, he wouldn't have put me and Dr. Harland here at the same time."

He studied his fingernails. "So, you're a God-fearing, Christian man, are you, Jimmy?"

"I am, First Sergeant. That's the highest calling there is."

He let his feet fall from the corner of the desk. "Do you know what I was doing before you came in here and interrupted me, Sergeant Grossmann?"

I shook my head, and he pulled open his desk drawer. A second later, a well-worn, leatherbound Bible landed on the center of his desk. "I was reading the third chapter of Colossians about forgiving people, just like God forgives us. And that's what I'm going to do. I'm going to forgive you for calling me *just* a medic, and I'm going to tell you what your buddy, the eye doctor, told me."

I stared down at his Bible and felt the warmth of First Sergeant Pearlman's faith. His harsh, accusatory tone was gone, replaced by the gentleness of a humble man of God.

"Jimmy, he told me that it'll likely be thirty days or so before you get to the top of the transplant list and they find you a new eye. It'll take you about a month to recover from the surgery, and it'll take at least two more months before your sight will be back to normal, then he'll sign you off to deploy with your unit again. By my calculations, that's exactly enough time for you to complete the course and go back to Special Forces."

I wanted to be overjoyed by the timeline, but I wanted so badly to get my new cornea that afternoon and head back to sniper platoon the next day. "Thank you for telling me, and I apologize for calling you *just* a medic. But I'm not Special Forces, First Sergeant. I'm a Ranger."

He slid the Bible back into the drawer. "You may not be a Green Beret yet, but when they hear about a Ranger sniper who's also a qualified medic and too dumb to take a medical retirement when they offer one up on a silver platter, the boys from Fort Bragg will be knocking down your door to sign you up."

Apparently, the look on my face said I liked that answer because he waved a hand and said, "Get out of here before you do some kind of happy puppy dance and pee on my floor."

I hit my feet in the position of attention at the same instant his telephone rang.

He lifted the receiver and covered the mouthpiece with a hand. "Yeah, yeah . . . you're dismissed."

I executed an about-face and disappeared from his office with every corner of my heart and soul screaming with excitement. The future unfolding in front of me seemed as if it had been poured out directly from the gates of Heaven. But I was seconds away from news I wasn't prepared to hear.

From down the hall behind me, the first sergeant's booming voice bounced off the walls. "Grossmann! Get back in here, double time!"

I spun and almost sprinted back into his office. Standing at rigid attention in front of his desk, I demonstrated more of my epic lack of patience, and he dropped the receiver back into its cradle.

"I've got some bad news, Sergeant."

My heart sank. The green beret I wanted so badly faded from my mind's eye, and I braced myself for the coming blow.

First Sergeant Pearlman motioned toward his phone. "That was the hospital, and it doesn't look like you'll be starting the combat medic course this week."

"Why not?"

"Sit down, Sergeant."

His command only heightened my dread, but I followed the order and reclaimed my previous seat.

He took a long breath and let it out as if it were his last. "Sergeant Grossmann, you can't start my schoolhouse tomorrow because you'll be recovering from eye surgery. Four soldiers were killed in a training accident two hours ago, and one of them is apparently a perfect match." He checked his watch. "Do you have wheels?" Unable to speak, I nodded, and he said, "Good. Report to the hospital, double quick."

Without waiting to be dismissed, I bolted from the chair and through the office door, but before I made it two strides into the hallway, he said, "One more thing, Sergeant."

I stepped back into his office, and he said, "I'll check on you to-morrow morning. And Jimmy . . . the wife and I will be praying for you."

Chapter 22
Dreams Do Come True

Proverbs 3:26 NASB
*"She opens her mouth in wisdom, and the
teaching of kindness is on her tongue."*

* * *

"How long has it been since you had anything to eat, Sergeant Grossmann?"

The Army nurse reminded me so much of my mother with her gentle, confident voice, and dark, sparkling eyes. The heartache of having my mother murdered before my eyes as a child was an agony I'd never defeat, but knowing she was at peace in the arms of Jesus softened the burden I'd bear as long as I lived.

I tried not to look at her like a nine-year-old child, but I probably failed. "I had breakfast, ma'am, but I don't know how long ago that was."

She smiled just like my mother. "That's fine. Do you have any questions for me?"

"Yes, ma'am. I've got about a thousand, but maybe you could just explain to me what's about to happen, and that'll answer most of them."

She laid her clipboard on the desk. "The doctor will go over the particulars with you, but it will generally go like this. We'll give you a general anesthetic. Do you know what that means?"

I shook my head, and she smiled again. "You've never had surgery before?"

"No, ma'am."

"That's okay. Dr. Harland is the best eye surgeon in the Army, so you're in very good hands."

I raised an eyebrow. "I may just be a dumb old sniper, but I know Dr. Harland is the *only* eye surgeon in the Army."

She gave me a wink. "See? I told you he was the best one we've got. He's so good we don't need any more. Anyway, stop interrupting me. We'll put you to sleep with a drug that will allow us to perform your surgery without you feeling a thing, or even knowing you're having surgery. Depending on how much damage the doctor finds when he gets inside your eye, the whole thing shouldn't take more than an hour or so. When it's over, we'll wake you up, and you'll have a whole new outlook on things."

"That's one way to put it," I said. "But I've got something serious to ask you. What about the soldier whose cornea I'm getting?"

"What about him?"

"When will you tell me his name and how to get in touch with his family? It's only right that I go see them and tell them how sorry I am about their son, and how thankful I am for what they're doing for me."

She frowned. "I'm sorry, but you'll never know the donor. We're not allowed to tell you who they are. Sometimes the donor's family isn't receptive to meeting the recipients of their loved one's organs. It's too painful for them. So, I'm sorry, but you'll have to be thankful and trust they'll know."

I furrowed my brow. "Will you tell them who I am?"

"I don't know. That's not my department."

"Can you at least tell me how he died?"

She lowered her chin. "I'm sorry, but I can't tell you that either because I don't know. Please don't think I'm a heartless person, but there's nothing we can do for him. He's gone. But there's so much he can do for so many other people like you who need donor organs and tissue. Sometimes, they need them to survive. If you're not an organ donor, you should consider becoming one. It's one of the greatest gifts you can ever give."

Instead of explaining how I'd probably die on a battlefield a long way from any hospitals, I changed the subject. "Is it normal to be nervous?"

She stood. "I'd be worried about you if you weren't. Now, come with me."

I spent the next few minutes having blood drawn and signing some paperwork I didn't read. I figured Dr. Harland wouldn't do the surgery if I didn't sign, so to me, it didn't matter what the paperwork said.

The nurse was right. The doctor spent fifteen minutes with me and explained the surgery in detail.

"Do you have any questions, Sergeant Grossmann?"

"Just one," I said. "Are you a Christian, Dr. Harland?"

He laid a hand on the center of my chest. "I'm a very good surgeon, Jimmy. You've got nothing to worry about."

I guess I got my answer, but not the one I wanted.

The drugs they used to put me to sleep were very good at their job. I fought hard to keep my eyes open, but I was powerless to fight the drugs off. I was twenty years old when I went to sleep, and I never remembered having a dream before that afternoon at Brooke Army Medical Center on Fort Sam Houston. Even though I couldn't remember ever dreaming before, I'd never forget what I'd experience in the coming hour.

I heard her voice long before I saw her face, and I could feel my brother poking me in the leg, trying to get me to flinch while Momma told us about Joseph.

"Sit still, and listen up, boys. I'm going to tell you a story 'bout a boy who was 'bout your age, whose brothers did a terrible thing."

The dream was more vivid than any memory I could produce, and my mother's beautiful voice was crisp and clear.

"This boy's name was Joseph, and he was an Israelite. You boys remember what being an Israelite means, don't ya?"

Billy said, "Yes, ma'am. It means he was Jewish, just like Jesus."

She continued her story. "The Bible tells us this boy's brothers sold him into slavery in Egypt. We're the descendants of slaves, boys, so that means we've got something in common with Joseph, and just like God had a plan for him, I just know He's got something great in store for you boys."

"But how could God have a plan for somebody who was a slave, Momma?"

I'll never understand why I could still hear Billy's voice so clearly after so many years of him being lost in silence.

"That's the best part. Now, listen here. Joseph was a good man, a godly man, and he had faith, even though he was a slave. You hear me? It don't matter how bad things get for you boys, you gotta hold strong to your faith. Sometimes, all we got is our faith."

"Yes, Momma."

"Hush now, and listen. Joseph's master's wife tried to get that boy to act up and carry on with her, but he wouldn't do it 'cause he knew it was wrong. There's a lesson in that, boys. Do what's right, even when you're tempted to do wrong. Joseph coulda give up, you know—him being a slave and all. He coulda said it ain't nothing for me 'cause of me being a slave. My own family done turned again' me, so what's it matter now what I do? But no, that ain't what he thought. He held strong, just like I want you boys to do, and Pharaoh got to hearin' 'bout how this slave boy, Joseph, could make sense of dreams. Pharaoh was havin' himself some tremulous dreams, and he sent somebody to fetch him that slave boy, Joseph."

I watched Billy lean in and listen like Momma was telling us the secret to everything. And maybe she was.

"Pharaoh told Joseph 'bout his dreams, and that boy listened, and God 'splained to Joseph what them dreams meant. He told Pharaoh, and Pharaoh believed him. Next thing you know, Joseph is livin' in Pharaoh's house and runnin' the food distribution 'cause of famines that was a comin'."

Billy wasn't the only one engrossed in Momma's story. I could almost see Pharaoh and Joseph. Momma sure had a way of bringing Bible stories to life.

"Now's, here's the best part. It turned out that Joseph was right about everything he told Pharaoh, and that Israelite boy growed up to be an important man, and he forgave his brothers for what they done to him. And in the end, everything worked out just right 'cause Joseph did the right thing. He listened to God, and he used the gifts God gave him, and even though he had to go through a rough patch there for a while, at the end of the day, God made everything all right for Joseph. I want you boys to remember that. You always be faithful to God, even if'n it's hard, and God'll always be faithful to you. Don't you never forget that. You hear me?"

When the nurse woke me up, I wanted to ask if she'd give me some more of those drugs so I could hear my momma's voice again, but I was afraid she'd think I was crazy.

"How do you feel, Sergeant Grossmann?"

"A little groggy."

"That's to be expected. The surgery went perfectly well with no complications. The donor cornea was a perfect match, and Dr. Harland says in a few weeks, you'll never know you've got somebody else's cornea."

I spent the night in the Army hospital, and they released me the next day. I got to take off the eyepatch the day after that, and even though nothing was in focus, I could see shapes and light and motion in my left eye for the first time in months.

Even though I missed starting the combat medic course the day of my surgery, First Sergeant Pearlman put me in the next class three weeks later.

By that time, I could see well enough to read with both eyes, but if I was tired, sometimes my left eye would get a little lazy and forget how to focus.

I studied hard and listened to everything our instructors told us. Just like I'd done in most of the classes Willy and I had gone to together, I crammed the material into my head until it made sense, and I scored well enough on every test to stay near the top of my class.

My opinions of medics changed in the sixteen weeks I spent in the schoolhouse. I learned the brave men who were combat medics were every bit the hero that the Rangers and Green Berets are. They put themselves in harm's way to save lives every time bullets start flying, and that's bravery at its finest, if you ask me.

When we graduated and passed our National Registry exams, I was proud to call myself a combat medic, and I'd learned skills that would serve me and the brave warriors I fought alongside for years to come. Without the wound to my left eye, I would've never gone to Fort Sam, and if I hadn't gone there, I would've never met Dr. Harland. People say God works in mysterious ways, but I don't think that's true. God works in ways that are mysterious to nonbelievers, but for those of us who trust Him and keep the faith just like Momma taught Billy and me, God works in wonderful ways that make our lives better and fuller than they could ever be without Him. Those ways aren't mysterious. They're the ways of love, and when it comes to love, there ain't no love like Momma's and God's.

Part II
I Picked a Rose

Chapter 23

God's Rose

Ecclesiastes 1:7 NASB
*"All the rivers flow into the sea, Yet the sea is not full. To the place
where the rivers flow, there they flow again."*

* * *

Since the day I left Fort Benning for Fort Sam, almost six months
before, I hadn't touched a weapon. Other than in the holsters of
the MPs, I hadn't even seen a gun in half a year. No Ranger
should ever spend that length of time away from his weapon, even
if he's learning to save lives instead of taking them.

I checked in back at sniper platoon to find my team not only
home, but also gearing up for a second deployment back to the
same dingy corner of the world from which Willy had never come
home.

Sergeant McMillan shook my hand and pulled me in for a bear
hug. "It's good to have you back, old boy. How's the eye?"

"It's good, but it's not my eye. I'm just borrowing it."

He waved me toward the equipment cage. "Yeah, that's what I
heard. Can you see with your borrowed eye?"

"Not as good as I could with the one God gave me, but a whole lot better than six months ago."

He motioned toward my section. "Your gear's all there. Have you seen the doc yet?"

"Not yet. I figured I'd check in with you before doing anything else."

"So, did you get all schooled up? Can you do better than shoving the hole full of gauze if I get shot again?"

"Hey, it may not have been pretty, but you lived, didn't you?"

He laughed. "Touché."

"I learned a few tricks," I said. "But hopefully, I'll never have to use any of them."

"*Hope* ain't a plan, Sergeant. Now, get your butt over to see the doc, and make him sign off on you going back downrange with us. It'll be nice having you back in my hide."

"I'm not current, even if the doc signs me off. I haven't qualified on my rifle since October."

He chuckled. "Do you think Carlos Hathcock worried about staying current?"

The legendary Marine sniper who became larger than life in Vietnam in the late 1960s was a hero to every modern-day sniper, and I was no exception.

"I'm no Carlos Hathcock."

Sergeant McMillan gave me a shove. "Yeah, I know, but if you don't get yourself dead, something tells me they'll speak your name with reverence, right along with his in another thirty years."

I shrugged. "I don't do this to be a rock star."

"Maybe not, but that doesn't mean you're not one. Get over to the hospital and stop worrying about qualifying. I'll point to the trigger if you forgot where they put it."

The doctor didn't share Sergeant McMillan's enthusiasm to get me back on the battlefield. He studied my eye as if he'd never seen one before and concluded that I wasn't ready for a combat deployment.

"But, doctor, my platoon is leaving on Friday, and I can't let 'em go without me."

Without looking up from his clipboard, he said, "You can stand on the tarmac and wave bye-bye, but you're not deployable yet, Sergeant."

"You don't understand . . ."

That was enough to pull him from the clipboard. "No, Sergeant. I believe it's *you* who doesn't understand. You don't deploy until I say you're deployable, and that settles it."

Sergeant McMillan blew his top and marched up the chain of command in a wasted effort to find somebody who could overrule the doctor, but no matter how high he climbed up that chain, the answer was still the same.

"At least send me to another school," I pleaded. "Don't make me sit around here in garrison while you and the rest of the platoon are downrange without me."

Sergeant McMillan asked, "What school do you have in mind?"

"I'll go to any school you'll send me to, but it'd be nice if I got to shoot while I was there."

"Can you swim?" he asked.

I feigned offense. "Is that how it is? You think I can't swim because I'm black, is that it?"

"No, it's got nothing to do with you being black. It's just that your head is as hard as a rock, so I figured you probably can't float."

"You may have a point there," I admitted, "but I can swim. Why?"

"We've got two slots in the Combat Diver Course in Key West. Baker and Thompson were slated to go, but the deployment put that on hold. Do you want one of their slots?"

"Sure. Why not?"

He shook his head. "Singer, I'd love to have a dozen more just like you. Get settled in, and I'll get the commander to cut you some orders for dive school."

"I'm settled. I've got eight pieces of clothing the Army didn't issue me, so getting settled is a matter of hanging up my uniforms and making sure my key still works in the door lock."

* * *

Key West, Florida, isn't what anybody would call a bastion of morality. My first time on Duval Street, I saw things I never imagined, and some of them were things I never wanted to see again. But there was one exception . . . One beautiful, unforgettable, irresistible exception. Her name was Rose.

She smiled and cocked her head as if amused. "Can I help you, sir?"

I wanted to speak, but it felt like my mouth wasn't connected to my brain anymore. All I could get out was, "I'm Singer."

She leaned toward me across the linoleum counter separating us. "Okay . . . so you're a singer. Did you want some ice cream?"

In my childhood, there was never enough money for candy or ice cream, but at the preacher's house, we sometimes made ice cream on the front porch on hot summer evenings. I sat for what felt like hours turning that crank and watching the tub spin inside the packed ice and rock salt. When it was finally ready, the top came off, and inside of that frozen metal tub was one of the greatest treats of my lifetime. Sometimes, we'd cut up a peach and drop the pieces into the white, fluffy layers of ice cream, and the world around me would disappear. That's the memory that sent me inside the ice cream parlor at the corner of Duval and Front Street.

She was wearing a yellow and white apron with her hair pulled back in a ponytail, and everything about her made me weak in the knees.

"I, um . . . Yes, ma'am, please."

She giggled, and her dimple looked like the brightest star in the night sky. "Cup or cone?"

I knew she'd asked a question, but my brain couldn't process it. "Yes, ma'am, please."

She giggled again. "You're cute. Let's start over, okay?"

I nodded, and she said, "Ice cream? Yes or no?"

I kept nodding.

"Cone?"

And I still nodded.

She plucked a cone from the stack and rinsed off the scoop. "You're going to have to speak now. We've got like twenty flavors, so I don't have time to go through each one."

Somehow, I managed to say, "Peach."

Her smile grew. "That's my favorite, too."

I watched her delicate, practiced hand slide the scoop through the ice cream and press it into the cone, and I thought I could stand there forever watching her.

She wrapped the cone in a napkin and handed it across the counter. I took it from her hand and felt like I was going to pass out when our fingers touched.

She continued smiling and motioned toward the cash register. "That's three twenty-five."

I pulled a five from my wallet and held it out, desperately trying not to make it obvious that I wanted to touch her hand again.

She pulled the bill from my fingers. "It's okay. I'm not going to bite. What's your name?"

"I'm Singer," I said again, sounding more ridiculous than the first time I said it.

"Your name's Singer? Really?"

"I had a cornea transplant, and now I can see again."

What? Where did that come from? Why would I tell her that? What's wrong with me? Get it together, Jimmy.

She slid the five into the register and held out my change. "Okay, that's a weird thing to say, but let's get back to the name thing. I'm Rose, and you're Singer?"

I gathered my wits as best as I could. "You're beautiful, Rose. I'm sorry. I didn't mean to . . ."

She slid her hand into mine and shook it. "You're doing fine, and thank you for the compliment, Singer. You're sweet."

I closed my eyes and took a long breath. Behind a rifle, I was supremely confident, but standing in front of the beautiful Rose with ice cream melting in my hand, I was an idiot.

"I'm really sorry. It's just that . . . I mean, people call me Singer, but my real name is Jimmy."

"Why do they call you Singer?"

A thousand answers popped into my head, but the one that fell out of my mouth turned out to be the best possible answer. "God gave me a gift."

Rose closed her eyes and squeezed my hand. "That's beautiful. Would you like to sing something for me?"

I panicked. "I don't really know many songs other than hymns. I sing old Southern Baptist hymns when I'm working."

"I like hymns. What key do you sing in?"

"Well, I don't know."

I think my answer disappointed her, and she changed the subject. "Have you seen the sunset from Mallory Square yet?"

"No, ma'am. I'm staying on base, and—"

"Oh, you're in the Navy?"

"No, ma'am. I'm not in the Navy."

"You can stop calling me ma'am. It's just Rose, and we're probably the same age."

Trying not to sound like a smitten boy, I said, "Why did you ask me about seeing the sunset?"

She lowered her chin. "I thought maybe, if you didn't have other plans, we could watch it together tonight. I get off at five."

I'd been through a lot of things in my two decades on Earth, but I'd never experienced anything that felt like having Rose ask me to watch the sunset with her.

"I'd love that."

She grinned. "Cool. Meet me here at, say, six?"

"I thought you said you get off at five."

"I do, but I have to go home and change. I can't go on a date with a cute Navy boy dressed like this."

"I'm not in the Navy."

"Yeah, that's what you said. We'll talk about that tonight, but for now, the line's getting pretty long behind you."

I shot a glance over my shoulder at the dozen people waiting for ice cream and Rose's attention. "I'm so sorry. I didn't mean to mess up the line."

I shoved the change into the tip jar and stepped aside. The ice cream was delicious, but it wasn't as good as the ice cream on the preacher's front porch ten years earlier.

My watch said it was 2:45, so that gave me just over three hours to add some more civilian clothes to my humble eight-piece wardrobe. I went with a Key West T-shirt and shorts, and I bought my first pair of flip-flops but felt like a drunken baby duckling trying to walk in them, so my running shoes would have to do. I turned out to be way underdressed.

Rose walked up to the ice cream parlor in a yellow dress, white sandals, and a flower in her hair. If she'd been beautiful in the apron, she was breathtaking in the dress. I stood from the bench that had been my home for the past anxious hour and stuck out my hand.

She slapped it away and stepped in. "We've already shaken hands, Singer. It's time for our first hug."

She smelled like everything should smell, and I was intoxicated. "You look amazing."

She stepped back and did a twirl. "Thanks. And you look like a tourist. Come on. If we go now, we'll get there in time to get a good spot on the rail."

We walked side by side toward Mallory Square, laughing at tourists who were dressed a lot like me.

"So, you said you're not in the Navy, but you're staying on the base. What's that about?"

"I'm in the Army. I'm here for the Combat Diver Course."

"I didn't know the Army had divers, and I'm not sure I believe you."

I plucked my wallet from my pocket and handed it to her. She took it and looked at me with confusion in her eyes.

I said, "Go ahead. Check it out." She opened the wallet, and I pointed to the card in the clear plastic sleeve. "See? That's my Army ID."

She held up the card. "Sergeant Jimmy Grossmann. I'm impressed."

She snapped the wallet closed and did something that was probably supposed to be a salute.

I laughed. "That's not even close, and I'm not an officer, so nobody salutes me."

"Whatever. Now, about this diving class. Is it like scuba diving?"

I shrugged. "I'm embarrassed to admit that I don't really know. I've been in the Army for three years, and I go to every school they'll let me."

"What do you do in the Army?"

"I shoot."

She gave me a playful slap. "Duh, everybody in the Army shoots, don't they?"

"Not the medics."

"So, that must mean you're not a medic."

I rolled my eyes. "That's a long story. I'm sort of a medic."

"How can you be *sort of* a medic?"

"I'm a Ranger, but I got hurt, and they sent me to the combat medic course down in Texas while I was healing up."

She stopped in her tracks. "How'd you get hurt?"

I stared down at a piece of a conch shell between my feet. "It was nothing. I hurt my eye."

She laughed. "Okay, so that's what the cornea transplant thing was about. You were so cute in the store this afternoon. It was like you'd never seen a pretty girl before."

"Yeah, I'm sorry about that. I guess I'm more comfortable with my rifle than I am with people. I don't think I've ever seen anybody as pretty as you before today, and that left me a little tongue-tied."

She stared up at me. "You're quite the smooth talker, but I'll take it."

We rounded the corner, and more Key West weirdness was on display. A man on a unicycle that must've been ten feet tall was juggling knives that were on fire. The gathered crowd stared at him in awe, and I was just as mesmerized as they were.

"Look at that. Have you ever seen anything like that?"

She huffed. "I see it every day."

"Well, it's my first time, and I'm impressed."

"Wanna try it?" she asked. "I know him, and I'm sure I could get him to let you try."

"No, I don't think so, but it does look amazing."

We continued our walk down the array of street performers until we came to a tiki hut with coconuts hanging everywhere.

"Let's get a drink," she said.

"I don't drink."

She looked up as if I'd just chewed the head off of a small animal. "Sure, you do. Everybody has to drink."

"I mean, I don't drink alcohol."

She hooked her hand inside my elbow and pulled me toward the tiki hut. "Two lemonades, please."

The lady behind the coconut bar filled two plastic cups and slid them across the bar. "That'll be nine dollars."

Rose looked up at me with expectation in her eyes, and I said, "I can't help you. You've still got my wallet."

She laughed and shoved it back into my hand. I paid for the lemonade, and we found a spot by the railing on the seawall.

She took a sip. "Pretty good, huh?"

Over the next thirty minutes, the square turned into a carnival. There must've been a couple thousand people milling around and waiting for sunset. Sailboats cruised by with the wind filling their white sails, and a massive cruise ship pulled away from the dock.

She watched the ship sail away. "Have you ever been on a cruise?"

"No, I've never really done anything except what the Army had me do."

"That's too bad. You've got to have a life outside of work."

"Being a Ranger is kind of a full-time thing. We're gone a lot, and even when we're home, the hours are long. We spend a lot of time in the field on training exercises, and like I said, I go to a lot of schools."

She played with her straw and then pointed to the west. "Here it comes . . . Your first Mallory Square sunset."

I stared into the bright-blue sky with wispy clouds changing color with every passing second. The lazy sun touched the water to a chorus of oohs and ahs, and even a few drinks were raised into the air. Watching the ocean absorb the sun was like watching Creation.

Rose was right. It was a sunset I'll never forget, but probably not for the reasons she expected.

Just before the final sliver of the sun sank out of sight, a boy pulled away from his mother a few feet from us and slipped through the rail. He fell ten feet and collided with the surface of the water, flat on his back. An instant later, he was gone, and the next moment of my life happened without conscious thought.

I bounded across the rail with my feet and knees together and hit the water like an arrow. When I resurfaced, I looked toward the spot where the boy had landed, and I swam as hard as my arms and legs would propel me toward the place I'd last seen him. I filled my lungs and dived hard, kicking, pulling, and praying I'd bump into the child. There was no visibility and no chance of finding him without divine intervention, but that didn't slow me down. I dived, surfaced, and dived again in repeating cycles until I felt my hand brush against something that shouldn't have been underwater.

I grabbed it, pulled it against my chest, and assessed the situation. *Two arms, two legs, a head.* I kicked for the surface and broke from the dark water a few feet downstream from the seawall in the receding tide. Kicking as hard as I could, I raised the boy from the water and gave him a squeeze. He coughed, gagged, spit up a lungful of water, and cried like a newborn.

Flashlights shone from the seawall, and a small boat drifted alongside me. I handed the boy up to the man in the boat and caught my breath before climbing over the gunwale.

By the time I'd climbed the steel ladder on the face of the seawall with the boy in my arms, firemen and police officers were everywhere. The frantic mother shoved everyone out of her way and positioned herself at the top of the ladder. She ripped the boy from my arms as soon as we reached the top.

The commotion lasted way too long, but I finally escaped the crowd to find Rose standing beside a lamppost with tears streaming down her face.

I ran to her and knelt at her feet. "It's okay. The boy's alive, and I don't think he's hurt."

"That's not why I'm crying . . . That was the bravest thing I've ever seen. You didn't even think. You just reacted. I'm speechless."

"Now you know how I felt the minute I saw you in the ice cream shop this afternoon."

She pulled me from my knees and collapsed against my chest with her arms wrapped around me as if she were holding on for dear life.

I tried to squirm away. "I'm getting you all wet."

She squeezed me even harder. "I don't care. You're amazing, Jimmy."

When we finally separated, she said, "I guess we both need some dry clothes now, huh?"

"Yeah, I guess so. I'm sorry I messed up the sunset."

She took my hand. "You didn't mess up anything. You were perfect."

"Nobody's perfect. I'm just glad we were here."

We walked back to the ice cream shop in silence, leaving a soggy trail behind. When we got to the Conch Train stop, she said, "You have to go get changed. And please throw that shirt away. It's terrible."

I pulled at the cheap cotton shirt with the water gluing it to my skin. "What? This is my new shirt."

She drummed her palms against my chest. "Yeah, well, throw it away anyway, and I'll take you shopping tomorrow after church. You are coming to church with me in the morning, right?"

Chapter 24
Music Lessons

2 Chronicles 29:29–30 NASB
"Now at the completion of the burnt offerings, the king and all who
were present with him bowed down and worshipped. Moreover,
King Hezekiah and the officials ordered the Levites to sing praises to
the Lord with the words of David and Asaph the seer. So they sang
praises with joy, and bowed down and worshipped."

* * *

When I arrived at Rose's church the following morning, I pulled
my worn, ragged Bible from the seat beside me and stepped from
my truck. To my surprise and delight, I saw Rose skipping down
the stairs with the most beautiful smile on her glowing face.

Before I'd taken two steps, she threw her arms around me.
"What's your favorite song?"

I returned the hug and said without hesitation, "He Walks with
Me."

She took my hand and led me beside the church where no one
could see or hear either of us. "Okay, sing the first couple of lines
for me."

I cleared my throat. "Okay. Whatever you say." I sang the first two lines of my favorite hymn to a woman I met less than twenty-four hours before, and she closed her eyes and listened to every word.

When I stopped, she asked, "Can you sing it one full step lower?"

"I don't know what that means."

She said, "Sing the line that goes, and He tells me I am his own."

I did, and she said, "Now, the note you sang on the word *tells* is an E note. Sing it again, a little lower."

I did, and she grinned. "That's it. When we sing it together this morning, I want you to sing every note one step lower than you sang it the first time. Can you do that?"

"I don't know. I don't really know anything about music. I just sing what feels right."

She looked up at me with her perfect dark eyes sparkling. "We're going to sing it in D because that's where it's easiest for me. My voice isn't as good as yours, so you have to make the change, okay?"

"We're singing together this morning?"

"I told my daddy we would."

"Your daddy? He's here?"

She gave me another playful slap on the arm. "Of course he's here, silly. He's the preacher, and Mom plays the piano."

I don't know what I expected the morning worship service to be at Rose's church, but I never dreamed I'd get a music lesson and be asked to sing in front of the congregation. But that's exactly what happened.

The choir sang three hymns that didn't require opening the well-worn red hymnals in the pockets of the pews, and the worship leader announced, "Thank you, choir. That was beautiful to God's ears. Now, we have a special duet. Everybody knows our sweet, beautiful Rose, and we've all heard her raise the roof by singing to the heavens, but this morning, she's not alone. Come on up here, Rose. Bring your friend and praise the Lord in song."

She took my hand and "encouraged" me to stand with her. I'm not shy about serving the Lord, but my earthly shell was a nervous wreck that morning.

What if I can't remember to sing everything a full step lower? What does a full step lower even mean? What if I forget the words? What if I look at Rose and forget who I am?

Rose's mother played the introduction, and I listened intently to every note, praying I could match the sound and not make Rose look like a fool for inviting me to join her.

On the first note of the old, familiar song, I heard the voice of a thousand angels pouring out of Rose's mouth, and my soul cried out in perfect praise. I never thought about singing in the wrong key or making the beautiful, godly woman beside me uncomfortable. Our voices rang out in praise and celebration, and I wondered if that was how David felt when he played and sang praises to God for King Saul.

I can't remember any particular moment of the song, but the experience of standing beside a woman unashamed of her faith and sharing a tiny instant in all of eternity together was a feeling I'll never forget. After the last stanza, the choir director leapt to his feet and waved his arms, encouraging the congregation to stand. Then, he motioned to the pianist to play the last chorus again, and the whole church joined their voices with ours in praise, thanksgiving, and celebration. When it finally ended, my face was dripping with tears of overwhelming joy.

Rose's father stepped to the pulpit. "Praise God this morning. Amen?"

The congregation erupted, and the pastor's sermon was more powerful than the music. It was a Sunday morning that will never leave my memory. I relive it in quiet moments when I'm alone and still. Feeling God's hands reaching down from Heaven to embrace us as a hundred or more of us praised Him in song and worship was a feeling I long for every day of my life, and I'll always believe that's how Heaven will feel. We'll join as one voice and one heart to worship and praise the God of love, mercy, and goodness for all eternity.

The day was full of unexpected beauty for me. An hour after the altar call and dismissal prayer, I found myself sitting between Rose and her fifteen-year-old sister, with a heaping plate in front of me.

From the head of the table, Rose's father said, "We're proud to have you in our home, Jimmy. Would you mind asking God to bless the food for us?"

Praying publicly isn't specifically forbidden in Scripture, but Jesus Himself encouraged His disciples to pray privately without showy repetition like the supposed Jewish leaders of His day. I'd always believed prayer to be an intimate conversation between a living soul and the one true God, but I felt honored to have such a powerful man of God ask me to pray at his table.

I offered thanks, prayed for strength and direction, and closed in a humble plea for daily forgiveness. Seconds later, the only sound in the room was forks hitting the Sunday china.

After lunch, just as she'd promised, Rose took me shopping, and I learned that I knew nothing about fashion. On that Sunday afternoon, I spent more money than I would make in the coming week, but my eight-piece wardrobe multiplied itself exponentially. I would need another bag to carry everything we bought back to Fort Benning.

That's when it hit me, and I motioned to a bench beneath an oak. "We have to talk."

She squeezed my hand. "Oh, no. Was it too much? I knew I

shouldn't do that to you. I'm so sorry. I shouldn't have asked you to sing and come to lunch. It was all too much. I'm—"

I pressed my finger to her lips. "Stop. It was perfect. It was the best Sunday of my life. I'll never be able to thank you for all of it, but we have to talk about the reality of tomorrow."

She leaned against me and wrapped her arms around my shoulders. "Oh, Jimmy . . . It's like you fell right out of Heaven just for me. I don't know what you're going to say, but please don't break my heart already."

I took her hands in mine. "I wasn't supposed to be here, Rose. I'm supposed to be in Northern Africa in a war zone with my sniper platoon. So many things had to happen in exactly the right order and at exactly the right time for me to end up in your ice cream shop yesterday afternoon. I know most people think life is just a bunch of coincidences stacked on top of each other, and maybe they're right, but I sure believe something different. If I could've asked God for the perfect girl, you'd be who He created just for me."

A tiny tear escaped her eye and rolled across her cheek. "I feel exactly the same way, Jimmy. It's almost too good to be true."

"I want to keep seeing you, Rose. I don't want to be without you. But . . ."

She froze with horror in her eyes. "Jimmy, no. No buts. We're meant to be together. You can't walk away."

"I'm not walking away, Rose. I wouldn't do that. But I do have responsibilities and demands of my time. I start the Combat Diver Qualification Course tomorrow at four a.m., and I don't know how long my days will be. I don't even know if I'll be allowed to leave the base during training."

"How long is the school?"

"It's about four weeks, if everything goes like it should, but if I get hurt or have to retrain on a section, it could be longer."

"So, you'll be here at least another month? That's good, I guess, but what happens after that?"

"I'll go back to Fort Benning to my unit."

"But you can take time off, right? Like vacation or something?"

"Yes, the Army calls it *leave*. In fact, I plan to take at least two weeks when I finish the course."

Her eyes brightened. "Here? Are you staying here after you finish?"

"I'd like to, if that's all right with you. I'd like to spend as much time as possible together, especially since I don't know how much free time I'll have while I'm in school."

She threw her arms around me again, and I did the same. We sat there holding each other as the rest of the world turned without us.

She abruptly hopped up and reached for my hand. "Come on. Put your bags in your truck and come with me. I want to show you my favorite place on the island."

We walked down Truman Avenue to Whitehead Street and through a pair of swinging gates. Eighty-eight iron stairs later, we were staring out over the breathtaking water where the Gulf of Mexico meets the Atlantic on the iron catwalk of the Key West Lighthouse. We watched sailboats and fishermen coming and going on the timeless ocean, and Rose wrapped her hands around my arm.

"You said you're a sniper, right?"

"That's right."

"Does that mean you kill people?"

There was no way to avoid the conversation, but that didn't make me look forward to it. "Sometimes."

She stood in silence for a moment, then asked, "What's that like? I mean, how does that make you feel?"

I squeezed the rail in front of me. "I don't kill innocent people.

It's not like that. My job is to protect American soldiers and innocent civilians from terrible people who are trying to kill them."

I expected to spend the rest of the afternoon defending my profession and explaining how a man of God could lie behind a rifle and pluck human souls from their earthly bodies, but for the moment, Rose seemed satisfied with my answer.

Her only follow-up question was, "Why does a sniper need to learn how to be a combat diver?"

I let go of the railing and laughed. "I have no idea, but the Army sent me, so I came. And best of all, I met you."

After taking in the unforgettable view in every direction for several minutes, that beautiful woman looked up at me and slid her hands around my neck. She stood on tiptoes and pressed her lips to mine, and the world around me dissolved into meaningless oblivion. The kiss may have lasted a second or ten thousand years, and in that moment, I couldn't tell the difference, but there was no question in my mind that I never wanted it to end.

When she pulled away, she whispered, "I know we just met yesterday, and it was probably presumptuous of me, but I wanted to kiss you when you were all wet after saving that little boy last night."

I'm sure I was grinning like an idiot, but I couldn't turn it off. The most beautiful woman I'd ever seen just kissed me a hundred feet above Key West, and suddenly, the Combat Diver Qualification Course was the last thing on my mind.

Chapter 25

An Honest-to-God Hero

Psalms 69:1–3 NASB
Shoshannim: A Psalm of David.
"Save me, O God, For the waters have threatened my life. I have
sunk in deep mire, and there is no foothold; I have come into deep
waters, and a flood overflows me. I am weary with my crying; my
throat is parched; My eyes fail while I wait for my God."

* * *

My introduction to the Combat Diver Qualification Course began at one minute past four the next morning. Standing at attention in our BDUs, thirty-five of us waited for the first day of the most challenging month of our lives. A soldier in khaki shorts, a skin-tight black T-shirt, and dive booties marched in front of our formation with four identically dressed men following in his wake. They walked within inches of each of us, studying our faces and memorizing our name tags.

Once that intimidation tactic reached its end, the first man centered himself on the formation and held a rolled newspaper above his head. "How many of you soon-to-be washouts read the *Key West Citizen* yesterday?"

No one flinched, so he yelled, "I guess you ladies didn't hear me. I want to know how many of you read the newspaper yesterday!"

Still, no one moved, so he said, "Oh, I get it. You probably don't know how to read. Is that it? Are we going to have to teach you to read at the same time we're teaching you to stay alive underwater?"

No one said a word, so he slapped the rolled paper into the palm of his hand several times, making a sound like the crack of a rifle. "Okay, then. Since you little dropouts can't read, I'll read it to you."

He unrolled the paper and held up the front page for everyone to see. "On second thought, I can't read, either, so I'll just tell you what the fine local newspaper had to report. Ladies, we have in our midst a true, red-blooded, all-American hero. I'll bet you didn't know that, did you?"

He glared at the class still standing at attention. "One of you decided to jump into Big Blue last night and pull a snot-nosed little brat out of the water while a thousand people watched. I guess that makes you think you're a big-shot hero, doesn't it, Mr. Hero-Man? Where's my Hero-Man, huh? Come on, Mr. Hero-Man. Step out and give us all a good look at what an honest-to-God hero looks like. That's what we all want to be, isn't it? Heroes? That's why you're here, because this is a hero school. Get up here, Sergeant Grossmann. Let's have a look at you."

I swallowed the sour taste in my mouth, stepped out of formation, and studied the rank insignia on the instructor's hat. "Yes, Master Sergeant. I'm Sergeant Grossmann. But I'm no hero, Master Sergeant."

The lead instructor motioned to the remaining four instructors and ran toward me as if I were on fire. Three of the five carried five-gallon buckets of the coldest water I'd ever felt and doused me with them. I gasped for breath, but there was no relief in sight. The remaining instructor stuck a hose in my face and sprayed water directly up my nose.

The master sergeant yelled, "Since you like being in the water so much, hero, why are you gagging like a sick little baby? It's just water. You're the one who loves to jump in. You're the one who got your picture on the front page of the Sunday paper. Now the whole world knows Ranger Grossmann is attending the Combat Diver Course. Now the enemy knows your face and your name and your weakness. You apparently have a soft spot for rebellious little kids, don't you, Ranger Grossmann?"

I tried to catch my breath through the barrage of water, but my words came out as if I were drowning. "Yes, Master Sergeant."

He turned to the formation. "How long have you Girl Scouts been in the Army? If you've been in the Army longer than thirty seconds, you know everybody has to look the same, and one of these things is not like the others. Fix it now, or pay the price!"

The formation broke up, but no one seemed to have any idea what to do. *Confusion* was obviously the word of the day, and I was right in the middle of it and realized I was the only student who was wet. Our options were for everyone to get wet or for me to change into a dry uniform.

I broke away from the hose torture and ran for the barracks. Three minutes later, I was back and wearing a clean, dry uniform, but everyone else was on their backs doing flutter kicks while the instructors sprayed them with hoses.

I threw myself to the ground beside my fellow students and stuck my hands under my butt. It only took seconds to get in rhythm with the flutter kicks, but I was soon to learn just how serious the instructors were about all of us looking the same.

The master sergeant yelled, "Oh, goody! Hero-Man is back, and he's clean and dry. The rest of you are soaking wet, so guess where that leaves us? You guessed it, powder puffs. One of these things is not like the others. Fix it!"

I leapt to my feet, ran half a dozen steps to the pool, and jumped into the frigid water. Thoroughly soaked, I swam to the side and pulled myself up and out of the water. A black dive bootie landed on my shoulder and kicked me back into the pool.

"Our hero wants to be in the water. We've got ourselves a real Aquaman here. Since he wants to be in the water, everybody get in the water, now! Move! Move! Move!"

The whole class joined me in the pool, and we treaded water in full uniform and boots as we waited for our next command.

The master sergeant leaned over the edge of the pool. "Where are my manners? I forgot to introduce myself. I'm Master Sergeant Grand. That's right. Grand. As in larger than life, as in better than you, as in everything you want to be when you grow up. Now, get underwater, and the first head that pops up for a breath is attached to the body that's packing his bags and crawling back home to Momma."

I took a breath and slowly let it out as I sank to the bottom of the pool. The water was cold, but I was determined to make it through the exercise. I would not be the one going home. As a stream of tiny bubbles trickled from my mouth, I knelt on the bottom and thought about anything other than being underwater. It was peaceful, quiet, and serene. Above the surface was pure chaos, but the bottom of the pool was another world I enjoyed, and I made no effort to reach the surface.

Staying on my knees, I pictured Rose. The gentleness of her touch and the energy in her kiss made me believe I could do anything. Holding my breath longer than just one of my classmates was all that was required of me. It wasn't a physical challenge. It was all mental. My body would run out of oxygen and begin screaming for more, but my conscious mind knew I wouldn't die if I withheld precious air a little longer. My lungs would burn, and my diaphragm would spasm, but I wouldn't let myself surface. I couldn't allow myself to fail.

That's when the pain came. Everything inside me wanted a breath. My body shuddered, and my lungs felt like they were in a furnace, but I held my ground. I pinned my knees to the bottom of that pool as if my life depended on it. There was no way I could look Rose in the eye and tell her I failed the course in the first thirty minutes because I couldn't hold my breath long enough.

I'd never compared myself to those around me before that day, and until that pivotal moment in my life, I was my only competition. There was no question that I had the physical strength and endurance to complete the training, but only time would tell if I had the mental fortitude. And for me, time wasn't measured by the hands of a clock. It was measured by one eternity, and my time on Earth—and at the bottom of that pool—was but a tiny speck in that blanket of time.

I vaguely remember a figure in a black, skin-tight T-shirt and dive mask grabbing me by the shoulders and shaking me, but my vision had gone black in an ever-closing tunnel. The next conscious memory I had was of being on my side on the concrete pool deck with vomit and blood pouring from my mouth and nose.

"Welcome back, hero. Where have you been?"

I blinked to clear my vision and shook my head to clear the fog. "I didn't come up first, did I?"

The five instructors gathered around me laughed in unison. "No, hero, you didn't come up at all. We had to come get your drowning butt at the bottom of that pool. What were you thinking?"

I sat up and wiped my mouth. "I was thinking that I wasn't getting kicked out on day one."

One of the instructors shined a light in my eyes. "What day is it, hero?"

"Monday."

"Who's the chairman of the Joint Chiefs of Staff?"

I spat a mouthful of rancid acid and pool water. "I didn't know that answer before I drowned."

They laughed and pulled me to my feet.

Master Sergeant Grand grabbed a handful of my shirt and shook me. For the first time, he spoke in a calm, measured tone. "I want all of you to look at this man." He checked his watch. "We've been here for twenty-seven minutes, and if Instructor Brewer hadn't pulled him from the pool, Sergeant Hero here would've been dead. Some of you probably think it was the pool that almost killed him. A few of you probably even think it was me. I'm the one who ordered everybody into the water and gave that crazy ultimatum about coming up first. You can blame whoever or whatever you want, but it wasn't me, and it dang sure wasn't that pool that almost killed our hero. It was Sergeant Hero's stubbornness."

He pointed toward the beach. "Look out there! That's Big Blue, and Big Blue don't care. She don't care if you got kids and a wife. She don't care if you've got a mortgage and a car payment you can't afford. She don't care about anything. She's just a billion trillion gallons of salt water doing what salt water does. Big Blue will not kill you! Do you hear me? She will not kill you! But as Sergeant Hero demonstrated for us this morning, even before the sun came up, Big Blue will absolutely let you kill yourself."

Silence reigned supreme for a long moment until he said, "Don't ever forget what you saw this morning. Don't ever forget that Ranger, sniper, Purple Heart, Bronze Star, Sergeant Grossmann almost killed himself because he was too stubborn to listen to his body. Don't make that mistake, divers. You're the impenetrable wall between the demons at the gate and three hundred million sleeping Americans who depend on you to beat those demons back. If you kill yourselves because you're too stubborn to take a breath when your body demands it, you opened the gate and let those demons in."

Chapter 26
The Mighty Ocean

Matthew 19:4–6 NASB
"And He answered and said, 'Have you not read that He who created them from the beginning made them male and female,' and said, 'For this reason a man shall leave his father and mother and be joined to his wife, and the two shall become one flesh. So they are no longer two, but one flesh. What therefore God has joined together, let no man separate.'"

* * *

Week one of CDQC only got more challenging. To a civilian, it would qualify as torture, but to those of us enduring the ordeal, it was an opportunity to learn, grow, and become better guardians of the freedoms we love so much in America. The days were eighteen hours long, and the nights felt like they passed in an instant. I'd never been exhausted to that degree, nor had I ever crammed so many calories down my throat. Staying warm in the pool was all but impossible, so our bodies burned up whatever we ate in no time. I was deprived of everything outside the course, but the only thing I missed was Rose.

I had excelled in every course I'd attended since joining the

Army, but none had been like CDQC. I wasn't at the bottom of the class, but there was no chance I'd be the honor graduate. The academics were challenging, but most of them were mathematical, and math is exactly how my brain has always worked. The physical aspects of the course were even more demanding than Ranger School, but no one showed up at the class who wasn't in nearly perfect physical condition. The real challenges came in the form of psychological trauma. Operating in the unforgiving, unrelenting environment of the ocean took a mental toll no one could've expected. Master Sergeant Grand was correct. Big Blue did not care. Defeating the ocean wasn't possible, but learning to work with her to accomplish our missions was the core of the course. The instructors were master underwater operators, but even they couldn't teach us the lessons Big Blue handed out every day, and especially every night.

After evening chow, we typically ran at least three miles to help digest our five-thousand-calorie dinner before gearing up and rolling back into the ocean for a navigation dive of up to three thousand meters. It was grueling, and we were graded based on the number of feet we missed our objective on the beach. With every passing waterborne evolution, I gained a little more respect for what the Navy SEALs went through to earn their beloved trident.

When Friday's night dive ended, Sergeant First Class Brewer stood in front of the nineteen of us who hadn't washed out in the previous five days. "Congratulations, gentlemen. You've made it through the toughest week of your lives so far, but don't worry. Next week will be tougher, and when it's over, a few of you will still be here, and those few will be tougher than you ever believed possible. The weekend is yours, divers. I recommend studying, eating everything you can find, and sleeping until your body forces you out of bed. If you decide to hit Duval Street in pursuit of whatever you pursue, keep your hands out of the local honey pots.

There's nothing for you in those jars. I know they're pretty, and they smell good, but you're here to hone yourselves into the tip of the spear, gentlemen. Don't let a Key West fling distract you from that mission. Got me?"

"Yes, Sergeant," came our exhausted reply, but I'd never been less sincere with anything that came out of my mouth. I'd dreamed and fantasized about Rose since our moment at the top of the lighthouse, and there was nothing Sergeant Brewer, or anyone else, could say or do to keep me away from her.

The shower felt good, and my new clothes fit, but I spent as little time as necessary to get clean, warm, and out the door. I pulled into the driveway at ten minutes after nine that Friday night to find Rose sitting on the front porch swing with two glasses of lemonade resting on a small side table. She was down the steps and standing beside the door of my truck before I unfastened my seat belt.

When I stepped out of the truck and into her arms, I questioned the sanity of my decision to return to dive school on Monday morning. I never wanted to leave the spot I found right there on the crushed shell driveway in front of that simple home.

She leaned back and touched lightly at the bruises and scrapes on my face. "What happened to you?"

I shrugged. "Just school. We all look like this. It's a tough course."

"I've missed you so badly all week. I wanted to see you."

I took a step toward the porch. "I've missed you, too, but there isn't time for anything other than training, sleeping, and eating. I'm exhausted."

We climbed the steps, and she put a glass in my hand as we settled onto the porch swing. The sounds of the night hung in the air, and it felt so good to be warm, dry, and comfortable. But, by far, the best feeling was having Rose sitting right beside me on that swing.

I finished the lemonade in one gulp and asked, "Do you have anything to eat?"

She cradled my head in her hands. "You poor thing. What do you want? I'll make you anything you want."

"I don't care. Anything is great. I'm just hungry."

She disappeared, and by the time she returned, I was sound asleep on the swing. I don't know if it was the smell of the eggs and bacon or the sense of missing time with Rose, but something roused me, and I blinked back to consciousness. She put the plate in my hands, and I devoured the breakfast for dinner.

"Slow down," she said. "You're going to choke."

I wiped my mouth. "I'm sorry. I just can't get enough to eat. I've lost five pounds already, and I'm eating fifteen thousand calories a day. We're constantly running, doing flutter kicks, or swimming. It never ends. I can't get enough food in my body."

She took the empty plate. "I'm sorry you're having to go through that, but I'm so thankful it brought us together. Do you want some more eggs?"

"No, I just want you to sit beside me. I think about you when I'm underwater, you know."

"What? That's sweet, but shouldn't you be focused on diving or whatever you're doing down there?"

"Yeah, probably, but I can't help it. When it's quiet underwater, I can't stop thinking about you."

"I think about you all the time. I'll never forget that look you had on your face when you came into the store that first day. I get hit on by a lot of tourists, but nobody has ever looked at me like you did, and I love that."

I fought to keep my eyes open. "I love you, too, Rose."

She squealed. "What? Did you just say you love me?"

I was instantly awake, but I made no effort to retract the profession of my emotion. I'd never been in love, but everything about how I felt with Rose told me all of that had changed.

She gently placed a knee on the swing beside me, leaned close, and gave me the second kiss of my life that hadn't come from my mother. When we parted, she whispered, "I love you, too, Jimmy. I know it's fast, and I feel silly, but it just feels right."

The weekend blasted by in an instant, and if I was awake, Rose and I spent every second of it together.

Everyone in my class survived the weekend, and week two of waterborne hell turned out to be far less psychologically demanding than the week before. We began small-boat operations in which we learned everything that could be known about inflatable rubber zodiacs. We jumped from helicopters and airplanes, inflated our boats in the water, and powered across the surface far faster than a boat of that size should ever travel. The relentless diving didn't end, but we began learning skills and tasks to be accomplished while diving instead of just simply navigating and swimming.

My performance in the CDQC paled in comparison to how I'd thrived in every previous course. I wanted to blame the demanding complexity of the course for my mediocre performance, but the honesty I demanded of myself required that I admit it was my inability to keep my mind off the beautiful young woman in the ice cream parlor who loved me. I tried to focus on every detail of the class, but doing so was almost impossible.

Rose and I spent every weekend together, sharing the stories of our twenty years on Earth and falling deeper in love with every passing minute.

During my third weekend away from the base, her father met me at the door on Friday night. "Let's go for a walk, son."

I'd been yelled at, threatened, tortured, and tormented by every training instructor the Army had to throw at me, and I never trembled, but that night, that man terrified me more than any man ever had. It's likely that will remain true for the entirety of my life.

"She's my little girl, Jimmy. I'm sure you understand that."

"Yes, sir."

He wasted no time. "We know what's going on. Rose's mother and I remember how it felt twenty-five years ago when I was a poor seminary student and she was waiting tables at the local diner. I used to borrow seventy-five cents from anybody I could so I could go have a cup of coffee at that diner every night. Jimmy, I don't even drink coffee."

I wanted to tell him what his daughter meant to me, but he never gave me the chance.

"We see where this is going, and I'll be honest with you. We want you to know that we don't want you taking our baby girl away from us."

He paused only long enough to encourage an iguana to leave the sidewalk. "But we know we can't keep her here forever. A serviceman isn't my first choice, but you're different, Jimmy. I haven't spent much time with you, but we don't have to spend weeks together for me to know you're first and foremost a man of God, and that's exactly what we want for our Rose." He dropped his chin, and his voice cracked for the first time. "You're taking her away, aren't you?"

I had taken lives and preserved lives. I'd learned skills almost no one ever learns. I could survive alone for years in most environments without relying on anyone, but the thought of giving Rose the life she deserved almost crippled me. I lived in an Army barracks at Fort Benning. I had nowhere to take her and nothing of material substance to offer her, but I loved her. I wanted to give her everything she could ever dream of having.

With a trembling voice I wanted to sound confident, I said, "I love her, and I want to marry her, but I won't ask her without your blessing."

He stopped and kicked a rock back and forth between his feet. "Does she know?"

"No, sir. I've not told her. Like I said, I wouldn't dare ask her without your approval. God gave her to you first. It's up to you after that."

He threw an arm around me. "Jimmy, you're either the smoothest talking young man I've ever met or you're the sincerest. It better be the latter. I'm not going to threaten you. What kind of fool would threaten an Army Ranger? But I am going to charge you before God to take care of her and love her with everything you've got and everything you'll ever have. If you hurt her, you'll have to answer to Him and me, but I don't see that kind of man standing beside me. I'm sure the bad guys are scared to death of you, but I see the gentlest soul I've ever met in you. I've just got two conditions before her mother and I give you our blessing."

"Yes, sir. I'm listening."

"I get to perform the wedding, and her momma gets to name her first grandbaby."

I let the dream play out in my mind, and I couldn't stop smiling. "I can't make you those promises, sir. As for me, I'm fine with both of those conditions, but those decisions are up to Rose."

With his arm still around my shoulder, he gave me a squeeze. "That's the only good answer, son. I guess that means welcome to the family. Can you afford to buy her a ring?"

I swallowed the enormous lump in my throat. "Yes, sir. I've got some money. The Army pays me well, and I don't have anything to spend it on, so I can afford a ring."

He pulled a folded piece of paper from his pocket and laid it in my hand. "Go see Michael over at Key Jewelers. Every piece of jewelry Maddy owns either came from her grandmother or Michael. He'll know what Rose would like. It's a pretty good bet that her and her momma have already been in there looking. You tell him who you are, and tell him Pastor Randal sent you."

"Thank you, sir."

He gave me a shove. "Thank me by treating my daughter like the princess she is, son. That's all I ask. Now, go see that pretty girl before it gets too late. I'm going to continue my walk and spend a little time talking with God. I've got some stuff I'm gonna need His help dealing with."

* * *

Two weeks later, I graduated from the Combat Diver Qualification Course and earned the Special Operations Diver badge that Rose pinned to my chest. It was far from the longest school I ever attended, but having her pin that badge on my uniform was one of the proudest moments of my life. The Army granted me two weeks of leave en route, meaning I'd have two weeks off before reporting back into my unit at Fort Benning.

Tired, bruised, and in the best physical condition imaginable, I packed up everything I owned and moved from the schoolhouse barracks into the equivalent of a hotel room at the Navy Lodge at Trumbo Point. I changed out of my uniform, made a call to the airport to make sure everything was ready, and headed for the parking lot. Rose climbed into my truck through the door I held open for her, and twenty minutes later, we were aboard a seaplane and headed west.

"Oh, Jimmy, this is amazing. I can't believe you did all of this for me."

"Just wait," I said. "The best is yet to come."

I'd seen Fort Jefferson and the Dry Tortugas a few times during my training. It appeared on the horizon during our first parachute insertion, and we flew by it a few more times during the helicopter insertions. There was no better place on Earth for what I had planned.

The pilot touched down a couple hundred feet from the beach and taxied to the water's edge.

"Have you ever been out here?" I asked as Rose leaned across me to see the beautiful island.

"Once, when I was in school, we took the ferry out here for a field trip, but that's been a long time ago, and you weren't there, so this time is already my favorite."

The pilot sank an anchor in the sound and tied off the seaplane. He yelled over his shoulder, "I'm going to do a little snorkeling. Let me know when you're ready to head back."

I helped her down from the plane, and we strolled across the beach, letting the warm water of the Gulf lap against our feet.

She looked up at me. "Thank you for this. It's so nice."

"I've spent a lot of time in the water over the past few weeks, so this is a real treat for me."

We walked the length of the beach to the northeast and turned back. When we made it back to the anchored seaplane, the pilot said, "There's some masks and snorkels in the center compartment in that starboard float."

I asked, "Do you like to snorkel?"

"I love it," she said, and we dug through the contents of the float until we found masks and fins that fit us well.

We walked into waist-deep water and pulled on our fins, then we held hands and swam to a small rock formation with a piece of orange flagging waving in the gentle current. I bent at the waist and dived for the bottom in search of just the right rock. When I found it, I palmed it in my hand and kicked for the surface. I exhaled to clear the water from my snorkel and held out my hand with one special little rock set in a delicate gold setting and held it in front of Rose's mask.

Her eyes turned to beachballs, and she grabbed the ring as if it were everything she'd ever wanted. She spat out her snorkel and screamed so loud I couldn't believe my ears. Rose shoved the ring on her finger and threw herself around me as she arched her back to pull her head out of the water. I raised my head and pulled my mask down around my neck, just as I'd been taught.

I expected some form of yes, but that's not what I got. Instead, she bellowed, "Please tell me you asked my daddy."

"I did."

She squirmed like an excited child and screamed, "Yes! Yes! A thousand times, yes!"

Chapter 27

Can I Get an Amen?

Proverbs 31:10–13 NASB

*"An excellent wife, who can find? For her worth is far above jewels.
The heart of her husband trusts in her, and he will have no lack of
gain. She does him good and not evil all the days of her life."*

* * *

Rose and I spent every waking minute together for the next week,
and we fell deeper in love with every passing day. There was
nothing about her I didn't love, and she never mentioned anything about me that drove her crazy until Sunday afternoon.

We sang together in church and gave thanks for a million gifts
from God we could never deserve. Her father's sermon came from
Proverbs 31, and he began as if he were talking only to Rose. "The
Holy Bible tells us in no uncertain terms, the duties, characteris-
tics, and responsibilities of a godly wife."

Pastor Randal stood still in the pulpit and kept his tone soft
and pleasant as if he were teaching instead of preaching, but all of
that changed a few minutes into his sermon, and Rose got off easy.

His volume, tone, and animation accelerated when he said,
"But, church, listen to me, and hear me when I tell you that a wife,

no matter how godly or how pious she is . . . amen? A wife alone does not . . . listen now. A wife does not and cannot make a marriage and a home and a family alone, amen? No matter how good she is, it takes two. It takes the wife, oh yes, the Bible is clear on this, but there is another, and God Almighty on His holy throne expects even more of that *other*."

He paused to wipe the sweat from his brow and take in enough breath to drive the point home and directly down my throat.

"It takes a man, amen? It takes a godly man. It takes a man who is not only willing to be a *man* but who is *able* to be a man. The book of Ephesians, chapter five, tells us a husband is to nourish his wife. God expects us to provide for the woman we love. A man goes to work, and a man brings home the bacon! Hear me, church. Who doesn't love the bacon?"

That got a chuckle from the congregation, but there was no chance I would laugh at any point in his sermon.

He wiped his brow again and dug back in. "Stay with me, church. We're just getting started. Here we go. What else does Ephesians tell us about the God-given duties and responsibilities of the husband? I'll tell you what it says. It says we are to cherish our wife, and this isn't the kind of cherish we think of today. I'm telling you God demands us to *protect* our wife, the most important person in our life. Do you hear me? We protect what we cherish, and it ain't no kind of man who'll look away when somebody or something threatens his wife."

From somewhere in the back, a woman called out. "Preach on, preacher!"

Pastor Randal threw up his hands and declared, "I will preach on, sister, but I'm gonna take us down a road you may not like. It may not be a popular or politically correct road, but it's a Biblical road, amen? Ephesians chapter five commands a man to *teach* his wife in spiritual matters. Now, I'm gonna preach to me and to

Jimmy Grossmann back there—the man who's gonna be my son-in-law—and he and I better listen good. I mean to tell you my wife of twenty-five wonderful years . . ."

Rose's mother cried out, "We've been married twenty-*seven* years, Randal."

The pastor didn't miss a beat. "Oh, I know, Maddy, but twenty-five of those years have been wonderful."

That got another chuckle from everyone except Maddy and me.

"Listen to me when I tell you that when the Bible—the Holy Word of God—tells us to teach our wives in spiritual matters, you better know that God intends for us to bury ourselves in the Word until we know it inside out and upside down and every way it can be known so we can share that beautiful, blessed, benevolent Word of God with the beautiful, blessed, benevolent woman we love and treasure and adore and protect and cherish, amen? Can a preacher get an amen? I said cherish, uh-huh. And I said protect, uh-huh. And I said love. Somebody better get on their feet and give the preacher an amen!"

There wasn't just one. Half the congregation was on its feet with hands the air, and it seemed to embolden Pastor Randal. He drank half the glass of water on the lectern and kept preaching.

"We're not finished, but don't sit down. Here comes the good part. The book of Psalms tells us to show her mercy and grace. Don't you go yellin' at your wife when she burns them grits. You hear me? Get up out of that chair, turn off that television—ain't nothing worth watching on that thing anyway—and take your wife to Waffle House, where they cook a hundred gallons of grits a day. Show her some mercy and some grace."

He swallowed the rest of the water, ran down the three steps to the altar, and spoke just above a whisper. "First Peter commands us to know her and to honor her. How do you get to know somebody, preacher? I'm glad you asked, 'cause I'm gonna tell you how. You get to know somebody by spending time with her, giving her your ears—both of them—and listening to her. Don't just sit there quietly waiting for your turn to talk when she finishes telling you about her day. Listen to that woman. Listen with your ears, and your heart, and your soul. Hear *her*, not just her words, but listen to her soul crying out to the man she loves. Listen with all of you, just like God listens to you when you kneel down to pray. That's what it means to know her. Now, listen. Here comes a good one."

He ran back up the stairs and held his Bible over his head. "This book, this holy book of God's word, tells us to do what?" He paused and raised his eyebrows as if listening for an answer from his congregation.

Just like Master Sergeant Grand had pounded the newspaper into his palm on the first day of CDQC, Pastor Randal slammed his Bible into his palm, again and again, sending a thundering report through the church. "Here it is, church. Here it is, Jimmy Grossmann. Proverbs thirty-one. Remember that chapter? That's where I started this morning teaching the virtues of a godly wife, but there's more to that chapter. It's not all pointed toward the wife. Read it with me, starting in verse twenty-eight. 'Her children rise up and bless her; Her husband also, and he praises her, saying: Many daughters have done nobly, but you excel them all.'"

Hands went up, and amens bounced from the rafters, but Pastor Randal spoke over all of them. "Wait a minute, church. We're not finished. Verse thirty says, 'Charm is deceitful, and beauty is vain, but a woman who fears the Lord, she shall be praised.'"

He closed his Bible and slammed it on the lectern. "Did you hear me? And beauty is vain. What does that mean, preacher? I'll tell you what it means. It means she's gonna get old and ugly—not you, Maddy—but all the rest of y'all is gonna get fat and bald. And I'm talking to you men now. Look at me. I got my dose, but Maddy, beautiful Maddy, still looks like the angel she was the first time I saw her, and she still loves me and praises me and honors me, and it's a two-way street."

He wiped his brow one final time and sighed. "It comes down to this, brothers and sisters and Jimmy Grossmann. Love one another as Christ loves the church, amen?"

* * *

As we tossed corn chips to the flocking seagulls on the beach, Rose asked, "What did you think of Daddy's sermon this morning?"

"I agreed with every word he said."

She rolled the top of the chip bag and stared up at me. "You heard the part about providing, didn't you?"

"Of course I did, and I will provide for you, Rose."

She planted her hands on her hips. "When you gonna start?"

"What are you talking about?"

She held her pose. "I'm going to start by giving you a hint. How much is the Army going to charge us for me to move into the barracks with you at Fort Benning?"

I palmed my forehead. "We have to have a house."

"That's right, Jimmy. You can't move your new bride into the barracks, 'cause sometimes I like to walk back to my bedroom without any clothes on when I get out of the shower. Do you want your wife doing that in the barracks with a hundred Army Rangers standing everywhere with their tongues hanging out?"

"We have to have a house," I said again.

"Yes, Jimmy, we have to have a house so you can provide for

your wife and so she can do you good and not evil all the days of her life."

* * *

It took just over twelve hours to drive from Key West to Columbus, Georgia, and Fort Benning. I rented two rooms, side by side in lodging so I wouldn't be miles away in the barracks while my fianceé had to sleep in lodging. Sharing a room wasn't an option, and it wasn't a thought that entered my head.

The housing office had a listing of several houses and apartments for rent in the area surrounding the base, and Rose picked three she wanted to see. I called the agents and made the appointments, but it turned out that I'd made two too many appointments. We only needed one. The first house we saw was a two-bedroom, two-bath, and had a tiny, fenced backyard. The first bedroom was big enough for a bed, a dresser, and maybe a nightstand, but that's not what sold us on the place.

When we walked into the second bedroom, the agent said, "Now, don't be put off by the paint and wallpaper. This room was a nursery. The last couple who lived here had a newborn, but we'll have it painted before you move in if this is the one you like."

Rose nestled beside me and looked up with those deep, beautiful eyes that left me powerless.

I listened to her heart and soul, just like her daddy said, and I turned to the real estate agent. "There's no need to paint it. We'll take it just the way it is."

* * *

My platoon was still deployed to Africa, so taking leave wasn't a problem. Our wedding was small, and Rose looked like an angel descended from Heaven in her white gown and veil. Seeing her walk down the aisle of that little church beside the ocean left me weeping in disbelief.

How can a woman like that love me?

When her father put Rose's hands in mine, she kissed the tip of her finger beneath her veil and pressed it against the Special Forces Combat Diver badge she'd pinned to my uniform. Soldiers don't get married in tuxedos.

Pastor Randal performed a beautiful ceremony . . . as far as I know. I was too enamored by Rose to hear a word of it. I remember saying, "I do," and I remember kissing my wife for the first time in front of God and everybody.

Later that night, I learned two things. The first thing I learned is that it's almost impossible to get every grain of rice out of every pocket of an Army dress blue uniform, and the second thing I learned was that Rose Potter Grossmann could take me places I would never dream of going with another living soul, and that made me the luckiest man alive.

Chapter 28

The Army Way

1 Chronicles 12:21–22 NASB
*"They helped David against the band of raiders,
for they were all mighty men of valor, and were captains
in the army. For day by day men came to David to help him,
until there was a great army like the army of God."*

* * *

As an adult, I had known only one way of doing things: the Army way. Physical training before the sun came up was simply how every day of my life began. Twelve- to fourteen-hour days when we were in garrison, and twenty-four-hour days when we were in the field, were my idea of normal, but the Army way isn't so easy for the daughter of a South Florida preacher to embrace.

"Is it always going to be like this, Jimmy?"

I looked up to see my beautiful wife—with her hair still wet from the shower—standing in the doorway of our tiny bedroom. "Like what?"

She motioned toward the bed, where three dozen pieces of military gear lay in well-organized piles. "This . . . All of this. And you leaving again. It's too much sometimes."

I abandoned my packing project and took her in my arms. "This is my life, sweetheart. It's how we make a living. I'm sorry I didn't do a very good job preparing you for life as a Ranger's wife. I should've—"

She pulled herself from my arms. "It's been two years, and you've been gone more than you've been home. It's just too much, Jimmy."

She stormed from the room, but I didn't hear any doors slamming, so she wouldn't be hard to find. A glance back at my gear strewn across the bed reminded me of the two worlds in which I tried to live: the deadly battlefield chaos, and the quiet, peaceful life of a happily married man. Those two worlds spent more time colliding than coexisting.

When I found her, she was standing in front of the sink with her palms on the counter and her shoulders rising and falling with every sob.

I stepped behind her and laced my arms around her waist. "Tell me what's going on," I whispered.

She spun around and slapped her palm against my chest. "You know what's going on, Jimmy. I want a baby. It's been two years. Why won't God let us have a baby?"

I wrapped her in my arms and held her tight against my chest.

Through gasps and sighs, she said, "My friend said if the Army wanted a Ranger to have a family, they would've issued him one. Does the Army really say stuff like that?"

I squeezed my eyes closed. "They say some terrible things sometimes. It's just how the Army is."

"You don't think that, do you?"

I stroked her hair. "Of course not. You and God are the most important things in my life."

"If that's true, why are you leaving again?"

"It's my job," I said. "I don't have a choice."

She pushed me away and wiped her eyes. "Yes, you do, Jimmy. There are lots of jobs out there. Normal jobs. We shouldn't have to live like this. I shouldn't have to be alone seven or eight months out of every year."

I reached for her hands. "What jobs are there for a sniper out there in the civilian world? I don't know how to do anything else. I don't have any education or experience in anything except being a soldier."

"I don't know, Jimmy, but there's got to be something. What about private security, or the FBI, or even a police officer? What about jobs like that?"

I pulled her back against me and stared at the ceiling. The two deployments in the previous eighteen months had been hard on everybody, but with every trip downrange and with every field exercise, I got a little better, a little sharper, a little more deadly. But to Rose, I got a little more distant, a little less human, a little farther away from the husband that God and she wanted me to be.

"When I get home, it'll be almost time to reenlist, so we'll take a hard look at our options. You're right. You shouldn't have to come in second behind the Army. It's not fair to you or to us. While I'm gone, see if you can find some civilian jobs for people like me. If that's what you truly want, I'll separate from the Army instead of reenlisting, or I'll talk to them about getting assigned to a regular unit outside the Rangers."

She squeezed me and whispered, "I love you, Jimmy. I'm sorry for all of this. I just want a normal life with a family, and a dog, and a husband who comes home every night. That's not too much to ask, is it?"

I ran my fingers through her hair. "No, that's not too much to ask, and I promise to do everything in my power to give you that when I get back. I can't get out of this deployment, though. It's too late. I've spent too much time training up for this mission. I have to go."

She stood on her tiptoes, just like she'd done on the catwalk of the Key West Lighthouse, and kissed me gently. "Will you ever be able to tell me where you're going and what you're doing?"

I pulled a pair of chairs away from the table, and we sat down. After drumming my fingers for a moment, I said, "You can never tell anyone what I'm about to tell you, okay?"

She nodded and leaned in.

"We're going to South America. That's as specific as I can be. There's a cartel that's holding as many as eighteen American hostages, and we're going to get them back."

Her beautiful eyes widened. "That sounds really dangerous."

I sighed. "It's not particularly dangerous for me. I'm just there to provide overwatch for the ground troops who'll actually free the hostages. It'll be my job to stop anyone from stopping them from getting to the hostages."

"That means you'll have to kill people, doesn't it?"

I would never lie to her, even if doing so would protect her from pain, and sugar-coated truth is a lie.

"It's possible, but like I told you when we first met . . . I don't kill innocent people."

"No one is innocent," she said. "The Bible tells us that."

"Why did I have to marry the smartest, most beautiful woman alive?"

She touched the tip of my nose with her finger. "Because you deserve the best of everything. That's why."

"I love you, Rose."

She bowed her head. "I'm sorry I was . . . you know."

I curled a finger beneath her chin. "Don't be sorry. We're in this together. When things bother you, let's talk about them. I should've been more attentive. I'm amped up about the deployment, and I let that get in the way of giving you what you need. I can't promise I'll stop instantly, but I'll work on it."

She said, "I was just having a moment. Your devotion to your work is part of the reason I fell in love with you. Don't neglect work for me. I know what you do is important."

"I have to finish packing, but I'll be all yours in less than an hour, okay?"

I kept my word, and our bedroom looked normal again in the promised timeframe. Dinner was perfect, and Rose was beautiful, as always. My report time was four a.m., so we were drifting off to sleep before nine with Rose's head on my chest and her leg draped across mine.

"I'm really going to miss you."

I brushed her hair back. "I'll miss you every second we're apart."

"Maybe we don't need to think so much about getting out of the Army when you get back. I know how important it is to you."

I pulled her close. "Nothing on Earth is more important than you. I promised your father that you'd always be a priority."

"I love you, Jimmy."

"I love you, Rose."

My perfect wife dropped me off at the squad bay at fifteen minutes to four the next morning. We embraced, kissed, and promised to pray for each other every day. When she pulled away, I became a sniper again, because after all, that's the Army way.

Chapter 29
The Blood of Our Enemies

Proverbs 24:17–18 NASB
"Do not rejoice when your enemy falls, and do not let your heart be glad when he stumbles; Or the Lord will see it and be displeased and turn His anger away from him."

* * *

We landed in Tegucigalpa, Honduras, for fuel and a local intelligence briefing. The stop lasted two hours, and when the other twenty-four Rangers and I reboarded the plane, everything about the operation changed. No one was laughing. We were warriors on a mission to liberate at least eighteen American hostages. While we were receiving our intel briefing, the CIA and DEA were pretending to negotiate for the release of the hostages. Those so-called negotiations were merely a ruse to keep the hostages alive long enough for my Rangers to get in, free the prisoners, and get out under the cover of darkness. The entire operation should take less than forty-eight hours, and we'd be back on an airplane and headed north.

My shooter was a newly promoted sergeant named Barnes Blackmon from Ozark, Alabama, about a hundred miles south of

Fort Benning. He was a good shot and a good soldier. As an E-6 staff sergeant, I was one of the more senior men on the mission and in command of the four-man sniper element. The other sniper team consisted of a pair of Rangers who'd been downrange together twice and spent countless hours side by side on the practice range. I had every confidence our sniper element would not be the reason our mission failed.

With our maps folded and stowed, our weapons secured in their bags and strapped to our rigs, and our parachutes double-checked, the jumpmaster yelled, "Door coming open. Guard your reserves."

Everyone on the plane, except maybe the pilots, was airborne qualified and already had a dozen combat jumps under their belts. There's no such thing as a typical nighttime parachute insertion, especially over the jungle of South America, but this one was as close to routine as any. The wind was light. There was just a sliver of moon hanging overhead that would give our night-vision devices just enough light to magnify and paint a perfect picture of the jungle below.

There were two major clearings where we could easily insert without any problems, as long as everyone got out and got a good parachute over their head on time. A main parachute failure in the dark at low altitude was more terrifying than anything the jungle beneath us had to offer. I lobbied for a high-altitude, low-opening insertion, but I wasn't far enough up the food chain to make those decisions yet, and if Rose found me a civilian job, I'd never reach those heights. The commanders and mission planners decided we'd insert from twelve hundred feet. As the door came open, I watched twenty-four Rangers pop to their feet, and I prayed every one of them would get out the door cleanly and feel a perfectly formed chute over their heads in seconds.

Barnes was in front of me, and I was at the end of the line. He and I would be the last two Rangers out of the airplane. The other two snipers were number four and five, so they'd be on the ground sixty seconds before Barnes and me.

The jumpmaster yelled, "Thirty seconds!"

I tightened the chin strap on my helmet and gave Barnes's parachute one final look. Leaning forward until our helmets touched, I yelled, "I don't know who packed your chute, but it looks like a bedsheet stuffed in a sausage skin. It'll never open."

He threw a playful elbow at my reserve hanging in front of me. "That's okay, Sarge. I'll just hang onto you."

I gave his shoulder a knock. "I'll see you on the ground, kid. We've got work to do."

The jumpmaster yelled, "Go! Go! Go!"

The first man stepped through the door, and we left the plane like a long centipede with twenty-five pairs of legs. Barnes disappeared into the darkness, and I yelled to the jumpmaster, "Last man!"

He slapped me on the shoulder, and I stepped into the humid night air. Just as I'd been taught and done countless times, I squeezed my legs together, ducked my chin, and waited for the main to open above me, but instead of the pleasant jerk of the chute when it deploys, I felt like I'd been hitched to a freight train doing two hundred miles per hour.

I slammed into the fuselage of the airplane as if thrown by some furious giant, but the beating didn't stop there. I bounced off the skin of the plane and slammed back against it again and again. The shock of being hung up on the static line and beaten like a rag doll against the plane almost overwhelmed me, but my first instinct was to force my head around to count parachutes beneath me. It was a wasted effort, and the necessity of either getting back inside the airplane or finding a way to get free of it became my sole concern.

I believed the jumpmaster and any volunteer from the Air Force crew he could recruit would be trying to haul me back in by the yellow, nylon static line connected to the pin that should've deployed my main chute. My first decision was to try and help the jumpmaster's efforts, so I reached above my head, found the static line, and fought against the wind stream to pull myself back toward the door. The harder I pulled, the harder the task became until I abandoned that plan and reached for my knife. Cutting myself free was the logical decision, but taking inventory before severing the only cord holding me at altitude had to happen first.

My reserve was still in place. Both of my boots were still on my feet. My helmet was . . .

Where's my helmet? Where's my night vision? Where's my rifle? Stay calm. Make good decisions. You can survive without a helmet, nods, and a rifle. You just have to get away from the airplane.

The decision was made, and I pushed my knife over my head until I felt it connect with the static line. Four strokes later, I was plummeting away from the airplane, and the roar of the engines drifted into the night. I gripped the ripcord on my reserve and pulled it free. Three seconds later, the pull of the fully deployed parachute I'd expected just outside the door of the C-130 finally came. It was a good parachute. In fact, it was the most beautiful parachute I'd ever seen.

I had expected to drift into the jungle while watching the rest of the Rangers land safely, but there was no way to know where or how far away they were. I was still alive, and I had a parachute I could land, but I was hopelessly lost above a jungle I'd never seen before, and the only thing I could think of was how terrified Rose would be if she knew my predicament.

The landing wasn't graceful, but I didn't break anything except a few tree limbs. Most of my chute stayed in the tree I hit, but thankfully, my boots made it to the ground. I shucked off the harness and immediately drew my pistol with my ear focused on every sound in my environment. There was no evidence that anyone was coming to capture or kill me, so my priorities changed from security to rescue.

I tried to calculate how long I was hanging from the plane at a hundred fifty miles per hour. That's a little over two and a half miles per minute. If I was stuck up there for three minutes—that seemed reasonable—I could be ten miles from the rest of my team. A mental inventory of my assets reminded me that I had a radio on my left hip, so I reached for my lifeline only to find an empty pouch where the radio should've been. My next thought was to light my parachute on fire to signal airborne search and rescue, but doing so would tell everybody in the area someone was out there in the jungle where he didn't belong. Signaling for rescue to save myself could endanger my team miles away, and I wasn't willing to put my team at risk.

Come on, Ranger. It's just a jungle. Use your head. Use your map. Use your compass.

I unfolded the laminated map and laid my compass on top of it. Our jump was made to the southwest, so I plotted a line on the map from the jump site to the southwest for ten miles. I was somewhere on that line. The mission would continue without me, but I couldn't stay with my parachute. The benefits of it being easy to see from the air for search and rescue were far outweighed by the probability that the cartel would see it and move in before search and rescue could arrive.

I had a nine-millimeter pistol and two knives. Fending off well-armed cocaine cowboys with those weapons was a terrible plan, so I did the only logical thing left. I moved northeast, planning to rendezvous with my team, if my calculations were correct. I couldn't know if the pilots made a turn as soon as they thought the last man was out of the plane, and I could've been completely wrong about my location. But until the sun came up and I could identify some landmarks, I had to assume I was correct about my position.

Covering ten miles of jungle in four to six hours was possible if the undergrowth wasn't too thick, but in the dark without night vision, it was impossible to tell what lay ahead. I marked the map with a time and my assumed location and started my walk. An hour into my journey, my vision blurred, and my body felt as if it were begging for sleep. I shouldn't have been tired. The adrenaline of the jump wore off, but I was in good shape and well rested. With something clearly wrong with me, I took a knee and drank as much water as I could, then shucked my pack and pulled off my shirt. I was sweating but not clammy or cold. Ten seconds into my self-exam, I found a handful of blood from beneath my left arm. I didn't know if I'd received the wound during my collision with the airframe or the tree, but it didn't matter. I was losing blood, and it had to be managed. I lay on my right side and poured clotting powder on the area where I found the blood, then I placed a pressure bandage over the wound and did my best to wrap my torso with an elastic bandage. I couldn't see the wound, but I believed I'd done the best job I could with the tools I had. Worrying about the bleeding wouldn't stop it, so I soldiered on.

I crammed protein bars down my throat and drank water at regular intervals to fuel my movement and survival. Thankfully, the jungle offered little resistance to my progress. The undergrowth was light, and the terrain wasn't as steep as I expected. My spirits were high, and I was making excellent progress with the sun less than an hour from rising. The canopy of trees blacked out the sky, but I grew more confident with every stride. I'd been well trained and conditioned, and my team was capable of managing the mission without me. We'd trained to exhaustion on scenarios just like that, and the primary objective would be achieved, but my team would not leave another Ranger alone in the jungle after the prisoners were free.

A comforting sound rose ahead, and I was reassured of my position when the rolling hiss of the river told me I was exactly where I predicted. Crossing the river wouldn't be easy, but it would be necessary. My team was less than two miles away, so it was time to get wet.

Fording the river turned out to be a far more demanding task than I expected. I had hoped to cross in waist-deep water, but unless I was willing to trek upstream or down, that was nothing but a foolish dream. If I had to swim, my bandage would undoubtedly become saturated and immediately lose its ability to keep me from bleeding out. As long as I made it across the water in one piece and kept my kit dry, I could rebandage the wound on the other side.

I moved upstream a few feet to put some large rocks downstream as backstops if the current swept me from my feet. As I slid down the muddy bank, my boots hit the water first and settled to the mucky bottom. At that point, I was in water almost to my armpits, but the current was manageable. Three strides ahead, that all changed. The bottom gave way, and I was underwater and being swept downstream far faster than I wanted. I twisted in the stream until my feet were leading the way and I finally hit a rock.

The pressure of the current pushed me onto the rock, and I climbed out of the water and leapt to another large rock, and then to a third. I was within ten feet of the bank and only a few swimming strokes to the other side. I took the plunge and stroked with all my strength until I dug my fingers into the slippery northern bank of the river. Sliding and clawing my way out of the river, I lay on my back, gasping for breath.

My body was too wet to rebandage, so I used the time to move far enough away from the river to hear the sounds of the night. As soon as I took a knee, shucked my pack, and pulled off my shirt, I heard a sound that could only be made by a handful of people in that jungle. The crack and report of a .308 sniper round pierced the pre-dawn darkness, and the urgency to replace my soaked bandage dissolved. I leapt to my feet and sprinted toward the sound of the rifle. As I settled into my stride, I heard a second shot followed by a dozen more. Then a flurry of gunfire filled the jungle air, and my heart sank.

My team was under fire and in a massive gunfight without me. The three remaining snipers could provide solid overwatch, but the sounds of the fight made me believe it was anything but a sniper's battle. The clear sounds of the 5.56mm M4s dominated the battle's staccato roar, but there were rifles being fired that I couldn't identify. Somebody was shooting back.

The more I ran, the harder my breath came until the cracks of the rifles were drowned out by my beating heart and pulsing lungs. I didn't feel faint, even though I was tired, wet, and running with all my strength. The thought of Rose's heart breaking when I got home with a hole under my arm stung almost as badly as hearing a gunfight that I couldn't get to in time to help. It would be over in minutes, and I was at least a mile from the hide position Barnes and I selected before leaving Fort Benning.

At that moment, I realized I had no way to let Barnes know I was coming. If he identified me as a bandit instead of a friendly, I could be the first friendly fire accident by a Ranger sniper in years, and I didn't envy the poor soul who'd have to tell Rose I was shot by my own teammate. With any luck, that conversation would never happen, and I would be able to approach Barnes's position undetected.

The rifle fire diminished until it sounded like the final few kernels of popcorn cooking off in the microwave. By the time I could see Barnes's hide, the fight was over, and the guns were silent.

I'd spent countless hours working with my shooter on the

range back at Benning, and we worked out a series of whistle signals as a ridiculous game to play during endless hours of lying in the prone position behind a rifle. With my eyes trained on his position, I whistled the three tones meant to ask, "Shooter ready?"

If the sound registered with him, he would return a long low tone as he exhaled slowly. The reply didn't come, so I asked again with the three unique tones.

That time, it hit him, and he called out, "Singer?"

"It's me. I'm coming up."

"It's about time."

I climbed into his nest and realized I'd abandoned my shirt and pack by the river when I heard the gunfire, and Barnes asked, "Where's your clothes? Are you hit?"

"It's a long story. I think I took a puncture wound from a broken tree limb, but I can't be sure. It may have happened when I was getting beaten to death by the jump plane."

He pulled his face from his scope. "What?"

"I got hung up coming out of the plane, and I ended up about ten miles away before I cut myself loose."

He shook his head. "Some people will do anything to get out of a shoot-out. Let me take a look at that wound."

"No, stay in your gun," I ordered. "Brief me up."

He pinned his cheek back to the stock and focused through the scope. "It's over now. We're just providing cover while they triage the prisoners."

"How many did we lose?"

He shrugged. "None that I know of, but it was exciting for a while. You missed a pretty good gunfight."

"There's no such thing," I said.

As the sun filled the sky, we loaded the last of the Americans onto the final Blackhawk helicopter in the clearing, and I slid in beside Lieutenant Sandburg.

"It's good to see you, Singer. We were planning to come get you when this was over. The pilots radioed your coordinates to me after you finally got the plane to let you go, but I should've known you'd make your way back to the fight. We've got five wounded Rangers." He paused and looked beneath my arm. "I guess we've got six wounded. Is that a bullet hole?"

"No, sir. I think it's a tree limb. It's a long story, but I'll tell you about it on the plane."

He motioned for the medic, and the kid with the med bag crawled across the floor of the Blackhawk.

The lieutenant motioned toward my wound. "Check that out."

He cut the dripping bandage from my side and inspected the wound. "It looks like you did a pretty good job. I'll clean it and dress it, but it's just barely bleeding."

We landed at an airfield that probably didn't appear on any map and surrendered our rescued hostages to some government agency who'd take them home and then take the credit for liberating them. That was okay with us. We didn't want or need the media coverage anyway.

As we waited on the tarmac to load up on the C-130 that would take us home, I watched two young soldiers—a specialist and a private first class—recreating the battle in animated excitement a few feet away. When their show was over, they leapt into the air and gave each other a flying high five.

The specialist leaned back and yelled into the morning sky. "We nailed those suckers! We put 'em down where they belong!"

I pushed myself from the wooden crate I was using as a chair and approached the young soldiers. "Cut it out, guys. We're professionals. We don't play in the blood of our enemies."

The younger of the two screwed up his face. "What's wrong with you, man? We kicked some—"

Before he could finish the misguided nonsense that was about to come out of his mouth, I hooked a heel behind his leg and shoved him to the ground. With my finger in his face, I said, "I'm not *man*. I'm Staff Sergeant Grossmann, and you're making a fool of yourselves. Look around you. Do you see any of us acting like you? Huh? Do you? No, you don't, and I'll tell you why. It's because we've been there and done that. It could just as easily have been our blood soaking in the ground out there in that jungle. Don't you forget that. What we do, we do with honor and dignity, and if you ever want to earn your Ranger tabs, you'd better get yourselves some military bearing and start acting like men of honor instead of hyped-up street thugs. You got me, Private?"

His camo-painted face sank. "Roger, Sergeant. This is our first real op downrange. It won't happen again."

I turned to the slightly older specialist. "And you, you've been here long enough to know better. Think about how your momma would feel if she saw our enemies dancing and celebrating after shooting you in the head."

He nodded but didn't speak, so I offered the soldier on the ground a hand. After he took it and brushed off his pants, I said, "Get on the plane. It's time to go home. They tell me you boys did all right out there tonight. You should be proud of yourselves, but don't forget how the seasoned operators around you behaved this morning."

The two trotted off toward the plane, and I followed behind with the hole in my side striking like lightning every time I took a step. It hurt, but all I could think about was how good Rose was going to feel in my arms. I just prayed she wouldn't squeeze me too tightly.

Chapter 30

Keep Your Seats

Psalms 34:17–19 NASB
"The righteous cry, and the Lord hears and delivers them out of all their troubles. The Lord is near to the brokenhearted and saves those who are crushed in spirit. Many are the afflictions of the righteous, but the Lord delivers him out of them all."

* * *

About half an hour before we touched down at Lawson Army Airfield at Fort Benning, one of the Air Force crewmen leaned down and told Lieutenant Sandburg something that brought our commander to his feet. He followed the airman to the cockpit of the Hercules and returned a few minutes later.

Standing in the middle of the cargo bay, he yelled over the roar of the engines and propellers. "Listen up! When we hit the deck, nobody moves. Got it?"

Groans and grumbles rose from the men who'd been awake for over thirty hours.

"That's enough," the lieutenant said. "Just stay in your seats when we land. We've got some stuff to take care of before anybody gets off the bird."

When his speech was over, he eyed me as if I were the reason the team was confined to the plane. Maybe I was in trouble for getting hung up outside the jump plane, or maybe it had nothing to do with me, but either way, I was no happier about it than any of my fellow Rangers. I wanted to get clean, debriefed, stow the gear, and get back to my wife.

The tires chirped as we touched down, and several men stood up, but the lieutenant yelled, "In your seats, men! I'll let you know when you can get up."

The soldiers reluctantly returned to their seats, and the lieutenant motioned to me. "Sergeant Grossmann, you're with me. Let's go."

I stood and made my way to the front of the cargo bay. "What's going on, sir?"

He shook his head. "I don't know, Singer, but the chaplain needs to see you before we let anybody off the plane."

"Why would the chaplain need to see me?"

He shrugged. "I've already told you everything I know."

The Air Force loadmaster opened the side hatch and deployed the stairs. I followed Lieutenant Sandburg down the ladder and onto the tarmac, where a pair of Army staff cars waited.

A lieutenant colonel with a silver cross on his hat approached and stuck out his hand. "Are you Staff Sergeant Grossmann?"

I shook his hand. "Yes, sir. What's this about, sir?"

He motioned toward a car, and I followed him onto the back seat.

I pulled the door closed and turned to the chaplain. "What's going on, sir? Those men are anxious to get off that plane."

"Don't worry about the men, Sergeant. They'll be fine. How are you doing?"

"I'm fine, sir, but what's this all about?"

The chaplain ran a hand slowly down his face. "I'm terribly sorry to tell you, but there's been an accident. It's your wife, Rose,

Sergeant. She was hit by a drunk driver last night, apparently on her way home from church."

My mouth turned to burning sand. "Is she all right? Where is she?"

He laid a hand on my forearm. "Sergeant Grossmann, your wife didn't survive the accident. I'm so very sorry."

My chest felt like it would explode, and I jerked my arm from the chaplain's grip. "No! There's some kind of mistake. It can't be Rose. It's not her."

The chaplain spoke softly. "I'm sorry, Jimmy, but there's been no mistake. I verified the details myself."

I broke down into wailing tears of horrific sorrow, and the chaplain put an arm around me. "Jimmy, again, I'm deeply sorry to have to bring you this unbearable news, but did you know Rose was pregnant?"

The weight of the universe collapsed onto my chest, and I died a thousand horrible deaths in the coming seconds. Like most people, when tragedy struck, I ran home, and my home was in God's loving arms. As I sat and sobbed, the chaplain and I softly prayed together. He asked for loving comfort for me and for Rose's family, but my prayer was quite different.

"Why, God? Why Rose? Why couldn't you have taken me? It's not fair. I've lost enough, God. Why are you doing this to me? First, my mother, then Willy, and now the one woman on Earth I believed you made just for me. Why?"

I stopped what wasn't truly a prayer and sobbed beside the chaplain. "What do I do now, Colonel?"

He cleared his throat. "You cry, Jimmy. Grieving is important, but in time—"

I cut him off. "Don't say it. Don't try to tell me something like time heals all wounds. No, it doesn't. Time only gives the world more opportunities to crush us."

I wiped my face and glared into the chaplain's eyes. "What's his name?"

"Who?"

"The drunk driver who murdered my wife and baby."

He lowered his chin. "Sergeant Grossmann, you can't—"

"Don't tell me what I can't do, Colonel. I want his name, and if I don't get it from you, I'll get it from somebody else. Please tell me he survived."

The chaplain hardened his tone. "Sergeant, if I believe you're on the verge of hurting yourself or someone else, I'm required to report that to the authorities. You cannot pursue the man. Is that understood?"

I put a finger on the center of his chest. "You made me a killer. You turned me into a man who's expected to take the lives of his enemies. You don't get to wear that uniform—the uniform of the country that taught me everything I know about ripping the life out of other humans—and then tell me I can't do precisely what you pay and expect me to do."

I shoved open the door and climbed from the car. Lieutenant Sandburg was waiting by the plane, and I said, "Dismiss your men, Lieutenant."

I don't remember the drive from the airfield to the convenience store a mile from my house, but I remember putting my boot through the glass door of the newspaper machine and yanking out the morning's paper. The story was on page two.

Twenty-seven-year-old Calvin James Conroy of Phenix City, Alabama, struck and killed twenty-three-year-old Rose Potter Grossmann of Columbus, GA, at the intersection of Highway 280 and 14th Street a few minutes past 8:00 p.m. last night. Officials say Conroy's blood alcohol level was measured at more than twice the legal limit when he arrived at Columbus Medical Center. Conroy is expected to recover from his injuries and will be arraigned on charges including negligent homicide, driving without a license, and driving while intoxicated, among others.

Every word of the article doubled the fire rising within me until I raged beyond control. So much of that night holds memories my mind will never let me retain. To this day, it comes back to me in flashes of irrepressible fury. What I do remember is the police officer guarding the door to Conroy's hospital room standing with one hand on his holstered weapon and the other on my chest.

"You can't go in there, sir."

With one swift uppercut, I sent the officer off his feet, and he was unconscious before hitting the floor. I broke the antenna from his radio and drew his weapon. Conroy lay on his back with one arm in a cast and the television blaring from its mount in the corner of the room. His eyes widened when I burst into the room, but it wasn't fear on his face. It was the face of man high on painkillers, but I was determined to make him understand everything that can be known about fear.

I forced the door closed and jammed a chair beneath the knob before crossing the room in four strides. I grabbed his swollen, bruised hand at the end of his cast and twisted his arm until the number of broken bones doubled. Suddenly, the painkillers lost their ability to do their job, and the man opened his mouth to cry out in agony.

I shoved the barrel of the unconscious police officer's pistol into his mouth far enough to pin his tonsils to his collarbones.

"You killed my wife, you miserable piece of trash. But that's not all you did. She was pregnant, and that means you killed my baby, too. Let's play a little game called 'guess what I do for a living.'"

He gagged, squirmed, and threw a wild punch with his free hand. I saw it coming and caught his fist. The next sound that echoed off the walls of the hospital room was that of several bones in his right hand, wrist, and arm succumbing to my rage.

Standing over him with the pistol shoved against his forehead, I stared down into the face of the man who'd taken my world from me—the man who'd robbed me of the person I loved most. But no matter how hard I squeezed the trigger of that pistol, it would not fire. I trembled in limitless rage and pressed the steel weapon tighter against his skull. Everything inside me cried out to pull the trigger a thousand times, but every time I contracted the muscle to drive my finger to take Conroy's life, I couldn't do it. I'd taken dozens of lives with that finger against a trigger, but above the roar of my anger, hatred, and murderous rage, the words of Christ in Luke 6 echoed above the chaos.

"Be merciful, just as your Father is merciful. Do not judge, and you will not be judged; and do not condemn, and you will not be condemned; pardon, and you will be pardoned."

With every fiber of my sinful, earthly being, I trembled as the timeless war between God—the ultimate good—and Satan—the epitome of evil—raged inside my chest. Submitting myself to the more powerful of those forces, I dropped the magazine from the pistol, racked the slide, and ejected the single round from the chamber. The gun fell from my hand, landing on Conroy's chest, and I collapsed to the floor of that hospital room—ashamed, terrified, and alone.

* * *

The next memory I have is my commander and first sergeant leading me from the brig at Fort Benning. I would be tried, and likely convicted by both the Army and the State of Georgia of more crimes than I could list, but the prospect of trial and conviction wasn't what loomed over me like a black cloud of dread and fear. The coming telephone call to Key West to tell Rose's family of the tragedy was the terror that haunted me most.

Pastor Randal's somber acceptance of the unimaginable news stood in stalwart testimony to his faith and comfort in God. "Bring her home, son, and we'll bury her here on the island."

I did exactly as he asked, and we buried Rose on an afternoon when the endless blue sky stretched to every horizon as if welcoming Heaven's new souls.

Evening came as I sat with Rose's family and cried until Randal pushed himself from his seat.

"Let's take a walk, son."

I wiped my eyes and followed him through the front door of their modest home. We walked in silence for half an hour until we came to the long, low wall where I'd asked him for Rose's hand— both an eternity and only seconds before.

We sat on the wall, and he placed a meaty arm across my shoulders. "It's not your fault, son. You didn't kill her. You love her, and I know you always will. We don't blame you, and we love you. You'll always be part of our family, and you'll always be welcome wherever we are. We own six plots in the cemetery where we laid our precious Rose. One of those plots of ground is yours if you decide that's where you want to be laid to rest."

I was without words. His faith and steadfast communion with God were astonishing. I remember begging God to grant me such faith and fill me with the peace Randal displayed that night.

"Listen to me, son. God did not take her from you and from us. It's easy for us to blame Him for things we're too weak to understand, but don't let that happen inside that head of yours. He didn't take her, but He accepted her soul and the soul of that baby inside her. We'll be reunited when our time comes, and there will be no more tears or sorrow. He never promised us we'd be without pain here on Earth. The paradise that awaits us when we shed this mortal body is His great promise."

I wanted so badly to say something of value, but I was empty.

He said, "Their passing left a void in you, and in us, but God wants us to praise Him for the great reward Rose and your baby are enjoying today. Weep for their loss, son. You wouldn't be a man if you didn't. But while your tears are falling, raise your hands and thank Him for holding our beautiful Rose in His arms."

Epilogue
My Family

James 1:17–20 NASB
*"Every good thing given, and every perfect gift is from above,
coming down from the Father of lights, with whom there is no
variation or shifting shadow. In the exercise of His will, He brought
us forth by the word of truth, so that we would be a kind of first
fruits among His creatures. This you know, my beloved brethren.
But everyone must be quick to hear, slow to speak and slow to anger;
for the anger of man does not achieve the righteousness of God."*

* * *

My trial by court-martial found me not guilty of the single charge
they brought against me, and the subsequent civilian criminal trial
yielded an identical result. There was no doubt I was guilty of everything they charged, but I was shown mercy where none should
have been.

Calvin Conroy was sentenced to eighteen years in prison, and I
prayed for him. God had shown him mercy by holding my trigger
finger in that hospital room, and the Alabama Department of
Corrections say Conroy accepted Christ and became a disciple of
God inside the prison walls. Forgiveness is a gift I'll likely never be

able to give Conroy, but I pray every time I hit my knees for God to give me the strength to do so.

* * *

My career in the United States Army was essentially over. The relentless drive I felt since the day I joined the Army alongside Willy was gone, replaced by an emptiness left deep inside my heart by the senseless murders of Rose and our baby.

I had a remaining commitment to the Army that was converted to an enlistment in an Army Reserve unit that required me to attend monthly weekend drills and a two-week active-duty training exercise during the summer. I served in the role of armorer and firearms instructor for the unit, but the thirst I felt to be down-range as a sniper was unquenched by service in the reserve, so I fulfilled my requirement and quietly left the service with the rank of sergeant first class.

My first job out of the Army was with Penfold Arms, a precision rifle manufacturer who loved to claim their rifles were developed by American snipers. The claim wasn't exactly true, but it wasn't a full-blown lie. The engineers consulted with us during the research and development phase of their rifles, but none of us shooters ever truly designed a rifle for Penfold. I continued to shoot thousands of rounds every month, but only at paper targets, and only under strictly controlled conditions. It wasn't exactly a dream job, but I earned a paycheck and got to shoot all I wanted.

Although it didn't result in a conviction, my episode in the hospital following Rose's death prevented me from qualifying as a police officer at any level, so essentially, I was left with only one option. I interviewed with three private security firms and was selected by all three as a contractor, implementing my skill and experience as a combat sniper in the military on the modern battlefield that was becoming more and more cluttered with civilian operators every year.

The best and worst firm I worked for was Brinkwater Security, one of the world's largest such companies. The pay was good, the equipment was solid and dependable, and the assignments were interesting. The rules of engagement for a civilian contractor are immeasurably different from those of the armed-services soldiers. I answered to civilian managers instead of military officers, and in some ways, that was a much better arrangement.

Losing Rose and our child left me cold and quiet most of the time. I still prayed almost constantly, but I spent almost no time with anyone else in social settings, and I believed I would never find anyone who could compare to the woman who'd been the center of my world. All of that began to change when I received a last-minute assignment to support an unconventional operation by a covert operative team in Eastern Europe. My assignment was to parachute into Kazakhstan, cross the Russian border, and provide sniper support for an operation to replace a Russian prisoner in the infamous Black Dolphin Prison with another Russian who could be the first woman's twin. I didn't ask a lot of questions. I simply did my job. But for the first time since leaving the Army, I felt the genesis of a brotherhood between the other operators and me.

The team I temporarily joined wasn't completely foreign to me. One of the most influential sniper instructors I studied under, Clark Johnson, was also out of the Army and working privately. However, he wasn't being paid by Brinkwater for that particular action. Clark wasn't the only familiar face on the team. Mongo, the giant Ranger who'd carried me off the helicopter in Northern Africa, was a fellow gunner on the op.

The commander of that operation was a civilian with no military service named Chase Fulton. During that mission, long ago, I had no way to know how important Chase would become in my life, but I knew from the moment I shook his hand, I had been delivered into his life for one specific reason. He believed in the God I worshipped, but he wasn't deeply devoted to His service. That would all change, and my existence in Chase's life would play a major role in making that change for the better. Not only was I there to teach and guide him back to God, but he would also come to serve a role in my life to help pull a defeated, empty man back from the depths of depression and ultimate sadness.

The Russian operation was brief but successful, and we went our separate ways afterwards. Fate, dumb luck, or perhaps the hand of God—as I prefer to believe—brought us back together for a partially failed operation that cost far more than the lives it took.

Brinkwater accepted a contract to provide security for a train carrying weapons and ammunition across the Khyber Pass between Pakistan and Afghanistan. Retired Major Smoke Butterworth, Clark Johnson, Mongo, a chopper pilot named Stump, and a former Green Beret named Snake Blanchard and I made up the security element. The equipment and ammo aboard the train was meant for Rangers and Special Forces teams on the Afghan side of the mountains, and we were devoted to delivering the cargo unmolested.

The mission was a breeze until we reached the steepest part of the pass where the train would move at its slowest speed, making that section the most attractive spot for an ambush from forces intent on capturing the train. I was in the chopper with Stump, providing close air support and recon at a hundred feet above the ground. We were well in front of the train when our greatest fear became reality. A massive force of aggressors hit the train, climbing aboard with AK-47s and bandoliers full of ammo. Their numbers alone made them a powerful force, but their weaponry upped the ante, and we were all in.

Clark called us on the radio the instant the gun battle began, and Stump spun the chopper in midair and headed back to join the fight at top speed. I laid down as much lead as my rifle could spit out, but it wasn't enough. We were hit by a barrage of rifle fire that all but destroyed the chopper. Stump took at least one round in the arm, but he kept the bird under control long enough for me to jump free of the dying machine before it struck the mountainside. My contact with the ground left me with a broken leg, but Stump and the chopper didn't survive.

I was able to stop the train with some well-placed shots, but the fight raged on. When the guns fell silent, the good guys won, but only based on the body count. I don't know how many people we killed that day, but we suffered horrendous losses of our own. Clark earned the worst punishment of anyone who survived that day. When the dust settled and the roar of gunfire fell silent, he was left with a broken back and massive internal injuries that could not be treated on the top of that mountain. Everyone was hurt, but with the exception of Stump, the pilot, we were still alive.

Twenty-four hours of calls to the Brinkwater operations center went unanswered and ignored. We were low on food, water, and batteries. Our satellite phone had less than thirty minutes of life left in its battery that we had no way to recharge. Clark was bad and growing worse by the minute. We had to find a way to get him off that mountain and into the hands of a competent doctor, or he wouldn't survive more than a few days.

In desperation, Mongo suggested we call the covert operative from the Black Dolphin Prison operation. "He and Clark are tight. If anybody can get him and us off this mountain in one piece, I think he's our guy."

Mongo was right. In the greatest display of brotherly love I've ever seen, Chase Fulton put together an operation involving a defense intelligence officer, a Tajiki pilot and flight engineer, and a Russian Hip helicopter at his personal expense. But he didn't just send someone to pluck us off the top of the world. He led the mission himself and saved all of our lives in the process.

Chase wasn't finished, though. Not only did he pull us off that mountain, but he also planned and executed an operation to capture and convict the politically motivated leadership of Brinkwater for abandoning a team eight thousand miles from home.

Chase could've stopped there, and he would've forever been one of the most powerful forces in our lives, but quitting early isn't something Chase does. Instead of delivering us home and wishing us well, he invited us into his home as long as we needed to stay, and then he hired us as full-time members of his covert operative team, earning more money per mission than any of us could've earned in our lifetime as security contractors.

That man saved my life, housed and fed me, made me wealthy, and gave me the second greatest gift I could've ever received. Having Chase in my life taught me how critically important my unencumbered relationship with God is. He gave me a home, and not merely a roof over my head. He handed me a team of operators who were thirsty for the spiritual direction my knowledge of the Bible and abiding faith could provide. God put those men in my life, and He put me in theirs.

After months of training together, learning from each other, and becoming a highly effective and cohesive unit, Chase, Clark, Mongo, a former combat controller named Hunter, and a pilot named Disco sat on the front row in the little wood-frame church in St. Marys, Georgia, while I stood at the altar for my ordination ceremony, officially making me a Baptist minister.

Although having those five men sitting on that old wooden pew doesn't sound like much to the rest of the world, to me, it was a pivotal moment in my life. Those five men had become the family I yearned for, prayed for, and believed I would never have. They showed me a kind of love that only men of God have to give. They took a broken, defeated man without a home and full of anger, and gave me a family—a family full of the gift of the Spirit, which, as our Bible teaches us, is *"Love, joy, peace, forbearance, kindness, goodness, faithfulness, gentleness, and self-control, against such things there is no law."*

When my life on Earth passes away, and my soul is united once again with Rose, our baby, and the God I faithfully serve, I will leave this world having known love without boundaries, and ultimately, the only gift that truly has any lasting value is that pure, honest, unselfish love that Christ Himself commanded in John 15. *"This is My commandment, that you love one another, just as I have loved you."*

Thank you for hearing the story of my life, and may God richly bless you in unimaginable ways as long as you live.

If you take nothing else from my story, please find a way to love others the way Christ loves us, and you will discover with enormous delight that such love is greater than any treasure we could ever acquire in this world. And ultimately, please remember the precious and priceless gift of salvation that awaits everyone in Christ's outstretched arms—first stretched in agony on the cross at Golgotha to pay the ultimate price for our sins, and now outstretched to each of us as He invites us into His kingdom, if we'll only accept, believe, and repent.

Love,

Singer

Author's Note
(Cap Daniels)

First and foremost, I'd like to sincerely thank you for reading this novel. The story is a dramatic departure from my typical writing, but I deeply believe the message of this story is one everyone should hear. Regardless of your faith or beliefs, the devotion of Singer—a fictional character—is admirable. I wish I could be more like him. He has long been inspirational to me, and as bizarre as it may sound, I've learned so much from Singer over the years of writing his character in the *Chase Fulton Novels*.

This story began as a study of the gift and fruit of the Spirit, but very quickly, it took on a life of its own and became a story that has already grown to mean more to me than I can put into words. It is my most sincere prayer that you found this fictional story inspiring, intriguing, and uplifting, but even more, I pray the message of this story will give you a reason and an opportunity to examine yourself and consider how your life could be fuller and more impactful to those around you.

Some unthinkably terrible events shaped and impacted Singer's life throughout this story, and as horrific as they may have seemed when poured out upon just one man, all of us suffer agonizing loss, disappointment, hurt, and personal pain from more directions than we can count. Singer's faith brought him through the lowest points of his life, even when he experienced ultimate loss and gave in to his own rage. We've all strayed from the path that God would have us walk, but even when we fail, His love never wavers, and the same faith, comfort, and healing our fictional character Singer experiences are available to each of us.

As with most fiction I create, I would ask that you forgive my compression of time and unlikely rapid progression through training within the U.S. Army. The career track I created for Singer isn't impossible, but it is highly unlikely. Likewise, you no doubt noticed I gave no specific locations for the combat appearing in this novel; instead, I gave vague references to Northern Africa and South America. I did this to avoid using actual historic battles in which some of you may have served. I would never wish to trivialize your service by fictionalizing it. I have enormous respect and gratitude for everyone who has taken up arms for the purpose of defending and supporting freedom across the globe, and I would never intentionally create any work of fiction that would lessen the true meaning and value of actual combat.

Finally, I wish to thank you, from the depth of my soul, for giving me the opportunity and platform to write a story such as this. I have written and published over two million words prior to this novel, but none of those words can compare to the ultimate truth within *Singer, Memoir of a Christian Sniper*. Writing this book with Dave and John has been a blessing beyond description for me, and I sincerely hope and pray it does the same for you.

May God bless you beyond your wildest dreams.

—Cap

Author's Note
(Dave Mason)

I have thoroughly enjoyed being a part of *Singer*. Being able to work together with my brother on this project has brought us closer together than we've ever been. It's a great joy to pray for those who will read this book, and I can only imagine the difference this book can have on so many around the world. All good and perfect gifts come down from the Father of lights.

Author's Note
(Pastor John Grossmann)

I met Cap Daniels over four years ago when I started reading his Chase series. He is such an excellent writer. We have developed a profound friendship through discussion about his books and just about every topic imaginable. It has been a great privilege to actually take part in the writing of this story. Along with Cap and his brother, Dave, I pray that you may be drawn to, or closer to, our Lord and Savior Jesus Christ as you read Singer's story. There is nothing more important than that.

Questions to Consider

Below are a few questions written by my co-authors, Dave and John, for thought after you've read Singer's memoir. The questions are broken down by chapter topic. We hope you enjoy the experience of pondering some of these important questions.

Chapter 1: Sons of Thunder

Singer reveals in his childhood, how he, his brother, and mother were repeatedly abused by an alcoholic father and that Singer killed his father.

1. Can you be a Christian and kill someone? Read Matthew 5:21–22. Does that impact your answer? Why or why not?
2. Singer shot and killed his father. Was his action right and justifiable?
3. Are there things in your life that deeply trouble you? How do you deal with them? Who, if anyone, do you turn to for help with them?
4. Are you there for others in your life? Do you seek to serve and help others? Should you? When you haven't been there for someone—a friend, family member, or whomever—what can or should you do about that?

Singer had to make peace with his past. Sometimes, in order for us to move forward, we need to look back—to look at the good, the bad, and the ugly in our lives. God uses all of it to make us who we are today.

5. What has happened to you in the past that you wished you could have avoided?
6. What hurt or pain have you caused that you wish you could go back and change?

Once we come to grips with the pain inflicted upon us and the pain we have caused, we can take it to God and give it all to Him. He already knows about it, so this is for our growth. Once we hand it over to Him, He will instruct us on how to use it and how to heal it.

2 Corinthians 5:17 NIV, "Therefore, if anyone is in Christ, the new creation has come: The old has gone, the new is here!"

Prayer: Father, thank you for everything that has happened in my life. There's been much good and some bad. Others have inflicted pain upon me, and I have inflicted pain upon them. Please forgive me and teach me to forgive them. Thank you that in Christ, I am a new creation. Please use my past to glorify you in the future. Amen.

Chapter 2: So Others May Live

Singer reflects on the importance of love, and we read about the thirteen POWs from the USS Pueblo who stood in for one another in daily torture by the North Koreans so they all might survive together.

1. What is love? Is it a feeling, an emotion, a passion, a choice, a sacrifice, or perhaps something else?

2. Are you a loving person? How can you be more loving? When you have been unloving, what should you do about it?

3. Can love get you saved? What does love have to do with being in a right relationship with God?

4. In their Yellow Submarine album, the Beatles sang a song, "All You Need is Love." Is that true? Why or why not?

Every person who has served in the military knows a little about sacrifice. Mothers of children, employees of a company or corporation, students, almost all of us can relate to the word sacrifice. In fact, love demands a sacrifice. One must give up something for the good of another.

5. What have others sacrificed for you?

6. What have you sacrificed for others?

7. Can you imagine putting yourself in the room with the men of the Coast Guard unit that took turns to be beaten, knowing their turn would soon come?

The greatest sacrifice ever made was made by Jesus Christ, the Son of God. He sacrificed everything. The Bible tells us that He willingly laid aside the glory that was His in Heaven to come to this Earth, take on human flesh, and then live a perfectly sinless life to become the perfect sacrifice. You and I deserved the penalties for what we have done wrong. Jesus took our place and became the perfect sacrifice to suffice the wrath of God against sin. Jesus died so we could live.

8. Have you accepted the free gift that God, our Father, offers to us through His son, Jesus Christ?

It's simply a matter of believing Jesus is the Son of God, that He sacrificed and took my place, that He died and was resurrected and has conquered death so we can live.

Romans 5:8, "But God demonstrates his own love for us in this: While we were still sinners, Christ died for us."

Prayer: Father, thank you for the sacrifice of Jesus Christ on my behalf. I believe Jesus is the perfect sacrifice and paid the price for my sins that I could not pay. I ask for your forgiveness, and I desire to know you and follow you all the days of my life. Amen.

Chapter 3: To Become More Than I Am

Singer finds his purpose in life, which seems to be military service.

1. Does your life have a purpose? What is it? Is the purpose of a person's life something that is developed through self-pursuit, or is it discovered outside of oneself?
2. Do you believe every person's life has a purpose? Do we exist for a reason, or are we here by chance? What difference does one's worldview make in answering these questions?
3. Where does purpose in life come from? Do you think someone's purpose in life can change? Would you like yours to change?
4. Singer says in this chapter that his faith and devotion to God is a greater purpose than all others. Do you agree with Singer? If so, how is it evident in your life? If not, do you have a greater purpose, or perhaps no discernible purpose? How do you feel about that?
5. Do you have questions about faith in God and living for Him? If so, we'd love to hear for you.

Cap: Cap@CapDaniels.com
John: John@CapDaniels.com
Dave: Dave@CapDaniels.com

Singer is challenged by learning what an Army Ranger is and what they do. The beret, the uniform, and the training were beyond his wildest dreams. Singer saw it as a challenge and was determined to live up to whatever it took to become a Ranger.

6. What is your greatest challenge? Is it to be the best parent, spouse, or grandparent, or to shake that addiction or bad habit?

Until Singer was exposed to the experience, he had no idea what a Ranger was. We all need to be challenged. Nothing great ever comes from what is easy. Every great accomplishment has been partnered with great work, pain, struggle, and a determination that would not allow for failure.

7. What area of your life needs to be challenged?
8. What dream can you dream that is so much bigger than yourself?

John 14:12, "Very truly I tell you, whoever believes in me will do the works I have been doing, and they will do even greater things than these, because I am going to the Father."

Prayer: Father, I have lived too small for too long. I need a challenge. I need to be a part of something so much bigger than myself. Please give me Your dreams for me. You know what I am capable of much better than I know. Stretch me, use me, let me make an eternal difference for You. I know it won't be easy, but I also know it will be worth it all. Amen.

Chapter 4: Gird Your Loins

Singer experiences military training and reflects on how God equips and leads us.

1. Have you sensed the Lord's leading in your life? Have you found that God's Word is the best and only flawless source of His guidance? Do you read and pray through the Bible daily?

2. What spiritual gift or gifts has God given you? How do you effectively put God's equipping into use in your life?

3. Do you see your talents and abilities as yours, or as God's gifts also meant to be used in His service? What difference does it make in your life when you live for yourself, versus when you live for the Lord to benefit others?

4. Do you always thank and pray for those who risk their lives to protect, defend, and serve us? (Members of all branches of the military, policemen, firemen, and so many others.)

Being trained is hard work. Trying to work without being trained is always harder. Singer and Willy were yelled at, teased, mocked, tortured, and pushed harder than they had ever been pushed, but there was a rhyme to the reason. Training only partially prepares us for the real thing. Sometimes, in life, God is training us without us even knowing it.

5. What was a time of training for you that prepared you for what was ahead?

6. What hardships did you endure that came in handy at a later time?

7. What training did you go through that at the time that seemed unnecessary and useless but turned out to be exactly what you needed and that you would someday put into practice?

2 Corinthians 12:10, "That is why, for Christ's sake, I delight in weaknesses, in insults, in hardships, in persecutions, in difficulties. For when I am weak, then I am strong."

Prayer: Father, thank You for the hard stuff because it has prepared me for what You have for me today. Thank You for my weakness, because in my weakness, You are strong. Thank You for carrying me when I couldn't take another step. Please teach me to lean into the hard times knowing that You are shaping me for the future. Amen

Chapter 5: RIP Doesn't Always Mean Rest in Peace

Singer and Willy endure Ranger Indoc Training, and Willy chal-lenges Singer's view that God is making them into what He wants them to be. Willy protests, insisting that they are the ones doing all the training and heavy lifting, not God.

1. In our lives, how do we distinguish what God is doing and what we are doing, or do we distinguish them?
2. Singer is concerned about Willy's disinterest in God. Do you pray regularly and specifically for non-believing friends, family members, acquaintances, and enemies to know Jesus? Do you love the lost as the Lord does? Do you share God's truth with them verbally and show them God's love in action? How can you improve in doing these things?

Chapter 6: A Higher Calling

1. Have you ever felt like you are made for more?

Singer didn't realize what "more" was until he was exposed to more. Too often, we live sheltered lives and don't stretch ourselves enough to try the new and exciting.

2. What are you passionate about?
3. What natural talents do you have?
4. What talents could you strengthen or develop?
5. Are there lessons you could take or adventures you could try?

Singer loved to sing and was good at it, but there's some difference in singing and calling cadence. He found the similarities and married them.

6. Now, can you go a little deeper? What would you do if time, money, and opportunity weren't objects?

Chapter 7: Soldier of the Year

Singer and Willy attend the U.S. Army Sniper Course, and Singer is told to be proud of making it in.

1. When is pride a good thing, and when is it a bad thing? We have all been guilty of sinful pride. What do you do to deal with it?
2. Singer says he could never deserve the love and forgiveness God has shown him, and he is right. What sorts of things do we deserve or do we have a right to? Are blessings, privileges, or honors truly deserved?
3. Singer wrestled with his prayer life. What can you do to be more consistent in prayer? 1 Thessalonians 5:17 says "pray without ceasing." How is that possible? How can we do that?
4. In this chapter, Singer pointed to what makes Jesus unique

and greater than all others. List all such qualities you can think of and why they're so important. What makes His love greater than ours?

5. Did Jesus die for everyone, as Singer affirms? If so, why isn't everyone saved? How does your answer square with God's sovereignty?

Chapter 8: Roman Lions

Singer attends Ranger School and discusses Exodus 20:13, "Thou shalt not kill." Many Christians have concluded from this that the taking of the life of another human being is always wrong. Singer explains that what is meant here is a prohibition of murder, not of all killing.

1. What do you think and why?
2. How does Jesus commanding His disciples to buy a sword impact your answer?
3. How do God's Laws concerning capital punishment in the Old Testament fit in? Do those Laws still apply today?
4. What about God's command to Israel to exterminate the Canaanites? Is it possible to believe that God is, in fact, good in light of such a command?

Sergeant Johnson and Singer discuss Matthew 11:28–30, in which Jesus invites the weary to come to Him with the promise that His yoke is easy and His burden is light. But Ranger training is hard, and no doubt there are many things in your life that are hard. If you follow Christ, He does not make all things easy.

5. How do we square that with His promise in Matthew 11?

Chapter 9: Atheists in a Foxhole

Singer and Willy discuss God after Ranger School.

1. The gist of Willy's question is worth considering: If God is good and loving, why would He send people to Hell?
2. God is the one who sends unrepentant sinners to Hell, Luke 12:4–5, and yet, how is it that unbelievers send themselves to Hell, as Singer says? What is the only way to avoid going to Hell? Have you availed yourself of it?

Chapter 10: How I Pray

Singer and Willy experience their first combat as Snipers.

1. Have you had nonbelievers ask you to pray for them, as Willy asked Singer? Are you diligent in doing so?
2. Do you ask nonbelievers how you can pray for them? *(This is a particularly helpful approach with Muslims who respect us when we pray.)*

Chapter 11: To Become More than I Am

Singer is in combat, firing long-distance shots.

1. Singer says that shooting or warfare will never end until Christ returns and brings true peace. What is the first thing that will happen when Christ returns? [Hint: it is not very peaceful.] Has your life ever really been at peace?
2. Read John 14:27. What is the peace that Christ gives that is not what the world gives? Have you experienced His peace? Would you like to?

3. Singer wrestles with taking lives in combat, albeit his actions save lives. Is warfare justified, and if so, when? Doing what is right is often not easy. Have you ever struggled with doing what is right, knowing that doing so would make some unhappy?

4. Do you thank God and pray for those who do hard things to protect and preserve the rest of us?

Singer possessed an ability that very few will ever know. His ability put him right in the middle of a great dichotomy: Do I kill to save others? Do I take a life to save lives? Most of us will never be faced with such questions in our lives, but all of us will be caught in the middle.

5. How do we decide what is best when pain will come with either decision?

6. What moral compass do we use when making decisions?

7. Is it always best to side with the majority, or are there times the majority is wrong?

In this chapter, it seems as if the fight is over, but it flares right back up.

8. Have you ever been in the middle of a crisis and thought you'd finally weathered the storm, only to discover the storm is still raging?

9. How can we believe the best but prepare for the worst?

Chapter 12: Were You Scared?

Singer and Willy experience an after-action report and discuss fear in combat.

1. What are you afraid of? How do you deal with fear?
2. What is courage? What does it have to do with fear?
3. What difference does a relationship with Jesus Christ and knowing where you will spend eternity make when you consider what you fear?

Singer shares his confidence in life beyond this earthly existence and encourages Willy to just ask God for it. Willy questions how it could be that simple.

4. Have you discovered that forgiveness of your wrongdoing and eternal life in Christ is actually quite simple to receive? Have you sincerely repented and asked God to save you?

Singer encourages Willy to pray with him about this.

5. Will you do that?

Willy thinks God doesn't have time to hear his prayers. He suggests God would listen if Singer prayed for him.

6. Does God hear the prayers of nonbelievers? Do nonbelievers have to have a believer pray for them? At the same time, are you diligent in praying for the unsaved? Is there a difference in God knowing the prayers of nonbelievers and God responding to so many things that nonbelievers may ask in prayer? What sort of prayers by nonbelievers does God always respond to?

One of the most endearing qualities of Singer is his humility. When given the opportunity to take the credit or to be recognized, he passed it up.

7. How do you handle compliments or accolades?

8. Who among us hasn't been scared?

9. What is your greatest fear?

10. Is there someone you can talk to about your fear?

11. What do you do with your fear?

Singer had the perfect place to put his fears: into God's hands. The Creator of the Universe and the One who has a great plan for our lives can handle our fears.

12. Can you turn your fears over to the God who loves you?

Chapter 13: Learning Without End

Singer learns to see a problem differently, and he reflects on God's love for Him in the process.

1. No matter how much you know or how expert you are at something, have you learned that there is always more to learn? God always has more to teach and show you. Are you willing to receive it?

2. Everyone is unique, but we all know how it is to feel alone— although maybe not in the same way a sniper does. Have you learned that with Jesus, through His Spirit, you are never really alone? Have you found His unfathomable and inexhaustible, sustaining love, even in the hardest things, and even when no one else seems to know or care?

In this chapter, Singer learns valuable lessons. He's faced with obstacles that were never an issue while training. The real world is always more challenging, and no matter how much training we have, there's almost always an element of surprise when we're faced with reality.

3. How do you handle obstacles?

4. What happens when what you expected doesn't happen?

5. Have you found the statement "What's easy isn't always right" to be true in your life? If so, can you give an example?

Chapter 14: Rules of Engagement

Singer provides overwatch in a battle at night.

1. In what sense is Satan the ruler of this world if God is the all-powerful sovereign?

2. Do you think Satan is subject to delusions?

3. Do you ever feel as if you're following one set of rules, and others either have no rules or have a different set of rules?

4. Do you feel that life is fair? Are we all on the same playing field?

5. Most of us would say that life isn't fair. There *are* different rules for different people. So how should we live in light of this truth?

6. Should we seek to live as God has instructed us? Should we follow the teachings of Jesus Christ that say, "humble yourself, turn the other cheek, go the extra mile"?

7. In this chapter, Singer mentions the overwhelming darkness several times. There is only one cure for darkness, and that is light. Are you living in the light or the darkness?

8. Does your moral compass still read the same when the world is caving in around you, or do you change your convictions in the heat of battle?

Chapter 15: The Taste of War

Singer continues in battle as his fellow soldiers are wounded around him.

1. Near the end of the chapter, Singer fights in anger and out of vengeance as his own men are hit. What is the difference between righteous and unrighteous anger? Who, by right, takes vengeance?

2. When you have acted in uncontrolled anger or vengeance, what have you thought and done about it?

3. Singer feels he has committed one of the darkest sins of his life. What was it? Are his actions forgivable?

4. What is the unforgivable sin? Mark 3:28–29 and Matthew 12:30–32.

5. How is it possible to stay calm in the midst of a battle?

6. Singer was part of a team, a family that would not abandon each other in their toughest of times. Who do you have in your life who will stick with you through your most difficult times?

6. If you don't have such people, where can you find them?

7. Singer knew that his best friend, Willy, couldn't have lived through the attack. What have you faced in your life when you knew your worst fears were about to become reality?

8. Have you ever expected the worst and it turned out to be better than you thought?

9. Have you ever wasted time and energy focusing on the negative when the positive was still possible?

Chapter 16: Hold On

Singer helps a wounded comrade, discovers that he is wounded, and goes to rescue Willy.

1. Have you ever sensed God's power, wisdom, or strength to do things beyond your capabilities? How did it go?
2. Have you lost a close friend or loved one? How did you get through it? To whom did you turn?
3. Do you know the love of God in the worst times?
4. Have you found Him to be what you really need?
5. Have you found anything better?

We are often in circumstances in which we only have an extremely short period of time to tell someone what really matters. Sometimes these circumstances are dire.

6. What must one believe and/or do to be saved?
7. Can you share the essence of the Gospel in two minutes, or even less?
8. Have you done so?

Chapter 17: The Roaring Silence

Singer reflects about Willy.

1. Are all human beings God's children? Explain.
2. Given that God hates sinners, Psalm 5:5, does He love all people? Does God hate and love at the same time?
3. In as much as we are to seek to be like God, how do we do this?
4. Is the common notion of loving the sinner and hating the sin a sufficient response?
5. Does Christ want to save all people? If He does want to do so, why doesn't He? In light of the fact that Christians have differed on this subject, what do you think and why?
6. Singer wishes Willy could've lived and that he instead

could've been killed. Do things happen by chance or luck, or is there a plan?

7. Do you see the hand of God at work, or is life often just confusing, frustrating, and purposeless?

Chapter 18: Guest of Honor

Singer is anxious to move on with being a sniper, but his injuries prevent him from doing so.

1. How patient are you? We all struggle with patience in various circumstances. What can you do to improve your patience?

2. How do you deal with life's unexpected turns? Do you turn to the Lord, or do you tend to try to bull your way through on your own? How has that worked out for you?

Chapter 19: Little Treasures

Singer is honored for action in combat.

1. When you are rewarded, promoted, praised, or honored, do you maintain your humility? Do you feel you deserve any such awards? Humble people always move us. What is humility, and how does one increase it?

Chapter 20: Go Fish

Singer thinks about the importance of submitting to God's will.

1. Have you learned the secret of successful living through faith in Christ and seeking Him first beyond yourself? Do you have a group of friends who are there for you to help in this?

2. How do you submit to God's will? What does obedience have to do with it? Obedience to what? To whom?

3. How do you know what God's will is? In big things? In little things? What about things where Scripture is not clear? What do you do when you don't know what God's will is?

Singer meets a surgeon who can perform the necessary surgery to restore his vision.

4. Has God worked in your life in ways beyond this world's explanation? How so? Afterward, how did you feel, and what did you do in response? Is there more you should do? Will you?

Chapter 21: Patience, Patients

Singer learns his first sergeant is a man of God.

1. Singer's dream of doing what he loved, of doing what it seemed as if he were born to do—be a sniper—looked as though it was coming to an end when he'd just begun. What feelings are you flooded with when circumstances seem to take a turn you were not expecting?

2. Singer could have taken a medical retirement from the Army but chose to stay and do whatever he could do. Are you committed in that degree to anything in your life?

3. Have you ever watched circumstances "fall" into your favor? Have you ever thought that the Sovereign God of the Universe is acting on your behalf? Reflect on the fact that rarely does our timing line up with God's timing, and God's timing is always the perfect time.

4. What does it feel like when someone tells you they're praying and you sense that they truly are praying for you?

5. Is there any greater act someone could do for you than to talk to the Creator on your behalf? Is there any greater act than for you to legitimately pray for someone else?

Chapter 22: Dreams Do Come True

Singer has eye surgery.

1. Singer asks Dr. Harland if he's a Christian, and the doctor says he's a "very good surgeon." Would you always prefer to have a Christian doctor, car mechanic, lawyer, etc. before a non-Christian? Do you feel the same about politicians you would vote for?

During the surgery, Singer dreams of his mother telling his brother and him the story of Joseph from the Bible. Joseph's brothers sold him into slavery.

2. Does God have a good plan, even in our bad circumstances and sinfulness? Is Romans 8:28 really true? Have you found this to be so in your life? If you're not a Christian and you see that Romans 8:28 does not apply to you, would you like for it to apply to you?

Again, any of us—Cap, Dave, or John—would love to hear from you if we might be of help.

3. When others have wronged us, do we have justification to wrong them in return? Can we apply an eye for an eye here? Leviticus 24:17–22.
4. Joseph forgave his brothers for selling him into slavery.

Should we always forgive those who wrong us? Can we? Does God do this?

5. Forgiveness is terribly important and desperately needed by all of us. Why? Should we forgive others, regardless of them repenting? Does God? What are we supposed to do? How does forgiveness on our part work when those who have wronged us do not repent?

Singer thinks about how combat soldiers are heroes. He then realizes that medics are also heroes.

6. Who have been the heroes in your life? What other categories of people can be heroes?

7. Have you found what God is doing that touches your life to sometimes be mysterious? Do you think we will understand it all in Heaven? Do you always find the Lord's work that touches your life to be wonderful, even when you don't understand it?

Have you learned to trust the Lord beyond your understanding, or are you blameful when unpleasant things happen?

Chapter 23: God's Rose

Singer meets Rose in the ice cream shop.

1. When Singer tells McMillan he hopes he'll never have to use his newly gained medical skills, McMillan says, "Hope ain't a plan." We get that, but is hope important? What do you hope for? Who do you hope in? Is your hope certain? If so, is it still hope? How?

2. Singer says he didn't become a sniper to be a rock star. Why do you do what you do? What are your motives and goals? Are they worthy, or should you change them?

When Singer is told he can't yet be deployed because his eye isn't fully healed, he asks to do something else. Ultimately, he is sent to Combat Diver school.

3. When you run into roadblocks regarding something you want or are pursuing, how do you react? And in the meantime, do you look for something else productive to do?

4. Do you live and engage in life with a positive attitude or a negative one? How can you change for the better?

5. When you met the love of your life, as Singer did when he met Rose, did you feel you were superbly lucky, or did you recognize God's orchestration in it?

6. When terrible things have happened to you, did you likewise see God's hand in it for your good, even then?

Chapter 24: Music Lessons

Singer sings with Rose at her church.

1. Do you live your whole life as worship? What is worship, in essence? Is it a temporary, glorious feeling of praise to God, or something much more?

2. Can you imagine the total joy of the oneness we will share in Heaven, worshipping the one true God together? Are you confident you are going to Heaven? Would you like to be?

3. When you are with those whose faith in Jesus Christ is strong, how does it impact you? Do you tend to think they're hypocrites, or do you see something wonderful in them that you want? Do you ask them about it? Feel free to ask us.

Chapter 25: An Honest-To-God Hero

Singer begins the Combat Diver Course.

1. A real hero is a rare thing, and none of the real heroes want any recognition for their heroism. Singer wasn't praised but rather criticized for his heroic act. How would you respond to criticism for doing the right thing?

2. Jesus was constantly criticized for doing the right thing. When he healed someone, the religious leaders criticized the way he did it, or when he did it, or even where he did it. How did Jesus respond?

3. When Singer refused to go to the surface to get a breath, was that a show of strength, stubbornness, or both?

4. Did Singer take it too far? Did he endanger others by pushing himself too hard?

5. Should we listen to our minds and bodies when they're screaming for us to respond? Is there a fine line between pushing yourself to the limits and knowing when enough is enough?

Chapter 26: The Mighty Ocean

Singer visits Rose for the weekend, talks with her dad about mar-riage, and gives her a ring.

1. Is love enough for a great marriage?

2. What are the keys to having a good relationship with your in-laws? Is asking the bride's father for her hand in marriage important? Why or why not?

3. Humanly speaking, who must be the most important person in your marriage? Does the answer change after having

children? Does the most important person in your marriage know that he or she is?

Chapter 27: Can I Get an Amen?

Singer hears Rose's father preach on the responsibilities of husbands.

1. Read Ephesians 5:21–33. What does God call for with regard to wives and with regard to husbands?
2. Men, do you own your responsibility to spiritually love, lead, teach, and sacrifice yourselves for your wives? How do you do these things? How do you cultivate your relationship with your wife? Do you only have eyes for her?
3. How do you wash your wife with the Word, Ephesians 5:26?
4. How do you love your wife like Christ loves the church? Ephesians 5:25.
5. Men, how do you balance providing for your wife and being there for her? Are you married to your work, or to your wife?
6. How do you guard your wife's purity? Ephesians 5:27.
7. After driving with Rose from Key West to Fort Benning in Georgia, Singer rented two rooms for them to stay in. How significant was this before they got married? Before marrying the woman you love, how do you guard her purity?
8. Singer and Rose looked forward to having children. Where do children fit in to your marital plans? Do Genesis 1:28 and Psalm 127:3 impact your thinking about this?

Chapter 28: The Army Way

Singer and Rose experience a disagreement in their relationship.

1. Singer and Rose loved the same God, and both were looking

to Him for life and hope. Is it possible for two such people to have a different understanding of the same issue?

2. Why didn't God give Rose a baby, the only thing she wanted?

3. How could Jimmy not see what his life as a Ranger was doing to their relationship?

4. Rose asked the question, "Is a normal life too much to ask for?" Is it? If we're following a call from God, should we expect normal or supernatural?

5. In the book of First Corinthians, the Apostle Paul makes the statement that it's better or easier for a person who is wholly committed to Jesus Christ to be single. Why is that statement true?

6. Does that mean in order to follow Christ completely, we need to abandon our spouses? Of course not, but we can see in the life of Rose and Singer that there was a strong pull in both directions on Singer to be a soldier and a dedicated husband. Do you ever feel pulled in different directions?

Chapter 29: The Blood of Our Enemies

Singer executes a parachute insertion into the Central American jungle but spends several minutes as a towed jumper when he experiences a serious gear malfunction.

In a serious crisis such as Singer found himself, being dragged by the plane, most people find it fairly easy to turn to the Lord for help, even if they don't believe in God.

1. Have you ever been in a real crisis?

The significant question is how you responded to the crisis after it passed. Afterward, many people carry on and think very little of how close they came to death or serious injury.

2. Do you thank God for protecting you? Does a crisis experience actually move you to think differently about life ongoing? Do you realize how much you always need the Lord? Are you grateful to Him in all the circumstances of your life?

3. After reaching his fellow soldiers, Singer sees two of the younger men celebrating with high fives after neutralizing the enemy. How do you react when you've been victorious in your work or in some game or competition? Are you prideful or humble? Are you respectful and gracious toward those you've defeated or bested? Do you display character or just excitement at your achievement? Do you live thinking first of others, or do you think primarily of yourself?

Chapter 30: Keep Your Seats

Singer reacts to an unthinkable loss.

1. How have you dealt with terrible tragedy? Compare and contrast Singer and Pastor Randal's responses. Was one right and the other wrong, or were they just different?

2. Are you able to praise God in the face of even awful things?

3. How do you deal with your raging anger when it occurs? How should you?

4. We understand, and are even sympathetic with, how Singer felt and why he wanted to kill Conroy. What held him back? Does the same thing keep your life in the right place?

5. Many people will compromise their principles or faith when something touches them personally, or something touches someone they love, while others do not compromise.

What is it that makes the difference? How has this played out in your life?

6. Why do we tend to question things the most when we're hurt the deepest?

7. Why, in the middle of tragedy, do we question a God that some don't have faith in to begin with?

8. Why do we feel we have to have questions answered at our darkest moments when there are so many questions every day for which we never get answers?

9. When we hurt, is it a sense of entitlement that allows us to demand answers?

10. Is it okay to question a loving God?

11. Why do bad things happen to good people?

12. Have you ever not known what to do or what you should feel?

13. Have you ever felt like you're the only one who knows the deepest, darkest depths of pain?

14. Do bad things happen to bad people?

15. Do the rich and the poor both feel agony?

16. Do the young and the old cross through death's door?

17. How much grieving is enough grieving?

18. Should we feel bad when grieving lessens or doesn't consume us as it once did?

19. Were Singer's actions when he went after the man who killed his wife acceptable or commendable? Or were his actions wrong?

20. Was the Army wrong in how they handled Singer's discipline?

Epilogue

Singer's life moves beyond the military.

1. Conroy converted to Christ. What if Singer had killed him? Does this give you some perspective on doing what feels right to us? Are there bigger things going on than what we see and understand? Are you able to do what God says is right, even when you strongly want to do the opposite?
2. Forgiveness is often very hard. How can you be a more forgiving person?

Having finished the book, Cap, Dave, and John would love to hear your thoughts, comments, etc. Please feel free to contact us any-time.

Cap: Cap@CapDaniels.com
John: John@CapDaniels.com
Dave: Dave@CapDaniels.com

About the Author

Cap Daniels

Cap Daniels is a former sailing charter captain, scuba and sailing instructor, pilot, Air Force combat veteran, and civil servant of the U.S. Department of Defense. Raised far from the ocean in rural East Tennessee, his early infatuation with salt water was sparked by the fascinating, and sometimes true, sea stories told by his father, a retired Navy Chief Petty Officer. Those stories of adventure on the high seas sent Cap in search of adventure of his own, which eventually landed him on Florida's Gulf Coast where he spends as much time as possible on, in, and under the waters of the Emerald Coast.

With a headful of larger-than-life characters and their thrilling exploits, Cap pours his love of adventure and passion for the ocean onto the pages of the Chase Fulton Novels and the Avenging Angel - Seven Deadly Sins series.

Visit www.CapDaniels.com to join the mailing list to receive newsletter and release updates.

Connect with Cap Daniels:

Facebook: www.Facebook.com/WriterCapDaniels
Instagram: https://www.instagram.com/authorcapdaniels/
BookBub: https://www.bookbub.com/profile/cap-daniels

Pastor John Grossmann

John Grossmann received his Master of Divinity degree from Trinity Evangelical Divinity School in 1980 and second Master of Theology degree in Old Testament studies in 1981. While at Trinity, he sat under the teachings of distinguished Bible scholars and theologians such as D. A. Carson, Norman Geisler, Gleason Archer, Warren Wiersbe, Walter Kaiser, David Wells, and Harold O. J. Brown. He has been the senior pastor of Grace Evangelical Free Church since 1984 and served as the leader of the Greater Cincinnati Evangelical Free Church of America ministerial association. Additionally, he is a former member of the tenure board at Trinity International University and the Divinity School. A native of Cincinnati, John graduated from Cincinnati Country Day School in 1973, then attended Miami University as a philosophy major, graduating in 1977. From 1982–1984, he served as interim pastor of Covenant First Presbyterian Church, Cincinnati. John and his wife, Mary Pat, are the proud parents of nine children, and they have six grandchildren.

Pastor Dave Mason

Dave received his Divinity Degree from Southeastern Baptist Theological Seminary in 1995. He began in the workforce immediately out of high school and worked in the printing and paper industry for fifteen years. While building his secular career, he worked in ministry as a layman, teaching Sunday school and assuming leadership roles in the local church, which are a large part his ministry experience. After graduating from seminary, he spent twenty years in pastoral ministry as senior pastor in small- to medium-size churches. For the past several years, he has served as an elder in the local church, while he and his wife are involved in premarital, marriage, and family counseling. He has traveled extensively on Evangelical missions in six different countries and several U.S. states. Dave and his wife, MeLissa, have three grown children and eleven incredible grandchildren.

Made in the USA
Columbia, SC
31 January 2024